Sarah Shatz

Jeremy Blachman is not a hiring partner at a major law firm, but he is the author of a popular blog called Anonymous Lawyer (anonymouslawyer.blogspot.com). Blachman is a recent graduate of Harvard Law School and lives in Brooklyn, New York.

www.picadorusa.com

Picador® is a U.S. registered trademark and is used by Henry Holt and Company under license from Pan Books Limited.

For information on Picador Reading Group Guides, as well as ordering, please contact Picador.
Phone: 646-307-5629
Fax: 212-253-9627
E-mail: readinggroupguides@picadorusa.com

Book design by Meryl Sussman Levavi

Library of Congress Cataloging-in-Publication Data

Blachman, Jeremy.
    Anonymous lawyer : a novel / by Jeremy Blachman.
        p. cm.
    ISBN-13: 978-0-312-42555-5
    ISBN-10: 0-312-42555-4
    1. Lawyers—Blogs—Fiction. 2. Blogs—Fiction. I. Title.

PS3602.L23A56 2006
813'.6—dc22

                                                                        2006041235

First published in the United States by Henry Holt and Company

D 10 9 8 7 6 5 4 3 2

Anonymous Lawyer

A NOVEL

Jeremy Blachman

Picador

Henry Holt and Company • New York

To my grandparents

Anonymous Lawyer

Monday, May 8

I see you. I see you walking by my office, trying to look like you have a reason to be there. But you don't. I see the guilty look on your face. You try not to make eye contact. You try to rush past me as if you're going to the bathroom. But the bathroom is at the other end of the hall. You think I'm naïve, but I know what you're doing. Everyone knows. But she's my secretary, not yours, and her candy belongs to me, not you. And if I have a say in whether or not you ever become a partner at this firm—and trust me, I do—I'm not going to forget this. My secretary. My candy. Go back to your office and finish reading the addendum to the lease agreement. I don't want to see you in the hall for at least another sixteen hours. AND STOP STEALING MY CANDY.

And stop stealing my stapler, too. I shouldn't have to go wandering the halls looking for a stapler. I'm a partner at a half-billion-dollar law firm. Staplers should be lining up at my desk, begging for me to use them. So should the young lawyers who think I know their names. The Short One, The Dumb One, The One With The Limp, The One Who's Never Getting Married, The One Who Missed Her Kid's Funeral—I don't know who these people really are. You in the blue shirt—no, the other blue shirt—I need you to count the number of commas in this three-foot-tall stack of paper. Pronto. The case is going to trial seven years from now, so I'll need this done by the time I leave the office today. Remember: I can make or break you. I hold your future in my hands. I decide whether you get a view of the ocean or a view of the dumpster. This isn't a game. Get back to work. My secretary. My stapler. MY CANDY.

#Posted by Anonymous at 1:14 PM

Tuesday, May 9

I can barely do anything this morning knowing there's a living creature in the office next to mine. Usually it's just the corporate securities partner, and he hasn't moved a muscle since the Carter administration. But today he brought his dog into the office. Ridiculous. As if there aren't enough animals here already. We had fish once. Piranhas. We overfed them. We threw The Fat Guy's lunch in the tank one day because he showed up to a meeting fifteen minutes late. The fish devoured it—turkey sandwich, brownie, forty-eight-ounce Coke—and then exploded. It made the point. No one shows up late to my meetings anymore.

But the dog arrived this morning and immediately everyone was in the hallway instead of where they belong, staring into their computer screens. Associates were getting up, out of their chairs, to go chase the dog, pet the dog, talk to the dog. Someone gave the dog a piece of his muffin from the attorney lounge. The muffins aren't for dogs. We don't even let the paralegals have the muffins. The muffins are for client-billing attorneys. They're purely sustenance to keep the lawyers from having to leave the office for breakfast. They're not for visitors. I made a note of the incident and I'll have a dollar-fifty taken off the guy's next paycheck.

The dog barked once. I told his owner to keep the dog quiet or I'd lock him in the document room with the junior associates who've been in there for six weeks, searching for a single e-mail in a room full of boxes. There's an eerie quiet that normally pervades the halls of the firm, punctuated only by the screams of those who've discovered they can use the letter opener to end the pain once and for all. I'd like to keep it that way. We don't need barking to drown out our inner turmoil. Noise is for the monthly happy hour and the annual picnic. Not the workspace. The workspace is sacred.

I overheard The One Who Doesn't Know How To Correctly Apply Her Makeup say the dog really brings some life into this place. "I don't feel so alone," she said. I gave her some more work to do. She's obviously not busy enough. She's supposed to feel alone. This isn't the kind of business where people can go into their co-workers' offices and fritter away the morning chatting about the weather or the stock market or their "relationship issues." Or playing with a damn dog.

We're a law firm. Time is billable. The client doesn't pay for small talk. Every minute you spend away from your desk is a minute the firm isn't making any money off your presence, even though you're still using the office supplies, eating the muffins, drinking the coffee, consuming the oxygen, and adding to the wear and tear on the carpets. You're overhead. And if you're not earning your keep, you shouldn't be here.

The dog shouldn't be here, except he's probably more easily trained than some of my associates. If I get him to eat some incriminating evidence we need to destroy, I can bill the client a couple hundred dollars an hour for it. If I can get him to bark at some opposing counsel and scare them into accepting our settlement offer, that's probably billable. If I can get him to pee on a secretary, it won't be billable, but it's entertaining nonetheless. Hardly matters. Having a dog in the office is almost as ridiculous as holding the elevator for a paralegal. Inappropriate, undesirable, and it WILL NOT HAPPEN when I become chairman of this place, I guarantee you that.

#Posted by Anonymous at 9:25 AM

To: Anonymous Niece
From: Anonymous Lawyer
Date: Tuesday, May 9, 1:40 PM

Great seeing you over the weekend. I'm glad you came down. I was just talking about you at lunch—another partner said his son is starting at Stanford in the fall, and I told him I have a niece who's graduating next month. I said I'd see if you'd let me pass along your e-mail address in case his son has any questions. His father is a tax lawyer, so the son's probably a nut, but at least I can get some points for being helpful to my colleagues. He'll owe me one the next time I need a swing vote at the partner meeting.

I took a quick look at some of those law student weblogs you told me about. They gave me some names to add to the list of kids I'm never going to hire. They also motivated me to start this new e-mail account. Maybe I'll write a weblog of my own. I'll be Anonymous Lawyer. You can be Anonymous Niece. How does that sound?

To: Anonymous Lawyer
From: Anonymous Niece
Date: Tuesday, May 9, 2:23 PM

Sounds strange, but you're the boss. Anonymous Niece is fine. Feel free to give the tax partner my e-mail address. I can tell his son which professors to avoid, where to get the best pizza, it's no problem. Besides, if I'm nice to his son, his dad will help me with my Tax assignments once I'm in law school, right?

To: Anonymous Niece
From: Anonymous Lawyer
Date: Tuesday, May 9, 2:37 PM

You won't need his help. I'm sure you'll do quite fine on your own. Not everyone can get into Yale Law School. I'm proud of you, you know. It doesn't look like either of my kids is turning out to be a genius, so you might be my only hope.

    Don't forget to call your grandma and wish her a happy birthday. We talked about you this morning. She's happy you're following in my footsteps. At least someone in this family is.

Wednesday, May 10

The Guy With The Giant Mole quit today. Associates usually quit in January, right after the annual bonus checks, but this guy had been trying to go on vacation for three and a half years and never got the chance. Apparently he woke up one day last week and decided to become a high school teacher. That's what happens when you can't cut it. The best part of my job is getting to watch people like him go from happy, energetic, eager-to-please young law school graduates to slightly older, frustrated, burned-out midlevel associates who can't stand to be here.

And then it falls to me to replace them. That's the power of being the hiring partner at one of the most prestigious law firms on the planet. Law students love us. We have to beat them away with sticks. Well, not anymore, at least not literally. In the old days, the story is they would get some sticks with the firm's logo screen-printed on the side and really have some fun with the recruiting process, but I think there's an American Bar Association rule against that now, and so we have to use the standard rejection letter. I bet it was a lot more fun with the sticks.

We have students lining up to hand us their résumés, yet we've got a 30 percent annual turnover rate. And it's not just us. It's everywhere, all our peers, the whole industry. That makes my job a bit of a challenge. How to stay positive about selling students on the excellence of this place when we have to make sure the boxes of copier paper aren't tied up with rope—because that rope is just too tempting. One hanging every so often is to be expected, but when there's another one every time we get new office supplies it starts to get a little difficult to work.

At least the ones who kill themselves are admitting the truth. Once you realize you can't hack it at a place like this—that you're not as smart as you thought you were, or don't have the discipline to make the sacrifices it takes to succeed—then obviously it's not really worth continuing the charade. But some don't get the hint. They stay until we push them out—with a polite suggestion that they might find more appropriate work at Denny's.

I've been informed we have a former associate driving a bus. Until someone said that, I didn't realize we still had buses in this country. I fired the person who told me. Lawyers at this firm shouldn't be riding the bus. They shouldn't be using any kind of transportation at all, actually. They should be here. Billing clients.

#Posted by Anonymous at 10:51 AM

To: Anonymous Lawyer
From: Anonymous Niece
Date: Wednesday, May 10, 10:58 AM

I'm just going to law school—I don't know that I'm following in your footsteps quite yet. I'm sure the work is very exciting at your firm, but I think I might want to end up doing something different. Maybe start a nonprofit, or even go into teaching. I think I'm too idealistic to do firm work.

To: Anonymous Niece
From: Anonymous Lawyer
Date: Wednesday, May 10, 11:14 AM

You'll change your mind. They all do. Everyone starts law school with stupid dreams like that but you can't make $160K your first year out of law school working for a nonprofit. I'll get you a job working here next summer and you'll see. Look at me. I didn't think I'd end up at a law firm, but here I am. I'm rich and successful and you can be too.

To: Anonymous Lawyer
From: Anonymous Niece
Date: Wednesday, May 10, 11:27 AM

I promise I'll think about it.

Thursday, May 11

I got here ninety seconds later than usual this morning, maybe a hundred, but definitely not even two minutes, walked into the attorney lounge, and saw The Jerk taking the last bagel. "Split it with you?" I asked.

"I don't think so," he said. "Just like the IBM deal. The early bird gets the worm. Or, in that case, a pretty major payday." He smirked as he walked past me and opened the door back into the hallway. And I'm stuck with a danish.

I hate that smirk. I've hated it for the past eighteen years. We both started at the firm on the same day, members of the same class of summer associates. He was already losing his hair back then. He tried to compensate by letting it grow long, but he wasn't fooling anyone. Now he thinks nobody notices when every three years his hairline is magically restored to where it hasn't been naturally for decades. Some sort of transplant surgery. My hair is 100 percent my own. No surgery, no nothing.

Eighteen years and I don't think we've ever had a civil conversation. On the very first day of the summer program I made some throwaway comment about how I couldn't believe we had to waste the first week in training and he replied, "Some of us are here to learn." And one of us was apparently there to be a jackass. Since then, it's been an open secret that we'd each like nothing more than for the other to die in a house fire. A brutal, painful, ugly death. Causing great misery, and not covered by insurance.

Early on, I got picked for the hiring committee. I thought I'd be the first third-year associate ever put on a committee. Three days later they told him he was on it too. I threw a chair when I found out. Broke it right in half. Well, dented it at least.

The only benefit was that I got a new chair. Usually there's a long wait. You need to file a requisition form, wait for approval, and then you're limited to a certain set of chairs no more expensive than any chair belonging to anyone with more seniority. There are thirteen classes of chairs in the catalog for associates and partners to choose from, but no second-year associate can have a class III chair until all of the third-year associates have chairs from that category. The hierarchy dictates that we manage the chair situation, or sixth-year associates will be getting chairs nicer than the ones the partners have, and that's obviously an untenable situation. But if your chair breaks, you get to bypass the rules, and so I got a partner-level chair even though I was still an associate. I still have that chair. It's a good chair.

A few years later, The Jerk and I both got corner offices. One time, emboldened by the satisfaction of having made the longest paper clip chain I'd ever constructed, I snuck in and measured. Mine's seven square feet bigger. That's fifty-two extra paper clips in each direction.

I've always taken that to be a sign. Seven square feet. I'm that much more valuable.

We were both named partner the same year, the first time our names came up for consideration. Of course, on the same day I got the call to be the hiring partner, The Jerk was named assistant head of litigation. I ripped up a paralegal's paycheck when I found out. Had to vent the frustration somehow.

The Jerk is everything I hate about the people here. He's smug and entitled and three inches taller than me. I'm not short, especially for a lawyer. But he's a mutant. I hate having to look up to him.

He fired his assistant on the day she announced she was pregnant—and he did it during the celebration in the conference room. Everyone was congratulating her, and he pulled her aside and told her he'd arranged the celebration so that security would have a chance to clean out her desk and pack her stuff in a box. She had a miscarriage later that night. He admits no responsibility. At least I wait until they come back from maternity leave before I tell them they're fired.

The Jerk is like a spoiled brat, in his custom-tailored suit meant to hide the fifteen extra pounds he's put on, still getting over the disappointment that he'll never be a Supreme Court justice. That's what they go to these top law schools hoping for, all of them. And The Jerk went to Harvard, the worst one of them all. Very few people go to Harvard just to become a lawyer. They go to Harvard to become chief justice. Normal kids grow up wanting to be firemen and astronauts and baseball players. One kid I interviewed this past fall told me he had a book of Supreme Court paper dolls when he was a kid, and played with them every day. That isn't normal. This is who these kids are, though. These mini-Jerks, Jerks-in-training, these Jerks who populate these hallways. I'd have happily shared the bagel with him. I'd have even given him the bigger half.

#Posted by Anonymous at 9:50 AM

To: Anonymous Niece

From: Anonymous Lawyer

Date: Thursday, May 11, 11:10 AM

I'm kind of embarrassed to tell you this, but I actually started one of those weblogs the other day, after I looked at the student ones you told me about. It's ridiculous, and I'm sure I'm not going to keep it going, but there's no one here I can talk openly to, and I thought it might be fun to have a place to write about life. I wrote a screenplay when I was in college—did I ever tell you that? I'm sure it was terrible. I probably won't keep the blog for long, but I've had some endless conference calls this week, and I've needed something to do.

I want you to check it out and make sure it's working, and also make sure no one can trace it back to me. No one can trace it if I'm anonymous, right? You know this computer stuff better than I do. I'm changing the details and not using anyone's name, but I just want to make sure. It wouldn't be good for everyone in the firm to start reading this and know it's me.

The address is http://anonymouslawyer.blogspot.com. Let me know if it looks okay.

To: Anonymous Lawyer
From: Anonymous Niece
Date: Thursday, May 11, 11:55 AM

The One Who Missed Her Kid's Funeral?? I hope you're exaggerating.

The blog's working fine. Graphically it's pretty basic, but I'm sure you don't want to spend your time playing around with that stuff. You probably do need to be careful. I'd imagine there are plenty of law students who would love to know what's going on inside a partner's head.

Definitely be careful about specific details. I know students at school who've been able to keep their blogs anonymous for a few years, but they're careful not to write anything traceable—never any names, they switch the genders and the dates, and they make sure nothing gives them away. It's a small world and if there are a couple hundred law firms like yours, you start saying too much and by process of elimination someone's going to find you.

But I don't think you have all that much to worry about. There are a million blogs out there. I sent the link to a couple of friends who are also going to law school in the fall. I didn't say you were my uncle, I just said I stumbled across the site. So it's nothing to worry about. I'll let you know if they say anything to me about it.

That tax kid sent me an e-mail yesterday. He wanted to know if people living in the dorms have to take communal showers. I think he may be a strange boy. Did you watch the Dodgers game last night? I told you they need a better bullpen. It's going to be a disaster like last year. I should be studying anyway.

To: Anonymous Niece
From: Anonymous Lawyer
Date: Thursday, May 11, 12:55 PM

Thanks for looking at the blog. I'm making sure to disguise things. The Jerk didn't take a bagel, he took a croissant. And the Dodgers will be fine, it's still early. Give them a chance. I'm leaving the office right after lunch and getting in a round of golf. I just saw The Tax Guy in the bathroom and he told me his son said you wrote back a helpful response. I appreciate it. He's so impressed you're going to Yale. He didn't get into Yale, and hopefully his son won't either. You're helping me win these conversations, so thanks.

Friday, May 12

There's a farewell reception for The Old Guy this afternoon in Conference Room 24B. He's been chairman of the firm for fifteen years, but he just turned seventy-five and the executive committee is forcing him out. They've got some chocolate truffle cake and an open bar, or at least that's what my secretary is telling me. You can tell how much we think of people by what kind of food we give out in their honor. We celebrate birthdays at the firm. For associates, it's usually some yellow sheet cake. For partners, we'll add some ice cream, maybe some brownies. For the support staff, we'll throw a box of Oreos on the table and see if anyone bothers to show up. Inevitably, people do. Partners making a million dollars a year will still leave their desks for a free cookie. There's not a partner here who can name one member of the custodial staff, yet when they get the e-mail that it's Karl's birthday, suddenly he's every partner's best friend because there's a package of Chunky Chips Ahoy in the attorney lounge.

I'll eat the cookies like everyone else, but at least it's not entirely a charade on my part. There are a lot of things I'm terrible at, like being a decent human being, but one thing I'm good at is remembering people's birthdays. It fools people into thinking I have a heart. I'll go up to a secretary and wish her a happy birthday, and she's shocked I even remember the month. Or that she has a birthday. Or that she's a person, who was once born.

It's a party trick. Birthdays, names, faces—I remember them. If I meet someone's kids, it sticks. "How're Roberto and Juanita?" I might ask, if we had any Hispanic lawyers at the firm, and Joaquin's eyes would open wide and he'd ask me how I could possibly remember the names of his kids when he can't recall ever even talking to me before. It's just something I'm good at. It fools clients too. And it especially fools summer associates—the naïve law students we bring on as interns each summer, who'll come back after graduation and replace all the attorneys who've left.

When I drop a detail into a conversation—something I learned about them when they interviewed back in the fall—they think I care. I don't.

"How'd the year at the law school newspaper finish up?"

"You remember?"

"Of course I remember. You're quite an impressive student. I'm so glad to have you aboard this summer."

"Thanks, I appreciate that."

"Now I know that another partner's got you working on that fascinating research assignment, but I was hoping I could steal you away for half a day to help me track down a piece of paper that's somewhere in a big room full of boxes. I'm asking you in particular because of that newspaper experience—I know how good journalists are at uncovering the scoop, and I'm sure you're one of the best. So what do you say you put down that other guy's files, help me out, and I'll take you for a reimbursable lunch later this week?"

It gets them every time.

This year's batch of summers will be here on Monday. But today it's all about The Old Guy. Truffle cake and vodka shots. It beats the box of Triscuits we had when the director of client services retired. Yeah, we didn't even spring for cookies that time.

The Old Guy has put in some good years of service. He led our global expansion to Europe and Asia. He streamlined the core practice groups to increase profits per partner and move us ten spots higher in *The American Lawyer* rankings. He left his wife for an associate a few years ago. A terrible associate. Shoddy work. Lack of commitment to the firm. She knew she wasn't going to make partner on her own merits so she figured she'd find another route. She's hidden away in Trusts and Estates now, where lawyers go to die.

The Old Guy's forced retirement is moving everyone up one spot in the hierarchy. The line of succession has been pretty clear for a while. The New Chairman, currently head of the corporate department, has been with the firm for thirty-three years, waiting his turn. He's from another generation. He remembers when the life of a lawyer wasn't quite so lucrative. He prefers a greasy cheeseburger to a hundred-dollar omakase sushi dinner. He's only got two houses. He flies coach. But he's sharp. He knew how to play the politics of this place and get himself into the chairman's office.

And I've got to do the same if I want to be next. The New Chairman will last no more than fifteen, seventeen years tops, and then it's going to be me or The Jerk. The problem is that they've been grooming both of us, and we can't both get that office. It seems like there's all the time in the world to prepare, but that's exactly what The Jerk wants me to think. While he tries to elbow his way ahead of me, I need to be vigilant.

With The Old Guy it was easy. I learned to play racquetball just to get that face time with him, and it got me to where I am today. The New Chairman doesn't play racquetball. He's built for brunch more than racquetball. I had my secretary send him a gift basket from Lobel's of New York. Finest steak money can buy. Hopefully he'll think of me while he eats it. The Jerk sent him flowers. I win.

Time for truffle cake.

#Posted by Anonymous at 3:54 PM

To: Anonymous Niece
From: Anonymous Lawyer
Date: Friday, May 12, 4:17 PM

You ever have truffle cake? It's good. Next summer, it can be yours.

To: Anonymous Lawyer
From: Anonymous Niece
Date: Friday, May 12, 4:33 PM

It sounds better than dining-hall food.

To: Anonymous Niece
From: Anonymous Lawyer
Date: Friday, May 12, 4:48 PM

Go out tonight, my treat. Just send me the receipt. It's the least I can do. You've given me someone to brag about. You can celebrate that I'm finally one step closer to becoming chairman of the firm.

To: Anonymous Lawyer
From: Anonymous Niece
Date: Friday, May 12, 4:55 PM

You sure? Thanks! That's so generous of you.

To: Anonymous Niece
From: Anonymous Lawyer
Date: Friday, May 12, 5:04 PM

You deserve it—I've got the world's smartest niece. Stanford is one thing, but Yale Law School is quite another. Especially looking at where you came from. I love your mom, but she was never the scholar growing up. I admit it—I'm jealous, just a bit, of all the opportunities you're going to have. I did fine going to Michigan for college and law school, but you're doing it the way it ought to be done. Stanford, Yale, and the most prestigious firm we can get you working for. I'll take advantage of every connection I've got, I promise. You'll go right to the top.

To: Anonymous Lawyer
From: Anonymous Niece
Date: Friday, May 12, 5:25 PM

I appreciate this so much, but like I told you—I'm not sure a big law firm is really where I want to end up. I want to help people.

To: Anonymous Niece
From: Anonymous Lawyer
Date: Friday, May 12, 5:35 PM

Don't worry. Give me a little time and I'll squeeze that "helping people" crap right out of you.

———————————

Saturday, May 13

The summer program starts on Monday, and I'm hosting a party this afternoon to thank everyone in advance for making this the best summer yet. I'm up early waiting for the guys with the tent to arrive. I undersold the party as a barbecue, but it's actually a surf-and-turf buffet, after a cocktail hour and some music from a three-piece string ensemble I dropped a few grand on. I made the maid stay late last night to ensure everything would be perfect. I realized this morning that the fringes on the rugs weren't lined up, so I got down on my knees and fixed them myself. It would have cost a client $275 if I was able to bill the time. The partners will get a tour of the inside of the house; the associates will be limited to the backyard area. My secretary helped me with the planning, and I'm sure she expected an invitation to come, but there wasn't a chance of that.

I don't need to have this party. On the surface, it's to thank everyone in advance for treating the summer associates well this year, and not letting them get too much of a glimpse of what working here is really like. But what it's really about is a chance to impress The New Chairman. To show off my house and finally get to exhibit the patio furniture that I had upholstered in the firm's color. When I'm chairman, I'll probably change our color. This cornflower blue isn't my favorite. It's not masculine enough. I'd like a forest green, maybe a hunter mixed with just a little note of midnight blue. I've thought about this a lot. We need to make a bolder statement in the marketplace to stand out against our competition. Cornflower isn't bold enough. It's on my list of things to address when I finally become chairman. Others:

1. Buy a new couch for my office
2. No more free food for overweight associates
3. Paralegals don't get health benefits
4. Fix the wobbly conference table in 23D
5. Switch to three-ply toilet paper

That's just the first five. I've got hundreds.

I've rented the deluxe tent, with the wind panels and the carpet floor. It cost a bunch of money, but it's worth it. Anonymous Wife is still in bed, of course—even though she knows how important this is. She's useless anyway. I had to hide her car in the garage because it's an old Honda with two dents in it, and I don't want the other partners to see it. I moved my Lexus out front. It's a better image. I'd get Anonymous Wife a nicer car, but she destroys them. She does her makeup while she's driving, or talks on the phone, paying no attention to anything. One day she's going to kill herself or the kids or, even worse, me. I don't drive with her anymore. The only thing I let her do is take the service providers home—the maid and the babysitter. If they get into an accident, it's a loss, but I'm willing to take the risk.

She doesn't understand the point of this party. She doesn't like the idea of a bunch of old men wandering through the living room.

But what can I expect? I read *U.S. News* and she reads *US Weekly*. If you can even call it reading. She's still pretty enough, sure. That's never been the problem. But she sits in the house watching reruns of *Press Your Luck* on the Game Show Network, and goes out with her friends for two-hundred-dollar lunches and to stroll through department stores buying dozens of things we don't need. The crap just ends up in the garage, never touched. An antique cuckoo clock, a towel warmer, a dog bed, a 24-karat gold chess set (as if she's ever played chess, even just once in her life), a cake decorating kit, and, the latest addition to the pile of junk, a four-foot-long rainstick.

We don't need a rainstick. It just gives Anonymous Son something else to break. Any day now, little grains of barley, or whatever's inside a rainstick, are going to be rolling all over the floor and someone's going to break his neck. I won't even call the ambulance if it's my wife. Maybe it'll teach her a lesson.

But I need her for today's party. Without her, people start to get suspicious. You can't be creepy like the real estate guy who goes home to his mother every night. Or fat. Those people don't have a future. They can't hope for the top. You need the image of a perfect family or you're not executive committee material. You don't get the best clients or the office with the ocean view. You need to blend in at the firm picnic and be part of the club. Or you're simply not an integral part of the future of the firm.

The people with the tent are finally knocking at the door. 7:39, almost ten minutes late. That'll be twenty bucks off the tip. At least.

#Posted by Anonymous at 7:40 AM

Saturday, May 13

What a waste. My chance to impress The New Chairman and he was here for all of fifteen minutes. The fancy tent, the string ensemble, the hundred-dollar surf and turf—all for him, and he didn't even have the decency to stay past the cocktail hour. He and The Jerk snuck away somewhere, too quick for me to intercept and make sure The New Chairman got the tour. Instead I was left with the B-team eating my food and traipsing around my backyard killing the grass.

If he'd left with anyone besides The Jerk, I wouldn't be so concerned. But every second of face time counts. I've synchronized my bathroom habits just to make sure I get in there right when The New Chairman does. It wreaks havoc on my system, but it's worth it.

Besides The New Chairman's quick exit, the party went off without a hitch—except for an early mishap with an associate during the cocktail hour. The Frumpy Litigator is allergic to shellfish, but one of the partners didn't know and offered her a bite of his lobster cake. Like any good associate, she knows the rules. When a partner tells you to do something, you do it, no matter what. Anaphylactic shock be damned. She politely took a bite, and as soon as she had the chance, turned and spit it into her napkin. But by then it was too late. She pulled me aside and said she thought she might need to go to the hospital. Of course I let her leave, despite the importance of the party. She handled the whole situation very discreetly. I'll be sure to send her an e-card on Monday wishing her a speedy recovery.

Anonymous Wife—who, thankfully, took her Wellbutrin today (I crushed it up and put it in her oatmeal)—led the partners on a splendid tour through the house, pointing out everything we'd rehearsed. Like the shelf of awards I've received from clients over the years—including the Lucite pin from the bowling alley conglomerate, the etched crystal corncob from the fertilizer company I helped out of bankruptcy, and the silver thumbtack from the office superstore. The awards spend three years on my bookshelf in the office before retiring to the house, displacing another one of Anonymous Daughter's ceramic monstrosities from art class or one of Anonymous Son's karate trophies.

My kids behaved themselves, which is more than I can say for the help. On his way out, The Guy With The Overbite, a sixth-year associate on the partner track, accidentally kicked over a wine glass. Like anyone would, he stood there, crossed his arms, and waited for one of the waiters to come clean it up. It took a waiter almost a full forty-five seconds to notice, even as The Guy With The Overbite was pointing and gesturing, and getting pretty upset. It was embarrassing, and I shaved another twenty dollars off the tip. Anonymous Son was about to go over and help, but of course I told him that wasn't his job. Maybe in twenty years, if he follows in his mother's footsteps. But he shouldn't be cleaning up glass when he's eight.

#Posted by Anonymous at 11:12 PM

To: Anonymous Lawyer
From: Anonymous Niece
Date: Sunday, May 14, 9:05 AM

Two posts in one day? You're like a thirteen-year-old girl.

To: Anonymous Niece
From: Anonymous Lawyer
Date: Sunday, May 14, 9:11 AM

It was a big day. I know I'm getting addicted to this. It's probably not healthy. But I've had no one to talk to about work for the past eighteen years, so it's kind of pouring out. I'm sure it'll get old, and I'm sure no one's reading it anyway. You're having an exciting weekend, I hope.

To: Anonymous Lawyer
From: Anonymous Niece
Date: Sunday, May 14, 9:18 AM

An exciting weekend studying, sure. Dinner on Friday was great—thanks. A couple of friends and I got some Thai food, it was like fifteen bucks each. It's okay if you weren't serious about paying for it. I can afford a $15 dinner. The friends I told about the blog said they've been reading and they love it. I think they passed the link along to some other people too. So that's cool—you've got some students reading. And I don't think there's any way they can link it back to you—no one even knows you're my uncle. Thank goodness—if it gets around at law school that my uncle is a hiring partner, I'll probably get more résumés than the people in Career Services.

Sunday, May 14

Twenty-eight messages on my BlackBerry this morning. The Black-Berry has absolutely revolutionized the way the firm works. It used to be that in times of crisis, associates were tethered to their desks, unable to leave for lunch, for dinner, for the bathroom, or for an emergency appendectomy—for fear that we wouldn't be able to get in touch with them. But now that they can receive e-mail wherever they are, twenty-four hours a day, their freedom has increased dramatically. Now it's okay for them to go to the hospital after their son's in an accident, or to take an hour to drive their fourteen-year-old daughter to the abortion clinic, or to go brush their teeth after they've been in the office all night. It's a great feeling to know that if I have a research question at three in the morning, I can e-mail an associate and expect an answer within minutes.

But to wake up to twenty-eight messages on a Sunday is unusual. All these messages are part of our long-running debate about the dress code for the summer program. You'd be surprised what some of the summer associates think they can get away with. Jeans, T-shirts, bold colors like green and brown, ties with unapproved patterns, and even open-toed shoes.

Last night one of the senior partners e-mailed to the entire hiring committee that he felt we should make a last-minute change to the memo we'll be distributing tomorrow and completely ban facial hair. This would be a change from the current policy, under which, with special permission, "neatly trimmed" beards and mustaches are acceptable. Apparently this senior partner spent the day with his grandchildren, was "alarmed by their sideburns," and wants to revisit the issue.

My take on it is that we want to be seen as a firm that's friendly to students who've made alternative lifestyle choices, including those involving facial hair. Besides, there'd be enforcement problems if any summer associates have to work through the night and won't have access to a razor. Luckily, cooler heads have prevailed and we won't have to reprint the memo before the summer associates arrive.

There's enough to do tomorrow anyway. I've got to lock the crazy partners in their offices and make sure they don't get out. There are certain attorneys that the summers are never allowed to see. The ones who hit, the ones who smell, and the ones who are just so high on the Asperger's scale that we can't risk letting them interact with law students we're hoping will accept our offers at the end of the summer and come back after graduation. Everyone here has Asperger's syndrome to some extent—it's one of the markings of a corporate lawyer. But the summers have it too, so it all works out okay. It's the ones at the tail end of the bell curve—like The Tax Guy—that we have to control. He'll start talking to summers about the consistency of his bowel movements.

#Posted by Anonymous at 9:46 AM

Monday, May 15

The Suck-Up was the first summer to approach me when I walked into the conference room this morning to see how many people had arrived early for orientation. He told me he spent last night reading the firm's Web site, memorizing all the partners' names, what we look like, and our practice areas, so he'd be ready to work right away. I told him that was very impressive, but it probably won't help. Most of the partners submitted photos that were already twenty years old when we put up the Web site a decade ago, and haven't updated them since.

"Like the real estate partner with the plaid jacket and the handlebar mustache?" he asked.

"No. That picture happens to be current. Unfortunately, he's not part of the summer program and you won't be getting a chance to meet him."

We get the same batch of kids every year. The Suck-Up, of course, and The Guy With The Bad Haircut, The Girl Who Dresses Like A Slut, Dopey, Ditzy, Drinky, Clumsy, and Oops, the one with the droopy mouth whom I definitely wouldn't have hired if her father wasn't a client. That Foreign Dude, from somewhere. It doesn't matter where. He's in America now. He should learn to assimilate. I hate hiring people with names we can't pronounce. It creates weeks of awkwardness on everyone's part. The kids don't want to correct us, and we don't want to be corrected. I'll spend the whole summer calling him

"Hey." It doesn't matter. I could call them all "Shitface" and they'd still respond.

"I'm excited to be in the same room where some of the country's most important merger-related conference calls have taken place," The Suck-Up continued.

"I didn't realize we were still talking."

He just finished his second year of law school at Cornell. It's hard to understand why law school needs to be three years long. If they wanted to be efficient they could teach everything in a couple of weeks and then send their students here to get the training they'll eventually need anyway. Kids waste too much time in law school thinking about justice and fairness, and not enough time learning what's important. They come here clueless about how to structure transactions in order to minimize tax liability, and how to appreciate fifteen-dollar pieces of fatty tuna. That's where we come in.

Our summer program introduces law students—most having just finished their second year of school, but if someone's father is a congressman, a client, or a partner at the firm we might take him after his first year—to life at the firm, and provides a critical pipeline of future associates to replace the ones who leave each year.

But hundreds of firms want the same students we do, from the top handful of law schools. We all compete for these students' affections—and this competition has meant that the perks we offer the summer associates have grown out of control.

We pay our summers $2600/week, the same salary as our first-year associates get. But the summers get to work normal hours, not the eighteen-hour days our associates work. And the summers have an action-packed schedule of events—baseball tickets, concerts, museum visits, a trip to Disneyland, a barbecue at the chairman's house, a helicopter ride, a scavenger hunt, lunches at some of the city's most expensive restaurants, a full-body massage, and more.

Plus, we give away an assortment of enough firm-logoed clothing and accessories to keep the Oriental Trading Company in business for a few more years. By the end of the summer, the kids will all have T-shirts, hats, fountain pens, coffee mugs, letter openers, cell phone holders, beach towels, throw pillows, canvas bags, leather portfolios, PEZ dispensers, and a limited-edition porcelain collector plate featuring an engraving of the firm's founders in front of a skyscraper-filled cityscape, signed by the artist. We give them so much junk that by the end they don't even want it. We throw out boxes of T-shirts at the end of every summer. Not me personally, of course. I don't touch garbage.

After all this, we hope the students accept our offer to join us after graduation, when the salary is the same, but the work hours are just a little longer, and the baseball tickets just a little harder to come by. It's a deal most of them are eager to take. There's nothing else out there that's going to pay them $160,000 a year at age twenty-five, with no job experience, right out of law school.

By now they're probably finishing up the bagels. Law students seem to get fatter every year. In a few minutes I'm heading back to the conference room to give my speech welcoming the summers to the firm. I have competing aims in mind. I want them to understand how happy we are to have them here, and how much fun we want them to have this summer, but I also want them to understand how lucky they are to be here, and how if not for us, they'd be living on the street, surviving on other people's trash. It's a tricky balancing act.

#Posted by Anonymous at 9:48 AM

To: Anonymous Lawyer
From: Anonymous Niece
Date: Monday, May 15, 9:53 AM

Do you really throw out boxes of T-shirts every year? The homeless shelter where I'm volunteering after graduation would love those, I'm sure. If you just wanted to ship them up here, I could take care of the rest and you wouldn't have to do a thing.

To: Anonymous Niece
From: Anonymous Lawyer
Date: Monday, May 15, 9:57 AM

Do you just want a T-shirt? I can get you a T-shirt if you want a T-shirt. You can't be serious about the homeless people. I can't have homeless people walking around wearing a T-shirt with the name of our firm on it. If a client saw that, he'd leave. I can't help it in every case—if a paralegal has a T-shirt, gets fired, gets evicted from her house, and then she becomes a homeless person wearing one of our shirts, well, there's nothing I can do about that. But to give them to people who are already homeless? That's terrible PR. You shouldn't be working for the homeless this summer anyway. I don't want you to get one of their diseases. I have to go give my speech. I'll send you a T-shirt.

———————————

Monday, May 15

"Good morning, and welcome. I hope you've enjoyed the bagels." I started my speech the same way I do every summer. "In life, there are winners and there are losers. Just by being here, you're already a winner. Surely you realize how much some people would give to be in your position. Last year, one student, from a very fine law school, offered his left arm for a chance to work for us. We took him up on the deal and he's now in a corner office on the eighteenth floor, typing with only one hand but being very productive about it.

"I'm kidding. But that's the kind of place we are. People want to work here. We're lucky to have you, but even more so, you're lucky to be here. Many of our partners started out in the very same seats in which you're sitting, and are now sitting in seats that are considerably more comfortable, helping some of the world's largest companies solve their hardest legal problems. This summer, you'll get a chance to meet people who talk directly to powerful corporate leaders, and to work with people who help other people help our clients engineer billion-dollar deals and navigate the sophisticated legal landscape of today's complex world.

"Most important, we want you to get to know one another. Look around. These are the people you will spend the rest of your lives with. Potentially thousands and thousands of billable hours. There are days these will be the only people you'll see. But I'm good at my job, and I've chosen you carefully, so I'm sure you'll all like each other just fine.

"We start the summer assuming everyone will leave with an offer to return after graduation. It's yours to lose. It's hard to lose. But it's been done before. Don't make us regret having given you the opportunity to work here. Don't make us wish you were instead working for the firm down the street, where the lunch allowance is ten dollars lower per person, where the Dodgers tickets are four sections farther from home plate, and where they don't even have a gym membership subsidy. You're one of us now. Welcome."

I then proceeded to the multimedia portion of the presentation. Anytime we can incorporate multimedia into our work it's always appreciated by those who have to sit through these things. Well, except for the fiasco last year when I showed a clip from Leni Riefenstahl's *Triumph of the Will* in order to inspire people to pledge their loyalty to the firm in the wake of a series of defections by several star associates.

This year, five film clips. I showed a clip from *Collateral* so they could see the dangers that await them if they leave the office and start driving around downtown L.A. It's not safe, especially in the sports cars they're all blowing their salaries to lease.

I showed a clip from *Rent* to illustrate that while there are indeed 525,600 minutes in a year, the important thing is that every one of those minutes is potentially billable to a client.

I showed a clip from *Brokeback Mountain,* which I think was done a tremendous disservice when they pitched it as a gay cowboy movie. I didn't see it, but it was fairly clear from the trailer that the point of the movie is that it's great to have a job that consumes most of your day. "Don't worry about how much time you spend in the office," I told them. "You might just fall in love with someone you're working with." There are far too few movies out there that illustrate the fallacy of work-life balance quite so well.

I showed a clip from *March of the Penguins* for an example of mindless work performed without complaint. The penguins march back and forth to and from the ocean, a long and arduous march in the cold on which many perish, yet none ever bitch and moan. They just do it. No whining, no trying to sneak out of the pack to find a shortcut, no escaping, no giving up. The penguins walk simply because that's what they're supposed to do.

That's all we're asking our associates to do. They don't have to make it more complicated than that. Just march. March to the library. March to the document room. March to the printer. All together now, mindlessly following the herd. That's all we need. Bodies, not brains. The penguins don't expect to be challenged. The penguins don't expect any individual attention. The penguins don't expect any praise for their work. They just do what they have to do. They march.

Finally, I showed a clip from *Independence Day* to illustrate that sometimes emergencies happen and you have to work over the holiday weekend.

The summers were pretty silent at the end, but the associates who snuck in to watch the presentation gave a big round of applause. These are the first movies they've seen in years.

#Posted by Anonymous at 11:43 AM

To: Anonymous Lawyer
From: Anonymous Niece
Date: Monday, May 15, 5:33 PM

Explain something to me. You say they all start out with a job offer that's theirs to lose. How many end up getting that offer at the end of the summer?

To: Anonymous Niece

From: Anonymous Lawyer

Date: Monday, May 15, 6:11 PM

Oh, virtually all of them. It's a stupid system, but we don't have a choice, because otherwise they go back to school and tell all their classmates that we didn't give everyone an offer. And then no one chooses to interview with us, because there are so many other firms and we're all so identical in so many ways. So it's a threat we hardly ever follow through on, but it scares them all anyway because the stakes are so high. You can't go back to school without an offer. No firm wants to take someone who's been rejected somewhere else.

And there are just enough stories of summers who didn't get offers—extreme stories about summers who slept with partners' wives, who got drunk on the boat cruise, stripped naked, and jumped into the ocean, or who accidentally sent e-mails to clients about their sexual escapades with underage strippers—to make these kids nervous. You'll see when you get to law school—everyone takes everything more seriously than they need to. But, luckily, that's what makes the system work.

Tuesday, May 16

We kicked off the summer events schedule last night with our annual bowling outing. We like to do something pretty low-key on the first night, just to ease the summers into the season. So we rented out a bowling alley, catered in some food, and got a luxury bus to take everyone over there from the office. The ride took about twenty minutes. We showed them the sexual harassment video.

I convinced a few partners to come out—Lives With His Mom, Closet Lesbian, Black Guy, and the cranky Old Yeller—and we made teams of one partner and three summer associates. The team with the highest score won lunch at any restaurant they want. It's not much of a prize, since they get restaurant lunches all summer anyway, but at least it's something. There's a limit to what we can offer. We gave cash prizes one year, but it gets messy to start handing out hundred-dollar bills at a bowling alley. The alley staff gets jealous.

As soon as we got there, The Suck-Up darted over to me and asked if he could be on my team. He's like a puppy dog. I asked him if he was any good at bowling. He said he was in a league with his mother when he was twelve, and they finished third. I reluctantly agreed that he could bowl with me, and I told him to pick two more summers to join us. I think he peed his pants with excitement over the opportunity to make a big decision like that. I saw a wet spot.

I should have let the recruiting coordinator pick the teams. That's a thankless job, recruiting coordinator. You're a grown person, and your job is to babysit a bunch of law students all summer. Thrilling. "I lost my electronic key card and can't get into the office." "A partner asked me to go to court today, and I don't have a tie." "I'm allergic to lunch and if you don't pick all the peanuts out by hand, I'm going to die. Also, I want you to do it blindfolded."

You put people in an environment where all of their needs are taken care of and suddenly they become incapable of doing anything for themselves. They can't make their own photocopies, they can't find the books they need on the library shelves, and they can't wipe themselves when they go to the bathroom.

For partners, this is understandable. We can't be expected to sharpen our own pencils, because we're charging clients over six hundred dollars an hour for our time and it's simply good business to get our secretaries to do it. Similarly, we shouldn't be wasting billable minutes cleaning up our lunch wrappers, picking up our dry cleaning, or holding the elevator for someone who's running to catch it. But the summers should be able to butter their own toast and change their own socks. They're not important yet.

Not that the recruiting coordinators are equipped to do much else. Most of them are former lawyers who were too weak to handle the demands of the job and had to "downshift" into a career in personal services. They wasted three years of their lives in law school, only to become nannies. It serves them right to have to vacuum the carpet in the attorney lounge after summers still drunk from the night before eat one too many muffins in the morning. Let the recruiters clean it up. What else are they good for? Certainly not litigating. Their parents must be so proud.

The Suck-Up brought over Chicago Guy and The Musician to be on our team. Chicago Guy spent the previous morning asking everyone in the room where they went to school. He got into a heated debate with Stanford Girl over whose school was better. Like it matters. Clients pay a premium for Harvard and Yale, but everything else is irrelevant.

I don't mind Chicago Guy. A little arrogance is good. It helps if it accompanies competence, but it's only the first day, so the jury's still out on that one. He claims he's never been bowling before, which won't help us win, but I'm not sure it's really a victory if I have to have lunch with The Suck-Up. "Bowling's not the kind of thing lawyers do too often, is it?" Chicago Guy asked.

No, it's not. I suppose it's ironic that we take everyone bowling when none of us would ever dream of coming to a place like this on our own. What lawyer goes bowling? We play golf, we go skiing, we build hockey rinks for our kids in the basement, complete with a mini Zamboni ice resurfacing machine. Things that require very expensive equipment. Not things that require shirts with our names stitched on them. We gave out bowling shirts, incidentally. Everyone got one on the way in. The Musician whispered to me, "How much you think I can get for this on eBay?"

The Musician's a wild card in the summer class. We always take a few. Wild cards, racial and ethnic minorities, and the disadvantaged kids who go to public universities. The Musician's résumé is a bit unusual. Most of the summers have been training for this for a while. They started legal newspapers in high school, they wrote theses in college about the 1933 Securities Act, and, most critically, there's no evidence they have any interests outside the law. Those are the kinds of students we like to see.

The Musician was in a band before law school. He interned for a record label last summer. A non-legal job. That's a red flag. In his interview, I asked him about it. "I needed to make sure the music thing was out of my system," he said. "I want something more intellectually challenging. The law engages a different part of my brain, and I missed that when I was just focusing on the music. Besides, a music career is too uncertain. I'm risk-averse. I want something more stable." And his grades were good, he's on Law Review, and he has nice teeth. So he convinced me. We took him. Heck, he goes to Yale, so of course we took him. But I'm worried.

The reality is that anyone who's got something else pulling at him is not going to be a good fit here. You can't spend a hundred and ten hours a week in the office if your heart is somewhere else. This is too all-consuming to leave room for passions. We know most of our associates don't truly love the law. We accept that. They're here because there's no job they can get this easily that'll pay this much money, and there's nothing else pulling at them to pursue something different. That's fine. But when we're the backup plan for someone with a creative dream, it's trouble. They wimp out on us. They start to imagine they deserve better. They don't deserve better. There is no better. This is as good as it gets.

The Jerk showed up twenty minutes late, as usual. My summer events are never as important as his precious litigation training sessions. You show up three minutes late to one of those and the food's all gone and you're stuck standing, hungry, for an hour and a half of mind-numbing PowerPoint. He puts out half the chairs he knows he'll need, purposely.

Just my luck, the only spot left in the bowling alley was the lane next to mine. The Jerk dropped his briefcase by my shoes and grabbed some food from the dinner spread. Steak frites with a pasta option for the morons who won't eat meat. We had no choice but to cater in—we certainly can't expect anyone to eat what they normally serve at a bowling alley. Maybe that's what truckers eat. I don't know.

The Jerk pulled Harvard Guy away from the spread and dragged him onto his lane, which was no surprise. School pride. The Jerk never misses an opportunity to remind everyone where he went to school. He owns a half dozen pairs of cuff links from Harvard, wears a Harvard ring, has framed pictures of the Harvard campus on his office wall, carries a Harvard pocket watch, has a Harvard wooden armchair in his office, uses Harvard pens exclusively, wears Harvard ties, has coffee table books about Harvard, goes back for every alumni event, and includes the word Harvard in every conversation he ever has. "Look at me. I went to Harvard. I'm important!"

He's not that important. At least not since Harvard fell a spot in the *U.S. News* rankings. He thinks that just because he went to an Ivy League school, it makes him better than me. I went to a fine school. No, it wasn't Harvard. But at least my law school isn't my entire identity.

Like the secretary who recovered from cancer. She has all these cancer walk T-shirts and wears a cancer pin and a cancer hat and all she can ever talk about is her cancer. No one wants to hear about it. Find something else to talk about.

"We're kind of mocking the people who take bowling seriously, aren't we?" Harvard Guy asked. He majored in sociology, or some other pseudo-science invented by the Communists. It's only the first week. By the end, he'll be converted. We expose them to a little taste of this lifestyle—a secretary, the expensive lunches, the visits to partners' houses—and suddenly these bleeding-heart liberals forget their concerns that making money is evil and that the underclass doesn't deserve to be poor.

The Jerk filled out his team with That Foreign Dude and Some Other Foreign Dude. I didn't even realize we had two.

Harvard Guy was a formidable opponent. He had a higher score than anyone else, even the public school kids: 146. That's not bad. I guess sociology majors like to bowl.

I remember Harvard Guy's interview. We do the Harvard interviews in suites at an expensive hotel in Harvard Square. We bring our most attractive recruiters and some personable Harvard-educated associates from the firm, set ourselves up in a large "reception suite," put some brochures out, and stock the place with drinks and snacks. The hotel has these chocolate-covered pretzels all the students seem to like, and the attorneys like them too. We have a rule. The attorneys can eat one pretzel for every two they persuade the students to eat. We want the students to eat our food. We're paying for it.

Some of the kids are reluctant to eat anything. They're reluctant to ask for a drink. They're reluctant to take a brochure. That's a fine instinct, but it's exactly the opposite of what we want. We want them to feel like they owe us a summer of work in exchange for some pretzels and a bumper sticker with our logo on it. And a stress ball. And a cup of coffee. And our full-color glossy brochure featuring associates from around the country, being paid to smile for the camera and approve the quotes our marketing staff writes for them.

"I thought it would be all work and no play, but I've made lifelong friends at the firm and wouldn't trade the experience for anything!" —Kathy, Litigation Associate, Stanford Law School.

"It's exciting to see the names of the companies I'm working with in the newspaper every day, and even more exciting to know that I'm playing a part in their success!"—Simon, Corporate Associate, University of Chicago School of Law.

"I get to work with some of the smartest people I've ever met, in a state-of-the-art office building with amazing views of the city. It's everything I imagined it would be, and more!"—Victor, Bankruptcy Associate, Harvard Law School.

They love the exclamation points over in the marketing department! So we throw some chocolate-covered pretzels at the candidates, and we have our friendly associates—happy to have a day out of the office—engage them in some light conversation. The firm's great. The summer program is great. The desk chairs are great. The antidepressants are working perfectly, thanks for asking.

When we interviewed up in Boston during the 2004 playoffs, there was an afternoon game going on during the interviews, so I kept the TV on mute during the sessions and tried to sneak some glances at the screen whenever I was getting bored with what the students were saying. It doesn't really matter. Most of it comes down to the grades anyway, and at a place like Harvard the grades aren't even that important. As long as they don't say anything stupid. Or ask silly questions about work-life balance. That's always a red flag.

Bowling last night all came down to the last frame. I didn't care about the team competition. I just wanted to beat The Jerk. He got a strike and finished with a 110. I threw a gutter ball and finished with a 98. Oh, who cares, it's just a game. And it's just one night. I've got my extra seven square feet every day of the year.

#Posted by Anonymous at 10:32 AM

To: Anonymous Niece
From: Anonymous Lawyer
Date: Tuesday, May 16, 1:10 PM

Can you bowl? Like, if I flew you down here for a rematch, could we beat The Jerk and whatever ringer he'd hire to be his nephew? Can your brother bowl?

To: Anonymous Lawyer
From: Anonymous Niece
Date: Tuesday, May 16, 1:40 PM

I can't bowl. I'm sorry. I don't know if Mark can bowl. I'll ask him. Should I have him call you if he can?

To: Anonymous Niece
From: Anonymous Lawyer
Date: Tuesday, May 16, 1:48 PM

No. It's okay. I just hate losing, especially to The Jerk. He's ugly. Did you know that? The ridiculous hair is only part of it. He has a double chin. Wrinkles around his eyes. He's too tall. It's awkward to watch him walk. Like Frankenstein. We're not going bowling next year. You'll see when you work here. We're playing Wiffle ball instead. I'm good at Wiffle ball. I can beat Anonymous Son. In basketball too.

To: Anonymous Lawyer
From: Anonymous Niece
Date: Tuesday, May 16, 1:56 PM

He's eight. Of course you can beat him.

To: Anonymous Niece
From: Anonymous Lawyer
Date: Tuesday, May 16, 1:58 PM

Some eight-year-olds are very athletic.

Wednesday, May 17

I passed The New Chairman in the hall on the way back from the bathroom. The stress of three days on the job looked like it was getting to
him. He seemed fatter than usual. "You didn't stay too long at my picnic on Saturday," I said to him. "I was hoping you'd get a chance to see
the house."

"[The Jerk] wanted to get me up to speed on what's going on in
litigation. Before I even knew what was happening, we were at The
Palm talking about new avenues of business for the firm to start ex-
ploring in the Asian market. I'll see the house some other time. I heard
the event went well."

"It did. I'd love to engage in the Asian discussions as well, if you
think my input would be useful."

"I didn't know you knew anything about the Asian market,"
he said.

"Sure I do. My neighbor's Asian. Chinese, I think."

"I'll keep you posted. Look, let me know when you want me to
make a cameo appearance for the summers. I saw one of them walking
around the halls this morning. I think he may have Down syndrome.
His eyes were kind of far apart."

"I'll look into it."

"Get him on the cover of the pro bono booklet. We'll win some points with the advocacy groups."

"Sure. Sounds good."

"See if your neighbor needs a job in accounting too. That Chinese guy down there just gave his notice, and we need a replacement. It would be great to keep up the diversity score."

"He's an investment banker."

"Perfect. Check with him about the accounting job and let me know."

And then The New Chairman waddled down the hall on the way back to his office. I know what The Jerk is trying to do. He's trying to angle his way in there. He wants to be The New Chairman's confidant. The guy he goes to with his problems. Almost like a friend. He wants to be the one The New Chairman calls after a client storms out of a meeting, so they can go out for drinks and he can reassure the boss that he's still got it. I can't let that happen. That's got to be me at the table, telling him all we need is to cut the secretaries' health benefits and we'll be back on top. That they're fungible, and there's no reason to pay them above-market wages, and that I'd be happy to do the dirty work and tell them. He can keep his hands clean, he can stay above the fray. I'll go down into the trenches. As long as he takes care of me.

If I really want this, I've got to make myself available to The New Chairman at every turn. I've got to join the same country club, eat at the same restaurants, and maybe even find myself a house in the very same gated community, like it or not. I guess I've got to find us a Chinese accountant. I've got to get myself as close to The New Chairman as I can. But it won't be easy. The Jerk has a head start. After all, they left my party together.

I hate this part of the job. I'm terrible at politicking. I can't lie with a straight face, and I beat myself up over too many things. I trip a paralegal in the hall, and, sure, it's fun for about ten minutes, but then I feel guilty. The Jerk doesn't feel guilty. That's my weakness.

I'm getting out of here early today to play golf. I want to try out my new clubs. I bought them on Friday. Every other Friday I splurge on something. When I was a young associate I developed a payday ritual. Twenty dollars, on the way home, on something stupid that I don't need. Or more, if I want. It's less exciting now that we have direct deposit, but it's still nice to get that pay stub and see how much I make.

A couple of months ago I bought ten containers of a Silly Putty–copycat called Thinking Putty, a bunch of different colors, just for fun. I put it all together into one big ball, brought it into the office, and found that bouncing it off the window—like that Toby character on *The West Wing*—is a very effective stress reliever. I like to pretend it's an associate's head. Bounce. Bounce. When I was a kid the putty used to do a great job lifting the print off the comics section in the newspaper. It does a terrible job lifting the print off legal documents. Unfortunately. That would be quite a trick. Could get us out of some sticky situations.

#Posted by Anonymous at 3:35 PM

To: Anonymous Lawyer
From: Anonymous Niece
Date: Wednesday, May 17, 6:47 PM

The summer doesn't really have Down syndrome, does he? And can I ask you for a favor?

To: Anonymous Niece
From: Anonymous Lawyer
Date: Wednesday, May 17, 7:11 PM

He'd better have Down syndrome. Otherwise there's really no excuse for him. What do you need?

To: Anonymous Lawyer
From: Anonymous Niece
Date: Wednesday, May 17, 7:16 PM

It's no big deal. I don't want to tell Mom, but I was borrowing a friend's car this afternoon and I hit something. It wasn't a major accident or anything like that, I just scraped the side of the car against a wall by accident, while I was parking. Nobody is hurt, but the car has some paint damage and I need to fix it before I give my friend back her car. I don't want to ask Mom for the money because she'll get all freaked out like she always does. But I don't know what else to do. I'll pay it back, I promise.

To: Anonymous Niece
From: Anonymous Lawyer
Date: Wednesday, May 17, 7:25 PM

Yeah, sure, whatever. We can treat it like an advance on your salary next summer.

To: Anonymous Lawyer
From: Anonymous Niece
Date: Wednesday, May 17, 7:29 PM

No, I'll pay you back before then.

To: Anonymous Niece
From: Anonymous Lawyer
Date: Wednesday, May 17, 7:33 PM

I'm only lending it to you if you promise to work here next summer.
I'm looking out for your best interests. No stupid decisions with a
résumé like yours. If I'd gone to Yale I'd be chairman by now.

To: Anonymous Lawyer
From: Anonymous Niece
Date: Wednesday, May 17, 7:38 PM

For the last time, I can't commit to anything this far in advance. I love
you, but I don't want to keep having this conversation. Can't you just
lend me the money?

To: Anonymous Niece
From: Anonymous Lawyer
Date: Wednesday, May 17, 7:43 PM

How much is it?

To: Anonymous Lawyer
From: Anonymous Niece
Date: Wednesday, May 17, 7:46 PM

$400.

To: Anonymous Niece
From: Anonymous Lawyer
Date: Wednesday, May 17, 7:50 PM

All this is about $400? I thought you meant real money. Why don't you
have $400? Of course I can lend you $400. What's easiest? Should I
just wire it to you?

Thursday, May 18

On my way in this morning, I peeked inside a few people's offices. I do
this for fun sometimes. See what secrets they're hiding. Associates
think they're fooling us if they leave the door open and a jacket draped
over the chair, but they don't realize I know when they're here. The

magnetic key card that lets them in and out of the building is linked to a database on the intranet, password-protected for partners. We know where everyone is at any given moment. I know who's in the attorney lounge, who's in the bathroom, who's left the building, and who's sitting at his desk, just waiting for a partner like me to call him up with a new assignment.

Candyman's office. I opened some drawers. Just as I thought, he's got a half dozen of my secretary's Reese's Peanut Butter Cups in there. Not anymore. Let him wonder what's happened to them.

The One Who Missed Her Kid's Funeral. She thinks she'll be a partner someday—she thinks she's earned it—but she won't. She puts in the hours, but no one thinks she'll ever be able to land a client. She doesn't know she isn't on the partner track, but we'll tell her eventually, after we wring a few more 2800-billable-hour years from her. We string the associates along sometimes. It's good business. There's twelve Diet Coke cans that I can count from outside the door, probably a dozen more I don't see, and an open file drawer with a bottle of Glenfiddich sticking out. Ever since her kid's funeral, she's become a drinker at work. It's irresponsible. There's a take-out sushi container on a shelf in her bookcase with a bunch of old pieces of California Roll still in there. Disgusting.

She's got a romance novel in plain sight on her bookshelf. Next to the tax code. Fabio on the cover, one of those trashy books about tearing off people's clothes in the heat of passion. Quivering loins. No one should be reading about passion here. It's not healthy. Anonymous Wife reads romance novels. Sort of. She listens to them on tape. We argue about this. I tell her it's not really reading if it's an audiobook. She tells me to go to hell. Instead of reading books, she buys underwear. I swear she doesn't wear the same pair twice. It's okay, we can afford it, but what a waste. She buys new sets of clothes for the kids each summer when they go to camp too. They're going to grow up thinking that instead of doing laundry, it's completely normal to buy entirely new wardrobes every three months.

The Bombshell. Her office is on the other side of the floor, but I figured I'd check it out. If I wasn't married . . . who am I kidding, I wouldn't have a chance. She gets away with a lot because she's beautiful, or at least that's always been the conventional wisdom around here. It's what people want to think, but it's not true. She does good work. Her memos are solid. Her work is airtight. Her clothes are airtight too. Nothing left to the imagination. But it's all for effect. Every year someone tries, but no one gets near her. She knows exactly what she's doing when she flashes that smile. She knows how to get what she wants. There's a putter in the corner of her office. Anonymous Wife won't play golf with me. She won't even try. A pair of stilettos over by the lamp. Anonymous Wife never seems to get dressed up anymore. Not like she used to. A couple of client files open on the desk. No week-old sushi to be found. Excellent.

We had a client meeting a few weeks ago, and The Bombshell leaned across the table to grab a file at just the right time, and everyone's eyes were glued to her chest. Her blouse didn't leave very much to the imagination. The client's very happy with her work and requested she be at every meeting. I don't blame him. Moving on . . .

My secretary's workstation has bright red nail polish, a bottle of nail polish remover, and three kinds of lipstick, all right on the shelf. And a pill bottle. Ambien. That probably shouldn't be left out where the associates can get to it. You never know what they'll do when faced with the long hours and growing pressures of the job. I put it in her desk drawer. Secretaries can't have any secrets. They sit right out in the open, easier to scream at from your office, easier to grab when you're running down the hall. They're the eyes and ears of the firm, although most of them do that job about as well as Helen Keller.

The One Who Loves His Kids. He's one of the ones who tries to sneak out early on Fridays, 7:00 or so, to make it home for dinner. Yesterday I saw him take off at 3:30—I was on the way to the bathroom when he was heading out, and he clearly took pains to avoid me. He did a 180-degree turn in the middle of the hallway, with his briefcase and the bankruptcy code under his arm. Never said goodbye, so how was I supposed to know he'd left?

So I went in there at about 4:00 and stuck a Post-it note on his computer asking him to see me as soon as he's back. I put the date and time on it. "Check in as soon as you get this," I wrote. "I have some important work for you to take home tonight. Hope it won't be much trouble. Thx." It'll put the fear of God into him when he gets in today, just a bit. This is one tactic e-mail and voice mail have almost completely destroyed. Even if there was a way to change the date stamps on there, you know they're checking almost compulsively from wherever they are. But a Post-it note on the computer? It's perfect.

Finally, The Jerk. And his office that's seven square feet smaller than mine. Sometimes I measure again, just to double-check. He has a couch that looks like it came from Sears. It's a bad image for the firm. At least I know how to pick out a couch. There's a pair of pants hanging on the inside of the door. They have an expandable waistband. I love it. He can't even buy normal pants anymore. They're cheap too. I opened his closet. There's a stack of copies of *The American Lawyer.* It's all the same issue. He was featured in a blurb a few years ago, about a case he was working on. He bought five hundred reprints. He gives them out to everyone he meets. I wish I had a match. I'd light the whole stack on fire. I suppose he'd just order more. Wouldn't really solve anything.

#Posted by Anonymous at 9:22 AM

To: Anonymous Lawyer
From: Anonymous Niece
Date: Thursday, May 18, 11:41 AM

Thanks for bailing me out of the car situation last night. I'm sorry I was a little freaked out about it. I was just worried. I got it fixed this morning, good as new.

To: Anonymous Niece
From: Anonymous Lawyer
Date: Thursday, May 18, 11:52 AM

Fine, great, anything else?

To: Anonymous Lawyer
From: Anonymous Niece
Date: Thursday, May 18, 11:59 AM

Not really. The Tax Guy's kid sent me another e-mail. He asked if there are garbage cans in the dorm rooms, and whether he'd be allowed to burn incense. Weird kid.

To: Anonymous Niece

From: Anonymous Lawyer

Date: Thursday, May 18, 12:05 PM

Write back to him quickly. His dad's a real pain and I don't want him to have any reason to get upset with me. I could try and set the two of you up next time you visit, if you want.

To: Anonymous Lawyer

From: Anonymous Niece

Date: Thursday, May 18, 12:13 PM

No thanks.

To: Anonymous Niece

From: Anonymous Lawyer

Date: Thursday, May 18, 12:17 PM

Think about it. I could win some real points here if I get his son a girl-friend. I imagine he doesn't have too much success on his own. We could consider it payback for the money if you want.

To: Anonymous Lawyer

From: Anonymous Niece

Date: Thursday, May 18, 12:20 PM

That's an interesting thought. Absolutely not. I need to get to class now.

Thursday, May 18

There's an associate in the office today who has the flu, or the avian flu, or something pretty terrible. She spent the morning coughing loudly enough you can hear her down the hall. I've told her twice now to try and be a little more considerate. She asked if she should go home. I told her that clearly wasn't an option given her workload, but she should definitely try and cut down on the coughing. That might even make it easier for her to get the work done.

At lunch she called me up and said she was out with some summer associates but she was really feeling terrible and she wanted to go "work from home." I know that scheme and I told her it's not going to work and she really needed to come back to the office. And, again, she's coughing, even after I told her not to. She's coughing out of spite because I wouldn't let her go home, obviously. And it's a game I just don't want to play today, with a deadline on a response brief and a bunch of other clients with time-sensitive work.

I saw her trying to sneak out at about 2:00—she said she was just going to the bathroom to throw up, but I didn't believe her. I asked her how far she'd gotten on that piece of research she's working on. She said she hadn't finished yet, so I told her to turn back around and finish it before she leaves, and to please use the service elevator when she finally does leave because I don't need her germs infecting everyone else. We're going to have to clean her office and get rid of whatever she's got, because she hasn't been smart enough to keep herself healthy at crunch time. They need to take care of themselves so they don't get sick, because you're not really allowed to get sick here. I'm making a note to play around at the end of the year with her billable-hour reports so she doesn't get a full bonus, as payback for this whole "sick" thing. I'm sick too. Sick of her.

#Posted by Anonymous at 2:15 PM

Friday, May 19

The New Chairman just e-mailed an idiotic memo to the entire firm. He's putting The Jerk in charge of an "expenditures committee," to reevaluate some of our practices. Until further notice the Friday afternoon happy hour in the conference room is canceled, and the birthday celebrations will all be consolidated into a once-a-month event.

Stupid. So we save maybe twenty thousand dollars over the course of a year. It's peanuts. I'd rather toss a summer off the roof, and then we'd save twice that—thirty thousand in salary and ten more in lunches and incidentals. I'm sure The Suck-Up would be more than willing to take one for the team. Or one of the Foreign Dudes. By the time the news gets back to their families in Pakistan or Cuba or wherever they're from, it won't be our problem anymore.

I don't care about the happy hour, and it's certainly not like anyone here needs more cake, but it's completely shortsighted. Associates notice these things. They affect morale. There's little enough for them to be excited about as it is—getting rid of the perks doesn't help.

And why is The Jerk getting put in charge of something when I'm not? This is what I was worried about. You work for all of these years with your eyes on that prize and now I can see it starting to slip away. Anything can happen in the next couple of decades. The Jerk can pull ahead, I can pull ahead, who knows. But every step matters. And he's been taking too many steps.

I've spent some time plotting his downfall. Nothing concrete, but in idle moments I've thought about what could happen. There's a folder in my middle drawer where I collect the ideas. He could get poisoned by a rogue bagel in the attorney lounge. Someone could tamper with the elevator controls and he could fall down the empty shaft, like that woman partner on *L.A. Law.* (Women partners. That's still kind of funny to type.) The designated emergency captain on his floor could misuse the cardiac paddles and shock The Jerk to death. An angry associate could strangle him. I could use my influence with the summer associates to get one to strangle him for me. I could concentrate throughout the interview process on finding a law student just crazy enough to be willing to strangle a partner. I could place an ad in the newspaper for someone willing to pose as a law student, for me to hire as a summer associate, who'd be crazy enough to strangle a partner. I'm not serious about any of these things, of course. But I've thought them through. It never hurts to be prepared.

I bill the time I think about these sorts of things. I call it "research." The clients never question it. "Research" is code for surfing the Internet, "drafting" is code for eating in your office, "misc. legal forms" is code for ordering gifts online, and "preparing for meeting" is code for taking a crap. Everyone knows. It's no big deal.

It's the uncertainty of my future that gets me. I can't be sure what's going on between The New Chairman and The Jerk, where the alliances are, who's in the best position. It's kind of like *Survivor* that way. It's like *Survivor* combined with *Big Brother*. With a little bit of *Deal or No Deal* thrown in—you never know when you're in the best position to cut and run. I admit it—I watch more television than I've let on. You need something to do when you get home, and I don't want to talk to my wife. It was her idea to get TiVo. That's what did me in. Before TiVo I watched the Dodgers and Ted Koppel and read the newspaper. Now I watch *America's Next Top Model* and feel the brain cells melting away. *The West Wing* was good when Aaron Sorkin was writing it. Then it became a disaster.

#Posted by Anonymous at 10:33 AM

Friday, May 19

I sent an e-mail this morning offering to take two summer associates out for lunch today, first two to reply. Lunch is big here. I can't overstate it. We allow a $50/person budget and let them go to lunch at least a couple of times a week, as long as they can find an associate or partner to take them. The associates benefit from this. All they need to do is grab some summers and they get a free $50 lunch. So every morning there's a couple dozen mass e-mails that circulate. "Associate looking for 2 summers who want Italian for lunch at 12:30." "Partner looking for a summer interested in Real Estate who wants sushi at 1." The summers have to figure out when to pounce. You never want to be left without a lunch, but you also don't want to say yes to the midrange Chinese buffet when twenty minutes later there's going to be a topflight sushi experience there for the taking.

By the end of the season there are always some summers complaining that $50/person isn't enough. You each get an appetizer, and maybe a couple of additional shared ones for the table, an entrée, a couple of iced teas, and you're already at $35 at most of these places. Add on dessert and cappuccino, and with tax and tip you start to come close. There are firms with a lower limit than $50. I've heard associates say they don't know how people can possibly manage lunch on $40/ person. Those are the ones we know are never, ever leaving the firm.

I like to make sure I take each summer to lunch at least once. This way I get a better sense of which kids were mistakes and should be assigned document review for a few years until they get disgusted and leave, and which ones may actually be useful enough to do real work. The first two to reply to my e-mail were The Musician and, unfortunately, The Suck-Up. The rest are probably already booked. The associates get to them early. I hear there's an eighteen-person lunch at a Brazilian churrascaria today. Nine associates, nine summers. Sounds pretty dreadful to me, but I guess some of them want to fill their monthly social-interaction quota in one afternoon.

I suggested we get steak at 11:30 in the morning. It makes me feel important, even though it's nauseating. They'll agree to it, I'm sure. For a $50 lunch, they'll agree to anything.

We had a student last summer who kept kosher. Or at least that's what she said. But anytime she got offered lunch at someplace exceptional, suddenly she wasn't kosher anymore. You asked her to go to a cheap Indian place down the street, oh, she can't, she's kosher. But if you wanted to drive up the coast for a long lunch at Nobu in Malibu, perfect, she'd eat anything. She'd eat raw shrimp wrapped in bacon with a glass of milk, off the naked stomach of a Palestinian, on Yom Kippur, if you told her it was expensive.

It's not just the cost. The summers want to be exactly like us. If they see a partner doing something, they do it too. I took some summers out for Chinese food last summer and started mindlessly folding my chopstick wrapper, just fidgeting. Suddenly I notice they're all folding their wrappers just the same, as if I'm doing it "the partner way."

They'll believe anything I say. I tell them it's going to rain, on a day without a cloud in the sky, and they reach for their umbrellas. I tell them I'd prefer they not take the elevator, and they gladly walk down twenty flights of stairs. I could tell them I'm pregnant, and next week they'd be throwing me a baby shower. Not to overstate it, but in a lot of ways I know how Jesus felt.

The Suck-Up must have had nine glasses of water. They kept refilling it. He was sweating it all out though. He was frighteningly nervous. Quaking in my presence. It's great. At one point, he knocked over the bread basket. He kept apologizing for it, throughout the meal. He stared at the forks in front of him, not sure which to use. As if I care which fork he uses. Well, it's a category on the evaluation form, so I do care. But still, he needs to commit. The fact that he drinks so much water is going to hurt his career. We can't have an associate who keeps going to the bathroom. That's billable time he's wasting. It's ridiculous.

When I took the bar exam, there were people who hooked themselves up to catheters so they wouldn't lose valuable time with bathroom trips. That's smart planning. Those are the kind of associates we need.

I haven't figured out The Musician yet. He said it was a relief to go to a steakhouse, because it was the only place he's been all week that wasn't serving miso-glazed salmon. He said he's noticed the more expensive the restaurants get, the more any claim of ethnic food converges into some sort of global fusion cuisine with the same fancy in-gredients. That the expensive Chinese food is the same as the expen-sive Greek food, and miso-glazed salmon is everywhere. Why is he thinking so much about the food?

He ordered the baby lettuce to start, and then went into what sounded like another routine he's been practicing about how the more expensive the restaurant, the younger the food, with baby lamb chops, baby octopus, baby scallops, baby asparagus, baby corn, baby back ribs, and that it seems like the price point goes down ten dollars for every ingredient that's been out of the womb for more than a week.

I don't need these kids trying to develop shtick out of the summer experience. I can't stand The Suck-Up, but I get more nervous about The Musician. He thinks too much. The music thing gets me worried. And at lunch he mentioned he likes to read too. Now I KNOW we shouldn't have hired him.

See, you're allowed one thing. Whether that's reading, hanging out with the friends you still have, or sleeping, there's time to balance the life of an associate with one outside interest. ONLY one. If you like to read, or if you like to go to the movies, or if you like to spend a bit of time with your family, we tolerate that. We're not evil. We understand. You need something. But you have more than one interest and we start to question your commitment to doing what it takes to thrive at a place like this. At a lesser firm, sure, you can spend time with your kids, and maybe also put together an occasional jigsaw puzzle. But here you have to prioritize.

#Posted by Anonymous at 3:19 PM

To: Anonymous Niece
From: Anonymous Lawyer
Date: Friday, May 19, 4:50 PM

Sorry about yesterday. I don't think you and The Tax Guy's son would
be a good fit. I'm just trying to make sure I have as much leverage with
the other partners as I can get. I need them to back me instead of The
Jerk in case it comes down to a power struggle someday.

To: Anonymous Lawyer
From: Anonymous Niece
Date: Friday, May 19, 5:13 PM

It's okay. I know you were only trying to help. I sent your blog address
to some more friends yesterday. They really like it. One of them wrote
back to me that it's making him rethink law school.

To: Anonymous Niece
From: Anonymous Lawyer
Date: Friday, May 19, 5:26 PM

If this is making someone rethink law school, he shouldn't be going in
the first place. Is there any way for me to figure out how many people
are actually reading this thing and what they think? Or would that com-
promise my anonymity?

To: Anonymous Lawyer
From: Anonymous Niece
Date: Friday, May 19, 5:33 PM

Well, you've already got the anonymous e-mail address. You could set
up a link in the sidebar so people could e-mail you. And you could in-
stall a counter to see how many people are reading the page. You
could enable comments, but I'm not sure you really want that. You'd
probably have to monitor it to make sure no one figures out your identity and posts it.

To: Anonymous Niece
From: Anonymous Lawyer
Date: Friday, May 19, 5:39 PM

Yes, that would be a problem. Let me think about it this weekend and
let you know. Your grandparents are paying a visit. I'll tell Dad I heard
you need money. He likes to take care of his grandkids. He'll send you
something, I'm sure.

To: Anonymous Lawyer
From: Anonymous Niece
Date: Friday, May 19, 5:48 PM

I'm okay. I don't need his money. Of course if he wants to send me
something that's great. But I'm not starving here, I swear.

To: Anonymous Niece
From: Anonymous Lawyer
Date: Friday, May 19, 5:55 PM

A Stanford graduate who's going to Yale Law School shouldn't be worrying about money. He'll send you something, don't worry. I'll take care of it.

Saturday, May 20

My parents are in town for the weekend, which is why I'm in the office on a Saturday morning. Not for me. For Dad.

He's here wandering the halls, looking for dust that the cleaning staff missed. He loves when he visits and I let him come to work with me. He misses this. I mean, it was never this intense for him, but he misses the atmosphere. He misses having a secretary. He misses having a reason to wake up in the morning, somewhere to go, someone to talk to. So I bring him here, let him run free, flip through stacks of paper, help me out on a case I don't really need his help on, make him feel marginally useful. I know he appreciates it.

He's holding court down the hall, with a few associates stuck wasting their weekends in the office, telling some stories about what it was like back in the day. "Before computers, we had to type out every contract by hand. . . ." Right, Dad, it was you at the typewriter, not some woman making four dollars a week and having to cope with your partner's unwanted advances at the Christmas party. Dad is a good guy. His partner was a creep. Dad tolerated him for way too long, never quite getting up the courage to confront him about the shoddy work he was doing and the way he treated everyone beneath him. They started the firm together right after law school. But his partner ruined the practice, drove it into the ground. They haven't spoken in years. So I'll indulge Dad's stories and his revisionist history. He doesn't understand the lifestyle today, the added pressures, the around-the-clock nature of the business. He's still stuck in the 1960s.

I have to admit he was a better father than I am. Mom says he was always at work, but that's not how I remember it. I remember him home, more often than not. At my birthday parties, baseball games, law school graduation. I don't even remember if I really knew what Dad did until I got to high school. It was just his job, not his life. Meanwhile, Anonymous Son knows the names of my top ten clients and how many hours I've billed each of them in the past fiscal year, and Anonymous Daughter knows how many times those clients have been cited for violations under OSHA. It's not as easy as it was before e-mail, before globalization, before this became more than a job. Dad didn't have to worry about a seven-figure mortgage, $25,000 private school tuitions, $180/person lunches in the backyard....

It's amazing what you can get for $180/person. Anonymous Wife promised a "delicious home-cooked meal." Only she isn't the one doing the cooking. These caterers even bring a picnic table. So the lawn furniture that I spent three thousand dollars on can remain in the garage, barely touched. Anonymous Wife can sit there painting her toenails, and we still get to eat.

I went to law school to make Dad proud of me. Or at least that's what I tell myself. Senior year of college I didn't have a plan. I didn't know what was next, and the thought of going out in the world and finding a job—of being an adult—was too frightening to seriously contemplate. Going to law school seemed easy. Dad pulled some strings and helped get me into Michigan. It made him happy, and it gave me three more years to figure out what I wanted to do with my life. He was more than willing to write the checks, so I was more than willing to spend three more years being a student. I knew how to be a student.

Being a student is easy. I have no sympathy for the ones who complain about law school. I'd give anything to be back in school. I didn't appreciate it at the time. I slept my way through it, doing enough work to get by but not much beyond that. It didn't feel like it mattered. I wasn't really going to be a lawyer. Who cared about the rules of evidence or the Uniform Commercial Code?

I worked for Dad the summer after the first year, and it wasn't horrible. I'd been out in California on vacation once and liked the weather, so when I got back to school I sent out résumés to some firms out here, did the interviews, and somehow ended up right where I am. The backup plan became the only plan. And it's too late to look back. It was good enough for Dad—and Dad's lived a fine life—so why shouldn't it be good enough for me?

My nephew is a sophomore in college. I called him on his birthday a couple of weeks ago to wish him well and came away feeling like college is turning him into a socialist. He thinks making money is wrong unless you do something good with it. He said I'm selfish. If he was trying to get me to offer to pay his tuition, it didn't work.

He sees his friends who are seniors start to get jobs, as investment bankers or management consultants, or decide to go to law school, and he said he's sad for them because they're going to waste their abilities and not do any good for the world. I think he has a lot of growing up to do. It's not all about doing good. Not everyone can do good. Some of us like having nice things. Some of us like being able to pay our bills.

He wants to paint. Not everyone who wants to paint can make a living painting. He doesn't understand that the world doesn't always let you do what you want to do. There are sacrifices and trade offs. You can't always follow your heart. He brought some of his paintings to Easter dinner last month. I don't know anything about art, but I know I didn't like them. They're terrible. He's wasting his energy. Too many kids are stupid these days. They have too many options. Too many choices. They think they can have ridiculous dreams and make them come true. How many people are making a living as painters? Five? Six? And how many of them really had the chance to be something better? I understand going for it if you don't have anything else you can do. But if you're smart enough to get a real job, and make some real money, you're just being an idiot not to secure your future. How do painters support a family? How do they afford health insurance? How do you ever know if your art is good enough? We win a case, I'm satisfied. The client's happy, I know I've done a good job. How does an artist know? I just want what's best for him.

It's not all about the money, but the money is society's way of saying that something's important. Not everyone can do what I do. Especially without losing his humanity. I occasionally kick the paralegals in the shins, we all do—it doesn't make me a bad person. I remembered my nephew's birthday. So how bad can I be? At least his sister's going to law school. She's the star of the family. She'll make it all worth it.

I see Dad now and I start to wonder if I'll end up like him, wandering the halls in search of meaning. But there's no time to ponder the meaning of life when I'm stuck here in Conference Room 23C watching the paralegals robotically place the "sign here" stickers on sheet after sheet of paper. I hope 3M charges a lot for these stickers, because they're invaluable. I'm typing this post, pretending to do work while Candyman, forced to skip his weekend, paces the room waiting for the paralegals to reprint sheet 74, screaming at them to get this done faster. I'm just babysitting.

This is what it's come to. I'm babysitting an associate and the paralegals, in a conference room I know better than my living room. I know where the cell phone reception is strongest, I know which chairs wobble, I know which cabinet the extra legal pads are in. Not that I'd ever get a new legal pad for myself. The paralegals bring them to me. That's their job. I know which window to look out if I want to see the homeless people, and I know which window to look out if I want to imagine a world where the homeless people don't exist. I like the conference room. Maybe I need one at home. For the kids to do their homework, for Anonymous Wife to hide the cigarettes I know she sneaks every couple of days, and for Dad to act out his own chairman-of-the-firm fantasies whenever he comes to visit.

Or maybe I just need a $180/person lunch, complete with its own picnic table. Can't possibly be worth it, but can't be worse than if Anonymous Wife cooked it herself, I suppose. Wouldn't really know. Maybe she'd be Wolfgang Puck if she tried.

#Posted by Anonymous at 11:45 AM

Sunday, May 21

I took my family to the Dodgers game this afternoon. The Dodgers lost, of course. There was a client using the firm's seats, so I had to buy regular tickets. I'd forgotten how far away the field seems when you're in regular seats, but it was a chance to remind myself how the ordinary people live. It's amazing how fat so many people have let themselves get.

We were on our way out, in the seventh inning, and I noticed one of the firm's secretaries and her family a little ways away, down the concourse, coming in our direction. I tried to avoid eye contact, and hoped she'd pass by without noticing me, but of course she noticed me and it was terribly awkward. I had to explain to her that the firm's seats were being used, and that I wouldn't normally be sitting in the upper deck but it was a last-minute thing, and then I had to introduce her to my parents and my kids, and it was a mess. I don't need her meeting my family. I don't need to meet her husband, I don't need to meet her son. I don't need them spending the car ride home talking about me, and about the firm, and now she's going to tell the other secretaries that my mom was so friendly, and how did she ever end up with a son like me, and about how Anonymous Daughter has a ring through her belly button—which was not something I consented to, but which Anonymous Wife let her go and do anyway. My wife said, "It's better than drugs." Well, yes, it's better than drugs, but skydiving is better than drugs and we don't let our kids do that either.

It's not even as if my daughter looks good with the belly button ring. She could lose twenty pounds. They say she's at the age when girls develop eating disorders. Maybe that's what she needs—get rid of some of the excess weight.

So it was a very uncomfortable thirty seconds and I felt like the secretary was waiting for me to say something nice about her in front of her husband but all I know about her is that she seems to have very good balance carrying two cups of coffee and a danish down the hall, and I didn't think that was a compliment worth saying in front of her family.

Plus, now she knows I own a pair of tennis shoes, and that's very sticky because it's not good for them to see us as normal people and the more we come down to their level the more difficult it is to maintain the hierarchy and treat them the way the secretaries need to be treated. It's very complicated. I should have just pretended I didn't see her and that it wasn't really me. A lot of people look like me. Not the fat people, but some of the people at the game could pass for me. Oh well, no use obsessing over it now.

#Posted by Anonymous at 7:55 PM

To: Anonymous Niece
From: Anonymous Lawyer
Date: Sunday, May 21, 9:18 PM

Okay. Are you at your computer? Let's do the e-mail address thing. I want to see what people think of what I've been writing.

To: Anonymous Lawyer
From: Anonymous Niece
Date: Sunday, May 21, 9:22 PM

Yeah, I'm here. Just give me your username and password and I'll post the address in the sidebar. Then you can post something saying it's there, and maybe you'll get a couple of e-mails from whoever's reading. On a Sunday night I'm not sure you'll get much of a reaction. Maybe in the morning.

Sunday, May 21

Small announcement. I've got an anonymous e-mail address now. I'm curious if anyone's reading this blog. So if anyone's out there, how about this: send me some ideas about how to torture my associates. Thanks.

#Posted by Anonymous at 9:58 PM

———————————

To: Anonymous Lawyer
From: David Merrigan
Date: Sunday, May 21, 10:02 PM

Here's what we do at my firm. Tell them you are worried that the computer is not correct and you want them to go through each client file and make a written list of client addresses, opposing counsel, statutes, etc.

   I like to watch the new employees' eyes glaze over when they realize just how many files they are going to have to go through by hand, and then I tell them we do this monthly. Great fun.

To: Anonymous Lawyer
From: Joseph M. Gordon
Date: Sunday, May 21, 10:07 PM

Torture? Have them find and summarize all the reported cases under the new Bankruptcy Code. Then send them to me. I need them!

To: Anonymous Lawyer

From: Rachel C. Applebaum

Date: Sunday, May 21, 10:19 PM

I've worked in the legal field for over twenty-five years and, son, the answer for how to torture your associates is simple. Assign them to work for a woman. Ha!

To: Anonymous Lawyer

From: Jonathan T. Brandt

Date: Sunday, May 21, 10:42 PM

There's no way you can really be who you say you are, but if you're looking for torture, once when I was a young associate, a partner at the firm had me sleep on the floor of his office "in case he needed me in the middle of the night."

And, even better: An unattractive, overweight, older male partner friend of mine used to call young female associates that he needed to fire into his office and ask them why there were "rumors all over the firm that he and she were having an affair." The effect was devastating. Of course, there were no real rumors, he just wanted to embarrass them into quitting. The fact that the entire office would believe that a cute young girl was having an affair with a very fat, very old guy was enough to get that letter of resignation out of her by noon. Always worked. You think I'm making this up, but I'm not.

To: Anonymous Lawyer
From: Pam Linberg
Date: Sunday, May 21, 11:02 PM

Have them unstaple and restaple all your documents because you want the staples to be perfectly straight and parallel to the margin. Then tell them you've changed your mind and need all the staples at a 45-degree angle. Then tell them they're in big trouble for wasting staples.

To: Anonymous Lawyer
From: Joe McReynolds
Date: Sunday, May 21, 11:36 PM

I'm at a firm in Australia. We had a junior start with us about a month ago. Total twat, on his high horse the entire time. After he left one night we superglued his phone to the cradle. By the next morning it had set rock-hard! Countless hours of fun ringing his phone and watching him race off to IT to get their help. Luckily we'd let them in on the joke, which meant there were no available phones for him to use!

   He killed himself two days later.

To: Anonymous Lawyer
From: J. Daniel Hull
Date: Sunday, May 21, 11:57 PM

Torture? Make them read your blog, jackass.

To: Anonymous Niece
From: Anonymous Lawyer
Date: Monday, May 22, 12:08 AM

Jesus. That post has been up for half an hour and I've gotten forty-three e-mails to the anonymous account you set up. Lawyers at firms I've heard of, lawyers at firms I haven't, a couple of Department of Justice guys, some law students, and someone with the e-mail address sexyfatgirl@hotmail.com, which besides being an impossibility is a terribly unprofessional e-mail address. If forty-three people e-mailed me in half an hour, on a Sunday night, lots of people must be reading this. I don't know if this is a good thing. It worries me just a bit.

To: Anonymous Lawyer
From: Anonymous Niece
Date: Monday, May 22, 12:18 AM

Why are you worried?? This is terrific—it's exactly what you wanted, isn't it? You're getting an audience. I told some people, they told some people, things spread. Calm down. If you weren't worried about getting caught before, there's no reason to worry now. You didn't do anything new except put up an e-mail address.

To: Anonymous Niece
From: Anonymous Lawyer
Date: Monday, May 22, 12:29 AM

I know, I know. I should be happy. Look, can you go back in and change all the Dodgers references to the Tigers? Put me back in Michigan. If there's anything else that gives away the ocean view, make it a view of a warehouse instead. That should throw people off. Just in case.

To: Anonymous Lawyer
From: Anonymous Niece
Date: Monday, May 22, 12:44 AM

You can't do that now, all of a sudden. Anyone who's been reading carefully will notice the changes and then they'll know you have something to hide. You think that if the Dodgers suddenly become the Tigers, no one will notice? And then they're going to think, "Oh, he must not want us to know he's in Los Angeles, so that's where he must be." You have no reason to be worried. After all, how many blogs were you reading before you started yours? You really think someone at the firm is reading this?

To: Anonymous Niece
From: Anonymous Lawyer
Date: Monday, May 22, 12:52 AM

You're right. I know. Nothing to worry about. Just the instant shock of the e-mails, that's all. I'm just going to post something quick and then I'll go to sleep and deal with it in the morning.

Monday, May 22

A lot of good suggestions so far. I have to admit I didn't realize so many people were reading. Some of you sent me great ideas. Someone suggested I shoot an associate as a warning signal to the rest of them. Someone else suggested I make an associate sleep with me. I think I know which one I'd choose. Someone else suggested I make them all shave their heads. We come close sometimes, we really do.

I did a performance review last year. I mentioned to one associate that his beard made him look a bit sloppy and it wasn't the image we were trying to convey to the world. In truth, I didn't care about his beard. But I always like to include something unpredictable in the reviews just to see how much power I really have. Sure enough, the next day he showed up clean-shaven—for the first time, he said, since law school. Turned out he wasn't a handsome man. Too bad. We made him grow it back. Sometimes even partners make mistakes.

We had a pregnant associate, and I joked that it would be a boon to her career if she named the kid after the firm. Sure enough, his middle name. It's a terrible name too. His initials spell out an awful word. She should have realized it. Lack of attention to detail. That's a career-killer.

We do all sorts of things to the associates to exert our power, sometimes for good reasons and sometimes just because we feel like it. I asked the IT department to remove solitaire from the computers on the network, because I went to talk to an associate who was supposed to be working on a project for me, and it was obvious what he was doing, and what he continued to do even as I was talking to him. As if I can't tell because I wasn't facing the screen. I know what it looks like. I've guest-lectured in law school classes before. Young people. We've given them too many toys. They can't focus on a task. They sit there facing the screen for hours, playing Freecell.

We should ban the whole Internet. Let them find the cases in books, like we did. Spending six hours in the library is character-building. Spending six hours playing solitaire is lazy, mind-numbing, and insulting to the partnership that pays them. I spread around the news about which associate was to blame for solitaire being removed. It got him ostracized by his colleagues, and he quit six months later. Apparently he's working for a public-interest organization now. They probably don't even have computers there. He couldn't get a job at another firm. Not after I had him blackballed.

I also wish I could ban this game that an associate showed me a couple of weeks ago called Snood. It's a computer game where they sit there and click on symbols for hours at a time to get them to disappear. I wish I could click on the associates who are wasting company resources playing it and get them to disappear too.

I'd also like to ban associates from putting pictures of their families on their desks. I've thought about this for a while. It's harder to yell at someone when you're looking at a picture of his kids. I'd like to ban tuna fish sandwiches. They make the hallway smell. I'd like to ban shoes that click when people walk down the hall. I have a whole list.

Chewing gum. Personal phone calls from the office phones. Whistling in the halls. Double-dipping dumplings into the dumpling sauce at firm receptions. It happens a lot. I notice it. Kettle corn. It's deceptive. You expect salty and you get sweet. I hate that. Secret Santa. Secretaries' Day. The chair massage guy. Talking about your elderly parents and which nursing home you're going to put them in. Debating the merits of the 401K program. It's not that hard. Just pick a fund. Stop talking about it. Lamenting the fact that you're working on Easter. The list goes on. And on.

In any case, I should probably be sleeping. Big day tomorrow. I just wanted to thank you all for the suggestions.

#Posted by Anonymous at 1:32 AM

To: Anonymous Lawyer
From: Emily Mann
Date: Monday, May 22, 2:22 AM

One of the IT guys at my company is rabid about the "no personal use of company computers" policy. To drive home the point, he searched through everyone's hard drives and e-mail inboxes, finding all sorts of personal photos (e.g., a photo of the CFO in his pajamas playing with his dog) and people's audio files. This contraband material formed the basis of a slide show projected at last year's holiday party. You should try it.

To: Anonymous Lawyer

From: Vanessa M. Zimmer

Date: Monday, May 22, 6:30 AM

Well, this may not be particularly creative, but it's a true story. Wait until
an associate has been staying late the whole week and is forced to
come in on a weekend. Pop by his office and ask if, when he has time,
he would mind cleaning the old and moldy food out of the fridge.
Always fun.

———————————

Monday, May 22

An associate e-mailed me at four in the morning and told me to call
her. Good thing, as a partner, I'm allowed to turn my BlackBerry off
while I'm sleeping. Turns out she wanted to tell me she's leaving. I told
her that was probably a good idea, because she was never going to
make partner. As I said it, I realized that had she been kidding—"Oh, I
was just teasing. I'd never leave you"—I'd have been in a bad spot. But
luckily she was serious. So off she goes. She and her pathetic number
of billable hours, her grating personality, and her obsession with pro
bono work.

I don't know why people come to large firms and then expect to be
given the freedom to work on cases we don't get paid for. If you want
to make the law firm salary, and live the law firm life, you should have
to do the law firm work. People shouldn't bristle when I say that. There
are lots of great organizations out there that do pro bono work, and if
that's what someone wants to do, they should work there. If you do
pro bono work from here, all you're doing is taking jobs from people

who really want to do pro bono work full-time, and you're costing the firm money. A little bit here and there is fine—when you're young, to get it out of your system, or when you're old, to help justify your seven-figure salary. But in between, I'm sorry. Office workers don't use company time and company resources to help poor people. You do it on your own time.

This whole culture of pro bono work at large firms—this fetishization, almost—is bizarre to me. If that's the kind of work you want to do, you're free to go do it—but leave my paper clips alone. Every paper clip you take and give to the battered women's legal defense association, or whatever it's called, is another three seconds your colleagues have to work to keep the firm's profitability at the same level. It sounds heartless, but we're a business. We give lots of money to charity. Heck, we're doing an auction tonight to raise money for the American Refugee Committee. We don't need to give them time too.

#Posted by Anonymous at 10:03 AM

To: Anonymous Lawyer
From: Irwin Magevney
Date: Monday, May 22, 10:27 AM

No torture idea from me, just a question about your most recent post. "Her pathetic number of billable hours." How many is that at a firm like yours?

Monday, May 22

I just got an e-mail from a reader who wants to know how many bill-able hours the pathetic associate had billed. 1600. Which is obviously ridiculous. Everyone here knows you won't make partner unless you're recording at least 2200 a year.

To bill 2200 hours, you have to be in the office a lot more than that, because you can be SuperLawyer and not bill every hour you're here. We have internal meetings that aren't billable. We have nonbill-able training sessions. Recruiting activities. Lunches. Dinners. Break-fasts. Office maintenance. Bathroom and e-mail. Masturbating. People do it. They close their doors, pull out a magazine. We've caught people. We caught two summer associates having sex in the bathroom once. I guess that's not the same thing. But people have to fulfill all of their needs here, because they're never home. People store entire wardrobes here. I have seven pairs of shoes in my office. They build up. You never know when you're going to need to go right from the office to the golf course, on a hike, to the gym, to court, to a casual dinner, to a fancy dinner, or horseback riding. Is that seven? That's seven. Good.

My secretary takes care of my billing for me. There's an online sys-tem I haven't bothered to figure out how to use. An hour on matter #97034, a quarter hour on the phone with client #43651, two hours writing a memo for #71273. All day you keep a running tally. Appar-ently some people don't like doing this. I don't see what the big deal is.

People cheat, of course. They don't cheat maliciously, at least not in most cases. The consequences are too high if you're caught, either by a colleague or by the client. But a half hour becomes an hour, and that break to read some movie reviews for a movie you'll never get the chance to see suddenly ends up absorbed into the hour you spent doing work. The hour at two in the morning becomes two hours, just to penalize the client, the hour on vacation becomes three hours, and the hour spent making a paper clip chain with the client's file open on your desk—well, you were thinking about the client, so that counts. And the hour you spent on the flight to client #43651, doing work for client #43652, gets billed to both of them. Because why shouldn't it? You have to take the hours where you can get them. I get billed out to clients at six hundred and seventy-five dollars an hour. That's a lot of money. This blog post is costing a client a couple hundred dollars. I take hundred-dollar shits in the bathroom. I think I feel another one coming on.

#Posted by Anonymous at 10:54 AM

To: Anonymous Niece

From: Anonymous Lawyer

Date: Monday, May 22, 1:20 PM

Nothing damaging has come through. Just a lot of e-mails from people with crazy (but useful!) ideas about how to torture my associates. Over a hundred so far. I don't have to write back to these people, do I?

To: Anonymous Lawyer

From: Anonymous Niece

Date: Monday, May 22, 1:42 PM

They'd probably appreciate it if you did, but they know you're a busy lawyer, so I think it's okay.

To: Anonymous Niece
From: Anonymous Lawyer
Date: Monday, May 22, 1:55 PM

Great.

Tuesday, May 23

The Musician is going to court with me this afternoon. It's an interme-
diate step in a bankruptcy case. Nothing of any great importance. He
won't learn much, except how much sitting around there is when
you go to court, how quickly I can do the *Los Angeles Times* crossword
puzzle, and how good I look in my suit. But I like to bring an associate
with me to do the menial work of the day like park my car, carry
around my briefcase, and open doors.

I knocked on The Musician's office door to let him know he was
coming. I told him to put on a suit. He looked at me funny.

"You have a suit in your office, right?"

"Uh . . ."

"You make any friends yet? Borrow a suit. Tell them you're getting
to do an oral argument. They'll crap their pants." Associates don't usually get to do oral arguments until they're eligible for AARP.

A lot of people come to a place like this thinking they'll get to
argue in court. I blame television for this misconception. On television, lawyers are always in court. They're cross-examining witnesses,
they're making closing arguments, they're getting interviewed by the
press, they're getting to be heroes. Maybe there are three or four
lawyers in the country who live lives like that. Maybe. But it bears very

little resemblance to the practice of law as it's actually done at a firm like this.

First of all, if someone really wants to go to court, they shouldn't be at a corporate law firm. They should be earning forty thousand dollars a year working for a district attorney. Public servants get to go to court. It's the only perk of a job that involves no free food, no gym membership (not that any of us use it), no secretary, and a salary fit for a public school teacher.

Sure, we have a litigation department, and the litigation department does, in theory, go to court. But in practice, the vast majority of our cases settle well before they get to the courtroom, after years of conference calls and memo-writing. On the rare occasions we end up trying a case, it's the partners who get to do it.

Our litigation associates mostly search through stacks of documents looking for evidence that would matter if we ever got to court, but since we'll never get to court, it turns out not to matter much at all. Except to scare the other side into thinking we'll one day go to court.

Not that it's any better to be a corporate associate. They write memos, draft contracts, and do their own equivalent of document review, "due diligence." Every company has lots of contracts in force at any given time—loan agreements, sales contracts, employment contracts, leases, etc. Some of these contracts specify that the company isn't allowed to sell a particular building without the bank's permission, or that if it gets bought by a larger company, the interest rates on its loans will go up. Due diligence means reading all of the contracts to see what will happen if the company does whatever it is it wants to do. I'm sorry I've bored you. Just think of what it does to the corporate associates.

#Posted by Anonymous at 2:54 PM

To: Anonymous Lawyer
From: Harold Kolb
Date: Tuesday, May 23, 3:04 PM

Do I work for you?

To: Harold Kolb
From: Anonymous Lawyer
Date: Tuesday, May 23, 3:08 PM

No.   *

To: Anonymous Lawyer
From: Harold Kolb
Date: Tuesday, May 23, 3:22 PM

Come on, you're Cary Goldsmith on 21, aren't you?

To: Harold Kolb
From: Anonymous Lawyer
Date: Tuesday, May 23, 3:25 PM

No.

To: Anonymous Lawyer
From: Harold Kolb
Date: Tuesday, May 23, 3:29 PM

I just walked by your office and you're in there, typing on your computer. You're writing a post, right? Tell me the truth. I won't tell anyone.

To: Harold Kolb
From: Anonymous Lawyer
Date: Tuesday, May 23, 3:33 PM

Not me.

To: Anonymous Lawyer
From: Harold Kolb
Date: Tuesday, May 23, 3:36 PM

I know it's you. Don't worry. Your secret is safe with me.

Tuesday, May 23

I just got home from our annual charity auction, where we raised money for some refugees far enough away that we never have to see them. Originally we were going to sponsor the Special Olympics but then we realized we'd actually have to send people to volunteer for it instead of just writing them a check. We do this charity auction every summer so the summer associates think it's the kind of thing we do all the time. It's our way of giving back to the community. I don't know what that means, but it's what we put on the flyers.

We turned it into a whole day of charity. We put a stop to the fifty-dollar lunches for a day and gave the money to a legal aid clinic. We invited someone from Habitat for Humanity to come talk to the summer associates about how they can spend a week after they're done here (but before they go back to school) helping to build houses in the San Gabriel Valley. And The Jerk's secretary circulated a petition soliciting donations for a walk-a-thon she's taking part in, in support of some disease called myositis. Her sister has it. It's a disease of the muscles. She can't walk. Ironic for them to do a walk-a-thon then, isn't it? If it were any other secretary, I'd give a couple of cents, definitely. But since she belongs to The Jerk, I'd rather not. I wrote The Suck-Up's name on the sheet instead and put him down for five dollars a mile. I'm sure he won't mind.

The myositis walk-a-thon is a bit of a waste. The people who really need a walk-a-thon are my colleagues. It's a sad state of affairs. We try to hire good-looking people—it helps on campus when the ones saying they worked at your firm are pretty and popular instead of fat and lonely—but once they get here it all goes down the drain. After about four months of work, they've lost their youthful glow. They're pale and puffy from lack of sleep. Their skin starts to react from the stress, harsh lighting, and lack of natural sun. Their bodies start to get used to the greasy takeout every night and they all begin to get a little soft in the middle. Not fat, at least not too many of them. Fat is sloppy. But soft. Soft is acceptable. If you're too fit, we know you're thinking about things besides lease agreements. If you have time to go to the gym, something's wrong. Unless it's your one thing. Then it's okay.

And for all the lip service people give to the glass-walled internal staircase that connects our seven floors in the building, only the young ones take the stairs. You get to be important, it's the elevator, every time. It's a status symbol. I see you on the stairs, I know you're insignificant. I see you take the elevator to go down one flight, I know your time and energy matter, and you can't be wasting it on the staircase, sharing space with the people delivering mail.

The physical degradation stops bothering the associates after a year or so. Who needs to look good when you're stuck in the office all day? It's not like they're going on dates or seeing their friends. There's no incentive not to look unpleasant. No one's looking.

Tonight's auction was a way for everyone to painlessly give something back. People donate items or services, we all gather in the conference room to bid, and all the money raised gets sent to charity. And usually billed back to clients somehow, so it isn't even money out of our own pockets—except for the support staff, who have no one to bill it back to.

It's not like this is the only charitable thing I do. After Hurricane Katrina, I donated a day's worth of binder clips and Post-it flags to the Red Cross, and sent out an e-mail encouraging others to do the same. Absent from the news media reports was any talk of the hundreds of thousands of dollars' worth of office supplies that were destroyed by the storm and went to waste. It's a shame. Office supplies are important.

We had a cocktail hour before the bidding started, to get everyone nice and tipsy and free with their money. It's fun when people wake up the next day, the buzz has worn off, and they realize they just spent a thousand dollars to be trapped in a hot-air balloon for a six-hour ride with the meanest partner at the firm.

The Jerk offered up a weekend at his beach house. I enjoyed the look on his face when The Mail Guy started bidding. None of us would ever want a member of the support staff trampling around our house. We don't even let the summer associates inside when we host a barbecue; there's no way any of us want a janitor, a secretary, or even a paralegal sitting on the couch or touching our things. Or sleeping in our bed. That one's the worst. It ends up costing a couple thousand dollars just to get everything fumigated.

The Jerk started to panic and wanted to ratchet the price out of The Mail Guy's range. He started throwing in some bonuses. "I'll cater in all your meals. You can use the pool. I'll include a bottle of wine from my private collection."

What he didn't know is that I was funding The Mail Guy's bid, just to watch The Jerk squirm. "Go as high as you need to," I pulled The Mail Guy aside and told him before the auction started. "It's my gift to you and your family. But if you tell anyone, I'm going to make sure your wife gets deported."

He ended up getting it for eight thousand dollars. An expensive joke, but at least it's a tax deduction, and the satisfaction of knowing The Jerk's towels are going to be used by The Mail Guy makes it all worthwhile. Best eight thousand dollars I've spent since I bought Anonymous Wife new breasts.

The One With The Birthmark donated eight hours of cleaning from his housekeeper. That went for forty bucks. Probably about the housekeeper's normal wage. Candyman donated a week of babysitting from his daughter's nanny. The Tax Guy donated a home-cooked meal from his personal chef. It's a gluten-free meal. The Tax Guy is allergic to gluten. And pollen. And people.

I offered an item just for the summer associates—the winning bidder gets to give me a list of up to five students from his law school that he doesn't want working here, and I'll make sure they don't get offers. That went for eight hundred bucks to Stinky, who probably doesn't have all that many friends regardless. I thought it was a creative item—and, best of all, costless to me. Much more inventive than the signed copy of the Bankruptcy Code that the head of the business reorganization group donated. It's signed by the vice president of the American Law Institute. Only at a law firm would that actually be a desirable item. And even here, its appeal is seriously limited.

The New Chairman donated a round of golf at his country club, followed by a steak dinner with him and his family. I hear he once ate a 48-ounce porterhouse. He had to preface the bidding with the disclaimer that it's a private club, and unfortunately not everyone in the room would be eligible to win. Luckily, the people to whom that was addressed understood exactly what he meant, and sat that one out.

An IT guy—the bearded one, I don't know his name—donated four hours of personal tech support. The woman who maintains the coffee machines donated flamenco dance lessons. The Word Processing Guy Who Used To Be Under House Arrest donated a midnight massage for an associate stuck late in the office, but no one bid on it. The secretary who offered up a "North African Feast" got a little upset when one of the partners asked if she'd be wearing some of her "weird African clothing" while she was cooking it. She explained that she's from Egypt, and the clothing they wear there is pretty much what she wears here, actually.

The Girl Who Dresses Like A Slut thought she was being funny and donated "sex" in the silent auction. It ended up going for $600.

She shouldn't worry too much about it. I know from previous years that most of the personal services end up unclaimed. People can't find a day when they're all free to go on a yacht, or take a salsa lesson, or learn to make pottery. Or they realize some weeks later that they don't actually want to play tennis with their boss and can't imagine why they bid $200 to do so. So they end up paying for nothing and the whole thing is just a complicated way to collect donations for the poor foreign kids, whoever they are.

The co-head of the real estate group donated a private real estate tour for the winner and his family, where they'll all drive around the city looking at buildings. Not even the movie stars' houses. Office buildings. Warehouses. Factories. All stuff we've helped our clients finance. Nothing sounds worse. There can't possibly be anyone here who really wants to do this. The partner isn't even a nice guy. He's a jackass. Yet every single first-year and second-year associate in real estate was all over that thing. It went for two thousand dollars. Just for a day of sucking up. It's like prostitution.

Except all the prostitutes I've ever met are a lot better looking than the head of the real estate group.

The Bombshell donated an extra ticket she had for a black-tie fund-raising gala. The winner would get to go as her date. I bid three hundred dollars but that was pocket change compared to what it eventually went for. Every guy at the firm was in the bidding, drooling over the chance. It went to Lives With His Mom for six thousand dollars. That should be a fun evening for them both.

The Musician donated a song. He said he'd write one for the winner, on whatever topic he wanted. I thought it could come in handy someday—perhaps we can fire an associate with a tender ballad—so I figured I'd bid a few bucks. And, sure enough, The Jerk saw my hand go up and started to raise his too. Out of spite. I went to $50, and he said $60. I went to $70, and he said $100. I went to $150, and he said $300. Meanwhile, Doc, the summer associate who donated some elective plastic surgery that only went for $250, looked on like he'd been hit by a truck. A song is worth more than a Botox injection?

It wasn't about the song anymore. It was a battle of wills. Who would cave first? It wasn't going to be me. I quickly rapped out a text message on my BlackBerry—learning how to type on that thing and send a message with one hand, without looking, while it's still in my pocket, has turned out to be a fairly useful skill—telling my secretary to have The Jerk paged on the intercom.

Just after the bidding was up to $750, the page came through, and he threw his bidding card down in disgust and left the room. So I got it for $775, enough for a nice dinner with the family, but some things are more important than family.

I passed The Jerk in the hall later and he scowled at me. "Enjoy your $800 song."

I will. I went back to my office to gloat. Me and my $800 song and my seven square feet. SEVEN SQUARE FEET.

#Posted by Anonymous at 11:15 PM

To: Anonymous Niece
From: Anonymous Lawyer
Date: Wednesday, May 24, 2:18 PM

Potential problem. I just got back from lunch with a summer associate. The Musician. The one who goes to Yale. He asked me at lunch if I ever read any weblogs. I told him I don't know what a weblog is. He looked

a little skeptical. He said he heard there's some hiring partner somewhere who's been writing one. He said he checked it out this morning.
He said he liked it. I tried not to react. I think he may know. Do you think
he knows?

To: Anonymous Lawyer
From: Anonymous Niece
Date: Wednesday, May 24, 2:32 PM

I don't know. If he brought it up, I think he might. But I don't understand
why he would mention it if he really thought it was you. He's got to believe that if you thought he knew, you'd either delete the whole thing or
you'd fire him. It seems like a pretty dumb move on his part. Especially
dumb for someone who goes to Yale.

To: Anonymous Niece
From: Anonymous Lawyer
Date: Wednesday, May 24, 2:40 PM

There's a way to delete the whole thing? Should I do that? If he starts
telling people about it, I'm a little concerned.

To: Anonymous Lawyer
From: Anonymous Niece
Date: Wednesday, May 24, 2:49 PM

You can't really delete it completely. Google stores everything on the Internet. So people could still find it. But I don't think you have anything to worry about yet. You should talk to him. Maybe. Unless he doesn't know it's you. How convincing were you at lunch? Although there's probably no way he doesn't know it's you, especially since you wrote about him. You changed the details though, right?

To: Anonymous Niece
From: Anonymous Lawyer
Date: Wednesday, May 24, 2:57 PM

Of course I changed the details. But he would probably still recognize himself. He's a smart kid. I don't think he has any reason to do anything stupid. Maybe I'll find some way to convey a warning in my next post, so he knows not to say anything. Then hopefully he'll never bring it up again. I'll be subtle about it, so it doesn't tip him off if he doesn't know it's me.

Wednesday, May 24

Summers do stupid things sometimes. They don't think about the consequences of their actions, and it gets them into trouble. A summer once parked in a partner's spot in the garage. That was a dumb idea.

The partner had the firm tow the girl's car, and he made life hell for her the rest of the time she was here. She got assigned to the employee benefits group. She didn't get invited to lunch. She didn't get an offer to come back after graduation. And the partner made sure his colleagues at other firms knew she was trouble, so she didn't get an offer anywhere. It ruined her life. She sells dishwashing soap now, on the Internet. Summers should think through their actions very carefully. Very, very carefully.

#Posted by Anonymous at 3:08 PM

To: Anonymous Lawyer

From: Frank Anderson

Date: Thursday, May 25, 3:05 AM

I'm a prisoner hoping for some legal advice. I'd like to sue my court-appointed attorney for malpractice, but I'm not sure how. I found your weblog. Can you help me?

Thursday, May 25

I just collided with a summer associate on the way out of the bathroom. The Prodigal Son. His father used to work here. I was coming out as he was going in, and he hit the door as I pushed it open and we both fell down. It's ridiculous. They should stay in their offices where they belong. I don't need summers cluttering up the hallways, drinking the coffee, or blocking the doorway to the bathroom. We had a partners-only bathroom for a while, which was a brilliant idea, but for some reason they decided to get rid of it a few years before I became partner. I don't understand why. Our time is obviously more valuable than anyone else's in the firm. If I need to use the bathroom, I shouldn't have to wait.

At the very least, anyone who's in the bathroom when a partner gets there should have to immediately leave. I hate when one of the two urinals is taken, and all the stalls are taken, and my choice is whether to urinate right next to a paralegal, or stand there and wait until someone leaves. I don't need the paralegal peeking over and looking at me. And I know they look. They all look. They want to see what a partner looks like. They're in awe of me. Every part of me.

There's a line of fraternization I don't want to cross, and the bathroom is a big part of it. It's not just the bathroom, though. We should have partners-only water fountains. The other partners may be weird but at least I know we all have good health care and live in respectable neighborhoods. Who knows what diseases the word-processing guy is going to pass along if he accidentally comes into contact with the spout?

We should certainly have a partners-only section in the attorney lounge so associates wouldn't hear us talking about them—and then we could get some more comfortable chairs and better food without feeling like we're wasting it all on the common folk. We rent a luxury bus every summer for the vineyard tour, and we have a hard-and-fast rule: partners in front, summers in the back. One year, a summer tried to sit up front. We fired him.

And partners should get better toilet paper. The kind the firm buys feels like sandpaper. It's okay when you're young but as you get older these things start to matter more. Plus this morning an associate used the last two sheets of paper towel in the bathroom, as if he was entitled to them as much as I am. Partners pay the bills. It's because of the partners that there are any paper towels at all.

The Prodigal Son will probably tell his father I ran him over. The kid's only here because of his dad. He retired a few years ago, and as a courtesy, we gave his son an offer. He doesn't have the grades to be here, but he doesn't know that, and instead he acts like he runs the place. He uses too many Post-it notes, he thinks he has a right to wander freely through the halls, and I even saw him pull out his cell phone the other day while the summers were all waiting in the lobby before their research training session. Just because they're waiting without anything to do doesn't mean they're off the clock and can take care of personal matters like checking their cell phone messages. That's for their own time, not the firm's time. It's a sign of disrespect.

I was heading up to the office on the elevator with The Prodigal Son after lunch yesterday and he had the nerve to push the button for his floor even though he knew that would mean he'd be getting off before me. That's an absurd inconvenience I shouldn't have to tolerate. We did have a partners-only elevator for a few years, but it kept getting vandalized by the support staff.

#Posted by Anonymous at 10:17 AM

To: Anonymous Lawyer
From: Anonymous Niece
Date: Thursday, May 25, 11:00 AM

Any more from The Musician?

To: Anonymous Niece
From: Anonymous Lawyer
Date: Thursday, May 25, 11:03 AM

No, nothing. I'm hoping I dodged a bullet there.

To: Anonymous Lawyer
From: Daniel Frank
Date: Thursday, May 25, 1:35 PM

Mr. Anonymous,

I was so glad you put an e-mail address on the site, because there's something I've been wanting to write in and ask. In the fall I'll be a second-year law student at Columbia. As I begin to think about the recruiting process, I'm realizing I don't know very much about how to tell one firm from another. I was hoping you might have some thoughts on that. I think your readers might appreciate it. And—who knows—perhaps I'll be interviewed by you in the coming months and won't even know it! Thanks so much for your help, and I look forward to hearing from you soon.

Thursday, May 25

I just received an e-mail from a 2L at a decent law school, asking how to tell one firm from another. Come on. This is crazy. If you can't tell one firm from another, you shouldn't be working at any of them. I do this for a living. You want to hear my pitch? You want to hear how well I can spin it? Here you go.

Let's start with the basics. We're a leading full-service international law firm with a proven track record for meeting the needs of our clients. They rely on us for top-notch service. You won't find a place with more interesting cases or more challenging work. Our clients are on the front pages of newspapers worldwide. Our work is unparalleled. Our practice is global. Our commitment to excellence is clear. We're on the cutting edge. We serve our clients domestically, and around the world. We have a strong presence in all of the major financial centers. Leaders in business count on us. Our success speaks for itself. Our list of awards is substantial and impressive.

Here, you'll find the atmosphere of a small firm combined with the resources of a large firm. The congeniality of a small firm combined with the diversity of a large firm. The one-on-one contact you find in a small firm combined with the kinds of cases you can only get at a large firm. It's the best of both worlds. It's the best of all worlds. It's the best, according to a recent survey. It's never been better. We're growing at an unbelievable pace. We have a five-year plan. We have a ten-year plan. Our finances are strong. Our client base is stronger than it's ever been. Our partnership is among the strongest in the industry. We just bought another floor in the building. The views are amazing. The artwork is unbelievable. The bathrooms are sparkling. We're in the best part of the city. There's so much to see. There are so many things to do.

And you'll want to do these things with the amazing people you'll be working with. We place a premium on collegiality. We strive to maintain an informal working atmosphere. We are committed to diversity. We treat each other with dignity and respect. We provide coffee. We provide bagels. We provide brand-new laptops. Our word-processing center is open twenty-four hours a day. Our client services department is there to meet your every need. Our support staff is magnificent.

And don't worry, we'll teach you everything you need to know. You won't be flying solo. We have a culture of collaboration. A commitment to cooperation. We have an open-door policy. You advance at your own pace. We give you as much responsibility as you can handle. You set your own hours. We treat you like the professional you are. We work hard, but we play hard. It's all about the people. We have great people. I'm constantly amazed by the people here. The people here are like nowhere else. It's the people that make all the difference. You will love the people here.

Except for you, Mr. E-mail, because you'll never be one of the people here. You e-mail an anonymous hiring partner without knowing who he really is and you're never getting a job here. Ever. Go badger the recruiting coordinators. That's why we pay them. Minimum wage.

#Posted by Anonymous at 2:51 PM

Thursday, May 25

I just got home from our summer associate dinner at Spago. It was a disaster, precipitated by my own mistake late this afternoon. I had a conference call and needed a summer to take notes, so I grabbed The Suck-Up from the hall—he's been lingering right outside my office for the past few days, waiting for an assignment. The call went on long enough that we ended up traveling to the dinner together and he sat right across the table from me. Awful.

Once again, The New Chairman couldn't be bothered to spend more than fifteen minutes at one of my events. He stopped by for drinks, and then he made some excuse about not feeling well and staggered out. He looked fine to me. It's just another slight in a growing list of slights. He saw me in the hall yesterday and didn't say hello. He left me off a list of partners he invited to lunch on Tuesday. And I saw him steal a piece of candy from my secretary's bowl as he walked past this morning. He thinks no one notices these things, but I do. I notice everything.

The Suck-Up spent the entire dinner trying to ingratiate himself with The Jerk, who was sitting two seats to his left. Even as I was mindlessly making ridiculous conversation with The Suck-Up, about his "girlfriend," as if he really has one, and about his "friends," as if anyone is really going to be friends with someone like him, all of his attention was on The Jerk. He kept looking at The Jerk, hoping The Jerk would turn his way so he could grab his attention. But The Jerk was focused on The Girl Who Dresses Like A Slut, seated on the other side of him. She brought a change of clothes for dinner. I wonder what her parents think of how she dresses. Have women stopped wearing underwear? Is that a thing these days? Are we not paying her enough to afford a bra? Not that I'm complaining. She's nothing compared to The Bombshell though. The Bombshell wore a strapless gown. And went home with one of the waiters.

In the middle of his crème brûlée with apricots and Persian berries, The Suck-Up reached over The Musician's plate and tapped The Jerk on the shoulder.

"I'm sorry to interrupt. That bittersweet chocolate truffle looks great. I just wanted to make sure I met you before dinner was done. I'm such a fan. I've been doing some research on the Bank of America matter, and I came across one of your old briefs. I think it's brilliant. I'd love to do some work for you, if you have any projects that need a summer's help."

"What did you say your name was? Come by my office tomorrow and we'll have a chat. You familiar with the Public Utility Holding Company Act of 1935?"

"The '35 Act? Oh, I'm a huge fan. I think it's brilliant."

"Perfect. I'll have my secretary send you some materials in the morning so you can get up to speed. Then stop by my office after lunch."

"Definitely. I'll get in early to wait for the materials. I think your secretary's brilliant."

Ugh. Sucking up to me is one thing. Sucking up to The Jerk is quite another. On the way out, I told The Suck-Up that I need a summary of today's conference call on my desk when I get in tomorrow morning. I don't. I don't ever need it. I'm just going to throw it out. But you can't act like The Jerk's more important than I am and expect to get away with it.

#Posted by Anonymous at 10:48 PM

To: Anonymous Lawyer
From: The Musician
Date: Thursday, May 25, 11:29 PM

You don't know the whole story. The Suck-Up pocketed The Jerk's napkin. On his way out, he grabbed it off the table and put it in his bag. I asked him what he was doing, and he looked a little embarrassed but he told me he just wanted a memento from the evening and it was so cool to have something that had touched The Jerk's face. The whole dinner was nauseating. I knew you'd write a post about it.

To: The Musician
From: Anonymous Lawyer
Date: Thursday, May 25, 11:41 PM

Who are you? I don't know what you're talking about.

To: Anonymous Lawyer
From: The Musician
Date: Thursday, May 25, 11:50 PM

You don't have to pretend, it's okay. I haven't told anyone, and I'm not going to. I don't think anyone else knows about it. I only stumbled across it by accident. I have a blog of my own, so I'm more plugged into this world than anyone else here, I'm sure. I think I'm better at the anonymous part than you are, though. I can show you some tricks. You should be posting using an IP address anonymizer, if you aren't already. This way the IT people won't be able to track you down. Also, you can change the time on the posts, so even if you write things in the order they happen, they appear on the page all out of sequence so people will be confused.

I knew yesterday at lunch it was you. I know I shouldn't have even said anything. The look on your face gave it away. When I mentioned the word "weblog," I could see you got very nervous, and tried to change the subject. I felt really terrible about it. I realized you'd probably be worried I would tell someone. And then I saw your post about how summer associates need to be careful about their actions, and I knew for sure that was because of me. I really apologize. I absolutely shouldn't have said anything, and I didn't mean to make you worry about it. I promise I'm not going to say anything to anyone. You can fire me if I do, really. I think it's fascinating that you're doing this. I would love to talk about it, if you're willing to.

But please don't kill me. I promise I'll keep this to myself.

To: The Musician
From: Anonymous Lawyer
Date: Friday, May 26, 12:05 AM

Okay, I won't kill you. But we need to talk. Come to my office tomorrow morning at ten. Bring me a cup of coffee. Milk and sugar. Regular sugar, not the fake stuff.

Friday, May 26

I'm posting at 5:30 in the morning because I have nothing else to do, and I'm awake for no reason. The phone just rang a few minutes ago. Anonymous Wife picked it up, half asleep. "Hello? Who? What?" She threw the phone at me. "Someone for you. I don't know who it is."

"Hello?"

"I hope I didn't wake you. I just wanted to make sure I caught you right when you got up. I figured you'd be awake by now, since I know how early you get into the office and how diligent you are about your work."

It was The Suck-Up. Christ. "Why are you calling me at 5:30 in the morning? How did you get my home phone number?"

"I begged your secretary. I wouldn't be calling, except it's an emergency. I sent you the notes from the conference call about an hour ago, like you asked. But I've been tossing and turning in bed ever since. I'm pretty sure I made a mistake, and I didn't know how to recall the e-mail. I didn't want you to wake up and read it and think I didn't know what I was doing, so I wanted to call just to tell you not to read it yet. I'm working on a revision. I failed to find an important case. I found it now though. I hope you didn't already forward the information on to the client. I'm so sorry about this. I hope I haven't destroyed your impression of my work product. I do good work, I promise. Nothing like this will ever happen again."

"I don't care. It was just busywork. It doesn't matter. Go to sleep."

"It doesn't matter?"

"No. I wasn't even going to read it."

"But I spent all night working on it."

"Make sure to bill it. And please don't call me at home anymore. I'm hanging up the phone now."

Now my wife is awake, my kids are awake, the dog is awake, all two hours before anyone needs to be up. As soon as I post this, I'm making breakfast, just to give the kids something to do. They won't eat it, but at least they can play with it on their plates. I'd make some pancakes if I could remember how. I used to be good at this. I used to cook more often. My wife stinks at it, so someone has to be decent. Lately I'm too busy to cook. I'll make some toast if we have any bread in the house, but that's about it. I have to do something about The Suck-Up. You can't call a partner at home at 5:30 in the morning. You just can't.

#Posted by Anonymous at 5:37 AM

To: Anonymous Lawyer
From: Bonnie Henderson
Date: Friday, May 26, 8:58 AM

My son would kill me if he knew I was e-mailing you, but I just had to write. I think he's The Suck-Up. I don't know how he got like this. We went on vacation to Washington, D.C., once and he tried to somehow escape from the White House tour, sneak up the stairs, and find the president to shake his hand. He was apprehended by security and we ended up spending the afternoon at the White House police station. I'd normally have chalked it up to kids just being kids, but this happened two years ago, when he was twenty-three. I'm sorry you're stuck with him this summer.

To: Bonnie Henderson
From: Anonymous Lawyer
Date: Friday, May 26, 9:02 AM

Does your son have the same last name as you?

To: Anonymous Lawyer
From: Bonnie Henderson
Date: Friday, May 26, 9:04 AM

Yes.

To: Bonnie Henderson
From: Anonymous Lawyer
Date: Friday, May 26, 9:16 AM

He doesn't work for me. Thankfully. He sounds dreadful. I hope you get
him some help. Of course, he probably got that way because of you.
What kind of mother e-mails someone he thinks is her son's boss with
a story like that? How did you even find my blog? No wonder your son
is so screwed up.

To: Anonymous Lawyer
From: Bonnie Henderson
Date: Friday, May 26, 9:24 AM

I just thought I was being helpful! If you knew he was like that at home,
maybe you wouldn't be so hard on him at the office. He's having a
terrible summer. The partners are all treating him badly, he hasn't made
any friends, he gets home every night and calls me in tears. I thought I
could help. You should be ashamed of yourself for treating him like
you've been. I should report you to someone.

To: Bonnie Henderson
From: Anonymous Lawyer
Date: Friday, May 26, 9:36 AM

Again, your son does not work here. Please stop bothering me.

To: Anonymous Lawyer
From: Bonnie Henderson
Date: Friday, May 26, 9:43 AM

Even so, I bet his mother feels the same way I do. You're all the same.
These kids are human beings, and for some of them this is their first
job. You should have more patience with them.

To: Bonnie Henderson
From: Anonymous Lawyer
Date: Friday, May 26, 9:48 AM

These kids need discipline, not patience. I wish we were allowed to hit
them.

Friday, May 26

The Musician has quickly become my favorite summer associate, despite his lackluster work ethic. I took him to lunch again today. Italian.
You can do pretty well with Italian food at fifty dollars a person. There

were leftovers. He has dinner now for the next three days. I've sometimes thought we'd get more goodwill out of our lunch budget if we took them all to the grocery store and let them spend the fifty dollars on food they could bring home. But that would defeat the purpose of exposing them to these fancy restaurants. We want them to get addicted to good food so they can't resist accepting the job offer, just for the money to buy good food, so they're not stuck eating ramen noodles like in college. Anonymous Son eats ramen noodles dry. Like noodle crackers. It sounds awful but they actually taste pretty good.

#Posted by Anonymous at 2:09 PM

To:　Anonymous Lawyer
From: Anonymous Niece
Date:　Friday, May 26, 2:16 PM

I just read your post. I'm guessing something happened with The Musician. Is everything okay?

To:　Anonymous Niece
From: Anonymous Lawyer
Date:　Friday, May 26, 2:25 PM

He knows about it. He says he won't tell anyone. I think I believe him, but I'm not sure. I took him to lunch today. He said if he tells anyone, I can fire him. That seems like a fair enough deal. He said he has a blog of his own. Do me a favor and try to find it for me. That way I have some dirt on him in case I need it. I'm still not sure whether to keep the blog up. Part of me thinks I should take it down and not have to worry about it anymore. I didn't even think it would last this long. But it's strange—it's like an outlet I didn't realize I even wanted. There's no one here to talk about this stuff with. So I'd rather not stop writing if I can help it. He told me some ways to change dates and times, and something about covering the tracks of my IP address, whatever that is. He wanted me to write a post saying that's he's single and handsome, but we ended up compromising with the post about how he's my favorite.

To: Anonymous Lawyer
From: Anonymous Niece
Date: Friday, May 26, 2:40 PM

Even if you stop the blog, you can still talk to me about work. This back-and-forth has been nice. I don't know any other lawyers to talk to about law school.

To: Anonymous Niece
From: Anonymous Lawyer
Date: Friday, May 26, 2:50 PM

We'll have plenty of time to talk once you're working here.

Friday, May 26

The Suck-Up just stopped by for another assignment. He wants to atone for his mistake. I don't care about the mistake, but I don't think there's much he can do to make up for waking me this morning. So I'm sending him to Belize. With one phone call. We don't have a client in Belize. I don't know what he's going to do in Belize. I don't know if the BlackBerry even gets service over there.

I just called the recruiting coordinator and said I need a summer associate to do some work in Belize. "Can you arrange the flight for tomorrow and I'll let him know the details? Thanks." I'll figure out some task later. But just like that, I'm ruining his Memorial Day weekend, sending him on a wild goose chase to the middle of Central America, and there's nothing he can do about it. Even if he wanted to do something about it, what could he do? He'll get there, I'll tell him the matter settled when he was on the flight, sorry to send him out there for nothing, and we'll turn him around and he'll come right back. An entire day, ruined. And all because I have power.

Why not exert my power? Why not have fun with it? I mentioned to Chicago Guy on Monday that I've never been sure which toilet on my floor flushes the best, and on Wednesday I had a memo summarizing the options. I wrongly accused a summer associate of taking my rubber band ball last year—turned out it was the janitor—and he made me a new one. That's the advantage of being in my position. I can make people do things. It's the one constant here, even as I worry about whether I'm ever going to become chairman.

There are a lot of things I can't control. As you get older, you can't control your body. My shoulder hurts from throwing a pair of scissors at my secretary last week. My elbow hurts from fighting for one of the swivel chairs at my department lunch in the conference room on Tuesday. My foot hurts from kicking a homeless man who was lingering around my car in the parking lot. I think he was homeless. He may have been a paralegal. I'm not sure. It's not important. But in the office, I have control. I can yell into the speakerphone. I can fire a messenger. I can berate an associate. I can demand a first-class plane ticket. I can order the shoe-shine guy not to leave any scuff marks.

In my fiefdom, I'm the king. I'm not the king anywhere else. You tell people at a cocktail party that you're a partner at a law firm, and it sounds okay, but it's nothing special. It's not like being a rock star or the third baseman for the Dodgers. But in this building it's everything. I wonder if Belize is nice this time of year. Actually, I don't even care. I hope it's snowing.

#Posted by Anonymous at 3:40 PM

To: Anonymous Lawyer
From: The Musician
Date: Friday, May 26, 4:03 PM

You sent The Suck-Up to Belize??

To: The Musician
From: Anonymous Lawyer
Date: Friday, May 26, 4:06 PM

Basically. Belize = Chicago. But otherwise it's true.

To: Anonymous Lawyer
From: Anonymous Niece
Date: Friday, May 26, 4:38 PM

You sent a summer associate to Belize??

To: Anonymous Niece
From: Anonymous Lawyer
Date: Friday, May 26, 4:42 PM

No, Chicago. See, I told you I'm changing the details. The kid's a pain
in the ass.

To: Anonymous Lawyer
From: Glenn Barrow
Date: Friday, May 26, 4:52 PM

I'm a partner at a major law firm in Belize. I would be delighted to give
your associate some work to do when he arrives in my country. We
have much work that an American law student could be helpful with. I
am more than eager to help. (By the way, the weather's very nice this
time of year. Also, if you are looking for another gift for your new chairman, we have delicious hot sauce available by mail order. Let me know
and I will send you the details.)

————————————

Friday, May 26

The Jerk charged into my office a few minutes ago. The Suck-Up apparently told him where he was headed. "Why did you send my summer associate to Belize?"

"He's not your summer associate. The summer program is my domain. Whatever I do with the summer associates is none of your concern. It happens to be very nice in Belize this time of year. And they have delicious hot sauce."

"You heard me say last night I had a project for him to work on. And now I find out he's halfway to the airport. We don't even have a client in Belize."

"Sure we do. You just don't know about it yet. Maybe The New Chairman's keeping you out of the loop on this one. It's top-secret. Guess you're not important enough. You need a summer associate? I have plenty. You can have Stinky. It'll be a perfect match."

"Forget it. I can't deal with you. I'm going back to my office."

Yeah, that's it. Go back to your office, Jerk. Your tiny little office. Seven square feet, and don't forget it. You can make it look bigger, with the mirror, and the little couch, but it's not. It's smaller. Noticeably smaller.

#Posted by Anonymous at 6:03 PM

Saturday, May 27

I woke up this morning and told Anonymous Wife we should do something with the kids, but she said she already had plans to take them to the beach and since I don't like the beach I shouldn't come. The beach is boring. I can't cope with just sitting there and doing nothing. I end up doing work on my laptop. And then sand gets in my dress shoes and it's a mess and I have to get someone to clean them for me.

She said we could spend time as a family next weekend if I saw a "life coach" this afternoon while she and the kids went to the beach. One of her vapid friends made her husband go see a life coach and she's convinced that it "strengthened their relationship." So that's where the idea came from. Just for my own amusement, I decided to go. Anonymous Wife was shocked. I never do anything she asks me to do.

What a waste of my (very expensive) time. Although it gave me an entirely new sense for what people do after they realize they can't function in the high-pressure world of corporate law. The irony is that these life coaches, claiming they can help people like me manage our lives and deal with the stress and figure out how to reach our goals, are the ones who couldn't hack it themselves. Instead they're leeching off people more talented than they are. It's sickening.

I walked into the life coach's office—which was smaller than our bathroom at home, and not even the big bathroom but the little one—and he immediately asked me to make a list of what I want in life, in terms of career, family, and personal satisfaction. Here was my list:

Career:

1. Find more associates to buy into the pyramid scheme and help me afford a new swimming pool

2. Figure out new ways to bill clients for work they shouldn't really have to pay for

3. Fire more people who are just like you and can't hack it

Family:

1. Effectively substitute time and energy with enough conspicuous consumption to make Anonymous Wife forget how little I care

2. Send Anonymous Daughter to fat camp

3. Have an affair with your wife, Mrs. Life Coach

Personal Satisfaction:

1. Buy a boat

2. Find a technicality in the law to enable me to force you to shut down your life coach practice

Mr. Life Coach was not amused. (He wasn't amused either when my BlackBerry kept buzzing.) How is this an industry? How shallow does someone have to be for this to be an effective method of life change? The sad thing about too many people at the firm is that this would actually do something for them. The Jerk would love this. He could list out some goals and feel like he's really accomplished something, and then come back to the office and be the same person he was when he left, only with even more conviction that he's a self-actualized human being and that the way he behaves is perfectly fine.

I really do want to run the firm one day. I have to run the firm. I have to run the firm to justify the years I've spent doing this. I know I'm ignoring the sunk costs. I know what's done is done and I can't take back the past. But even if it's not economically rational, running the firm is the only way this is ever going to pay off.

I never thought I'd get this far at the firm. It didn't start out well. I nearly failed the bar exam after law school. The day the results were released I was on pins and needles. I didn't study hard enough, I didn't focus, it was close. The managing partner at the time called us all into his office, one by one, with a copy of *California Lawyer* on his desk. You'd sit down, and he'd look at the list until he got to where your name should have been, and if it was there he'd shake your hand and congratulate you. If it wasn't, he'd launch into a fifteen-minute angry tirade about how the practice of law is something to be taken with the utmost seriousness. He'd throw things. He wouldn't stop until he saw tears. But the speech did its job. No one in my class failed the bar a second time.

Every year at the firm there's one or two who fail. People pretend it's okay, but that's all for show. You can't expect to fail the bar exam and then be respected around the office. You're mercilessly mocked, to your face and behind your back. More than everyone else is. You won't make partner. You won't rise to the top. You have two months after law school with nothing else to do but study for the bar exam. If you can't pass an exam like that on the first try, how are you going to do the kind of work our clients demand? You don't get a second chance to file a motion.

Well, you can amend the motion. So you do get a second chance. But that's not the point.

I came home and Anonymous Wife still isn't back. What's the point of being in the house all alone? They're still at the beach. I may as well go to work.

#Posted by Anonymous at 4:16 PM

To: Anonymous Lawyer
From: Anonymous Niece
Date: Saturday, May 27, 5:00 PM

Didn't you fail the bar exam the first time?

To: Anonymous Niece
From: Anonymous Lawyer
Date: Saturday, May 27, 6:04 PM

You're not supposed to know that.

I can't be admitting things like that to my readers. They'll lose all respect for me. I'm a hiring partner. I'm important. Important people don't fail the bar exam.

Except Kathleen Sullivan, the former Stanford dean. It's bad she failed, because it makes the associates feel like they can fail too, without consequence. It erodes our power. It makes it harder for us to punish them for it. I think her firm should fire her. Set an example. I also think Stanford should lose its American Bar Association accreditation for this. Their former dean can't pass the bar exam? How can they even call themselves a law school? Good thing you're getting out of there and going to Yale. Every time I write that I get even prouder.

I hope you realize how lucky you are. I've spent eighteen years at the firm proving myself so everyone would forget that I failed the bar exam, but even more so that they'd forget that I went to Michigan. Michigan's a fine school, but it's not Yale. You can do anything with a Yale degree. I've had to work really hard all these years. I've had to make sacrifices. You won't have to make those sacrifices. You can write your own ticket.

Sunday, May 28

I wasn't planning on coming into the office today. But I'm here. I went to Mr. Life Coach yesterday and so I thought today we could do something as a family. But Anonymous Daughter already had plans to go to a friend's house, and my wife was going to lunch with a neighbor. She joked that if I really wanted to be helpful I could take Anonymous Son and go to the grocery store. I called her bluff. Unbeknownst to her, I'm completely competent to go grocery shopping.

So Anonymous Son and I went to Ralphs. It's amazing how fat most of the people in supermarkets are. I suppose it makes sense, since fat people would naturally flock to where all of the food is sold, but the sheer size of some of these people, and their screaming, fat children, and the way they all clog up the aisles gets a little ridiculous. We got some turkey from behind the deli counter. The guy slicing the meat didn't have any gloves on. The woman behind me on the deli line had a cart full of generic grocery items. I think I'd have to be pretty desperate before I'd start eating Oatie-Os and Fruit Hoops. I saw the store manager stocking shelves in the soup aisle and complained to him about the broken wheel on my shopping cart, but he didn't seem to care. There was a puddle in the middle of the cheese aisle he didn't seem to care about either. I'm hoping it was water.

I don't remember supermarkets always having so many organic products. I guess it's these fat people's illusion that if they eat a whole box of organic cookies the weight they put on will be healthier than if it was a box of Oreos. I don't care how my meat is killed, how my vegetables are grown, or how the people on the assembly line are treated while they pack the English muffins into the plastic bags. I don't have time to worry about the process. If I don't care about how we treat people at the office, I certainly don't care how they treat people over at General Mills, or how they treat the animals over at the cattle farm. I bet the animals have it good compared to some of my associates. I bet they get a full night's sleep. I bet they don't get office supplies thrown at them. I bet most of my associates would gladly switch places with a cow. Just like the cows, we fatten up our associates with some good meals while they're summers, and then we squeeze all the milk out of them, and slaughter and eat them. Okay, we don't eat them. Not yet. Although no one really knows what's in the cafeteria's beef stew.

Anonymous Son insisted on some ice cream. Even the ice cream names acknowledge the size of the people buying this stuff. Chubby Hubby. Chunky Monkey. Anonymous Wife will be upset I let him get ice cream. But he's just a kid. Kids can eat ice cream. It's adults who should be avoiding it. And our daughter. Maybe I should put some of this back.

A confession: In case you haven't noticed, I have an issue with fat people. It comes through in this blog, I'm sure. But fat means lazy, and lazy means stupid, and stupid means I don't want anything to do with you. Smart people are smart enough not to be fat. It's the last remaining prejudice we're allowed to have. I love minorities, I love old people, I love foreign people, I love the deformed and the disabled. I hate fat. I don't know where that came from. Sorry. My daughter is fat. Well, pudgy at least. I love her despite that. My wife's already talking about getting her liposuction.

We got to the checkout. I figured I'd save some time and get on the express line. Fifteen items or less. I had sixteen. Some idiot in front of me looked at my cart, counted to himself—I could see his lips moving—and told me I had one too many items. "What do you do?" I asked him. "I run a business from home." "Well, I'm a corporate lawyer. My time is valuable. Yours clearly isn't. I'm in a hurry." "This line is for people with fifteen items or less." I ignored him. It took him a full minute to figure out how the credit card reader worked. It's not that difficult. He held people up a lot more than my extra item did. He used a coupon too. Like anyone's time is worth so little that they should be spending it clipping coupons.

I recognized the cashier. One of my former associates. This is what happens when you quit a good job at the firm. You eventually ring up groceries. She didn't recognize me. Maybe it wasn't her. They all look the same after a while.

As we were checking out, my cell phone rang. It was The Chairman. I mean The New Chairman. I'm switching his name. It's been two weeks. He's not that new anymore. He's never called me before. He asked me to come in for a quick meeting in the office. He didn't say what it was about. So I called my wife at lunch and told Anonymous Son to stand outside with the shopping cart and she'd be there to pick him up in a few minutes. Can't keep The Chairman waiting, especially when I know The Jerk wouldn't. I'm in the office now waiting for him to finish up with something. I hope my wife got there quickly. I don't want the milk to spoil.

I hope this meeting's not about The Suck-Up. I can't imagine The Jerk really told him I sent The Suck-Up to Belize. It would be a waste of his time. Maybe there's a summer associate who's done something wrong that I'm not aware of. Maybe The Ugly Kid scared away a client. I just got a call from The Chairman's secretary. Time for the meeting.

#Posted by Anonymous at 12:06 PM

To: Anonymous Lawyer
From: Anonymous Niece
Date: Sunday, May 28, 12:26 PM

I hope the meeting's not about your blog. Let me know how it goes.

Sunday, May 28

I walked into The Chairman's office. I hadn't seen the place since The Old Guy retired. He's changed the whole thing around. The desk is on the other side of the room. The couch is new. Used to be blue, now it's brown. New carpeting too. The artwork is different. The Old Guy liked patriotic war paintings. Delacroix's *Liberty Leading the People.* The new guy likes garbage. It's just blocks of color. I don't understand modern art. I can paint a whole canvas purple. It's really not that hard. But whatever he likes. It's not my office to complain about. Not yet.

He's a slob too. There's a half-eaten plate of food on his bookshelf, and another one sticking out from under his desk. It's actually kind of disgusting. Half a hot dog and the crust from a slice of pizza. He doesn't eat well. I keep my office immaculate. It's the only way I can focus and get anything done. I guess once you're chairman you don't have to do much besides eat. You delegate. So the sloppy office is okay.

"Thanks for coming in on a Sunday," he said.

"I was on my way into the office anyway, of course. Some client work to catch up on."

"Of course. How's the family?"

"They're doing well. How's yours?"

"Doing well. You're probably wondering why I called you in today. I'm just trying to meet with everyone on the management team and let you know the kinds of things I'm thinking about, so we're on the same page. I know we haven't always been the best of colleagues, and I know there's all sorts of political shifts when something like this happens and there's a new man in charge. I know there are a few of you trying to angle your way into my good graces now, and set yourselves up to be next in line. I got the steak you sent me. It was very good. Don't think I won't remember that."

"That's great. And I'm happy you called me in. I'm really just looking at how I can be most useful to the firm, and to you. I want to be a team player here."

He laughed an unpleasant laugh. "Don't play games with me. I did it, you're doing it, we all do it. We all want to think we're next. I don't give out praise easily. None of us do. Just wanted to tell you I think you're doing a great job as hiring partner, and I'm glad to have you on my team."

"I appreciate that."

"And it's certainly too early to handicap anything, and none of us know what the next few years will bring, but stay the course and after a good long run on my part, it wouldn't be a shock if you're the one I end up passing the baton to."

"That's terrific to hear. I definitely appreciate the support."

He stood up and walked around his desk, behind my chair, and put his hands on my shoulders. I had to resist the initial urge to recoil. "If I learned anything from The Old Guy, it's that people need to know where they stand. I don't want mass defections. I'm going to be cutting costs. I'm going to be instituting some new initiatives to cut the dead weight. But I want to make sure the people I want are the ones who remain, and that we have a top-notch team going forward. There will be some movement at the senior level."

"That's a bit vague."

"Well, I think you'll find it to your liking. There are people who, in the coming months, will be transitioning toward other opportunities. They may not be aware of this yet. Do you get what I'm saying?"

"I think I might."

Finally he took his hands off of me and went back to his chair. "Good. Stay the course. You're an important part of this firm. I hate interviewing. I hate summer associates. I hate cocktail parties. That's why I need you. Don't make me interview anyone, and we'll get along just fine. Now get back to work."

"Thanks for making me come in this afternoon. This meeting was definitely worth it."

"I thought you were coming in anyway."

"I was. Have a good holiday."

"What holiday?"

"Memorial Day?"

"There's no holiday."

"Of course. What was I thinking?"

And then he got up again and walked me out. I'm back in my office now, reflecting on what he said. I think he said The Jerk is leaving. It was vague, but I think that's what he was trying to tell me. I should stay the course. Movement at the senior level. This is my chance. He likes me. I'm going to run this firm someday. Time to open some bubbly.

#Posted by Anonymous at 1:48 PM

Monday, May 29

Too many people are out of the office this morning. The government has created a set of holidays without any legitimate significance at all—Memorial Day, Labor Day, Mother's Day—and a quarter of the people here think it's okay not to show up to work. They're lazy. I understand if an associate wants an hour off on Thanksgiving to go home and carve a turkey, or a few minutes to open the presents on Christmas. But what are people celebrating on Memorial Day, and why can't they do it at work? Wear a red, white, and blue tie if you have to. But clients don't ask less of us just because there's no mail delivery. Our job is to be here for them, no matter when they need us. It's a service industry.

I'm more flexible than a lot of my colleagues. If someone's Jewish and wants to go to temple on Rosh Hashana, I'll happily schedule the meeting for between the services. If someone needs an hour to take his daughter for a pregnancy test, he can participate in the conference call by phone, that's fine. But I don't know why people insist on needing to take their wives out for dinner on the exact date of their anniversary. If she leaves you for something like that, you're probably better off.

And I have no idea what Christopher Columbus has to do with the practice of corporate law, and why we'd even contemplate celebrating his birthday by staying home. If he'd stayed home, we wouldn't even be here. I honor Christopher Columbus by working. I honor Martin

Luther King by working. And on Easter Sunday, how better to honor Jesus Christ than by putting in a full day of satisfying labor? Anyone I see wandering the halls today gets a free T-shirt from the carton of extras from last week's summer associate dance contest. Their colleagues who return tomorrow will be jealous.

#Posted by Anonymous at 11:03 AM

Monday, May 29

Almost forgot. It's not like the holidays are my least favorite days of the year. My least favorite is the day in the spring when we turn the clocks forward. Daylight savings time. Individually, it's not a big deal, but think of it on a firm-wide level. That's hundreds of billable hours. Gone. Without a trace. And don't tell me we get them back in October when the clocks turn the other way, because by October everyone forgets about the debt they incurred back in April, and just uses the extra hour to sleep. Pathetic.

#Posted by Anonymous at 11:20 AM

To: Anonymous Lawyer
From: Anonymous Niece
Date: Monday, May 29, 12:18 PM

Sounds like yesterday's meeting with The New Chairman went really well.

To: Anonymous Niece
From: Anonymous Lawyer
Date: Monday, May 29, 12:42 PM

Definitely. I don't want to read too much into what The Chairman said, but I'm pretty pleased about it. Although once I got over the euphoria last night I realized he probably told The Jerk the exact same thing. That's their game. They build up just enough hope so that you're willing to put in the hours. But you never really know where you stand. It's the game I play with my associates. Nobody knows if he's making partner. It's a carrot we hold out for them. You'll make partner, though. Stanford, Yale, absolutely. No question. I don't want to scare you away with any of this. It's not that bad. I'll approach The Chairman in a few years, get some more clarity on his plan, get something on paper. I'm going to run this firm someday, I promise.

To: Anonymous Lawyer
From: Anonymous Niece
Date: Monday, May 29, 12:58 PM

I hope so. It sounds like it's the same thing as at school. I get a little bit of praise from a professor and it totally motivates me to work harder in that class, just to please them. Like, I'll spend more time studying for the final, or start writing the paper sooner than the night before.

To: Anonymous Niece

From: Anonymous Lawyer

Date: Monday, May 29, 1:08 PM

I understand what you mean, but this is work. You can't compare work to school. The stakes are higher here. These are important things we do. One day you'll understand.

Tuesday, May 30

The Suck-Up was waiting for me outside my office when I got in this morning. "Are there any extra toothbrushes around?" he asked. "I got back from Belize late last night and came into the office to catch up on another project. I was going to wash up in the bathroom, but I was hoping there might be an extra toothbrush around, and maybe a razor."

I can see where he would think there might be. Most of us have a toothbrush in a mug on the bookshelf somewhere. Law students notice it sometimes during interviews. They're answering an interview question and suddenly they do a double take. A few brave souls every year ask about it. "You never know when you're going to be called into court and need to look your best" is the standard answer. Associates might disagree. The truth is you never know when you might be spending the night.

We tell them in the interviews that they only have to be here when they're doing work, and if they want to come in at noon and leave at three in the morning, that's as legitimate as coming in at four in the morning and leaving by dinnertime. But we don't really mean it. There's an expectation that if I'm in the office, everyone who works for me should be here too. And no one wants to be seen sneaking out early. You get a reputation that way.

But the associates figure out tricks when they want to leave. It's easier here than in New York, where you can't very easily sneak out in the middle of winter, because everyone sees you with your coat and your gloves and your scarf and they know where you're going. Unless you want to risk frostbite, which some of them do. But that's why the firms in New York strike frostbite from the health care coverage. You sneak out early without your coat and your pinky falls off—that's money out of your own pocket, not the firm's.

It's easier out here. You pretend you're just going to the records department, or downstairs for a cup of coffee. Never get on the elevator to the lobby unless you're the only one inside. Get off at another floor, take a lap around the hall and try again. Take the fire stairs. Leave a coat on the back of your chair. Leave your computer on. Leave a book open. Leave a half-filled cup of coffee at your desk. Tell your secretary you're going to a meeting and won't be back until after she's gone for the day. Don't let anybody know. I hate the secretaries who think they're doing their associates a favor by covering for them. They work for the firm, not the individual. If The Guy With No Neck is on a three-hour lunch, I want the truth. There's no point in giving them secretaries if we can't rely on them to rat people out. We have the corporate tracking system anyway. So they're not really fooling us.

The Suck-Up said he had a great time flying to and from Belize. "It's too bad the matter got resolved before I got there. I'd love to go to lunch with you again and talk about some of the other cases you're working on. I know it's very important this summer that we find mentors at the firm, and I can't think of anyone I'd rather have mentoring me than you."

Mentor. I hate that word. It's how they manipulate us into caring about them. If I'm your boss, I can make your life a living hell without spending a single instant worrying about what you're getting out of it or how it affects your "career development." (Career development. Another pair of words I hate.) But call me a "mentor" and suddenly I'm burdened with having to think about you. I don't want to think about The Suck-Up as a real person. I don't want the responsibility of making sure that what I ask him to do is actually helping him. It's helping the firm. That's all that's supposed to matter.

We're a business. We're trying to maximize profits. If that means each year we take fifty law school graduates and burn out forty-eight of them before they turn thirty-five, well, that's what they're signing up for. We don't promise mentors.

Well, in the recruiting literature we do. But in the recruiting literature we also promise client contact, pro bono opportunities, and a work-life balance. We have a work-life balance. Scales balance in all sorts of ways.

What's the problem anyway? We're doing well. It's been almost seventy-five days without a work-related suicide.

"I'm flattered," I lied to The Suck-Up, "and I would love to take you to lunch again. Except I need you to head to Raleigh for some document review on a case we're working on with local counsel down there. You did a great job in Belize. I'll set it up with your secretary."

In a lot of ways Raleigh is worse than Belize. Law firms in second-tier cities are kind of ridiculous. I don't understand people who decide to practice in a place like Atlanta or Wilmington or Boston or Dallas. When I work with local counsel in places like that, I take an antihistamine before the conference call. That way I'll talk slower and slur my words a little bit so they understand me. Their minds work in a little different gear than the rest of ours. If they didn't, of course they'd be in a real city. No legitimate corporate lawyer chooses to be in Detroit or Columbus or Chattanooga or Richmond. Why would anyone choose to work with second-tier clients, with second-tier colleagues, and in second-tier office buildings with second-tier artwork on the walls and second-tier views from the balcony? Who cares if you can see the Hartford skyline? Who wants to see the Hartford skyline? Who wants to work where the most expensive lunch you can charge the client is twenty dollars at TGI Friday's? Anonymous Wife made friends once with a couple who invited us to eat with them at TGI Friday's. We weren't friends after that.

#Posted by Anonymous Lawyer at 9:46 AM

To: Anonymous Lawyer
From: The Musician
Date: Tuesday, May 30, 10:17 AM

I hate to ask, but do you have any work for me? I'm out of paper clips.

To: The Musician
From: Anonymous Lawyer
Date: Tuesday, May 30, 10:23 AM

Why don't you have any work? Which partners have you been working for? They should be keeping you busy.

To: Anonymous Lawyer
From: The Musician
Date: Tuesday, May 30, 10:28 AM

Um, no one really. I think I might have slipped through the cracks. I figured someone would realize it sooner or later and give me something
to do, and I didn't really want to say anything, but I've read the entire
archives of The Smoking Gun, every Bill Simmons column on ESPN,
and can solve even the hardest Sudoku puzzle in less than four minutes, so I'm kind of running out of ways to kill time. So if you have any
work for me, I'd love to help out with something.

To: The Musician
From: Anonymous Lawyer
Date: Tuesday, May 30, 10:32 AM

Come by my office after lunch. Here's a secret. Two weeks is nothing.
Last summer we had someone stop coming to work after three days
and it took us a month to notice. It's easy for summers to get lost in the
cracks, especially when there're people like The Suck-Up begging for
work every ten seconds. Obviously you already know too much for me
to hold this against you. Lucky you. Usually if I find out someone's
been hiding I make them stamp numbers on all the papers we're getting ready to recycle. I may have something more interesting for you
though. What do you know about corporate bankruptcy?

———————————

Tuesday, May 30

Crisis.

The whole firm just got an e-mail from The Chairman:

"I need someone willing to take over on the Consolidated case. I've been doing some work on the papers, but I think I'm currently in the midst of a heart attack and expect I may be dead before the case comes to completion. There are still a good number of additional billable hours left in the matter, and I want the transition for the client to be seamless. The files will be in my top drawer, and I'll try to save my work before I am overtaken by the pain. Your willingness to step up and take one for the team will not soon be forgotten. Please e-mail Barbara if you're available, and do feel free to charge any funeral expenses back to the client. Someone please call 911. I should have spent more time at the office. Godspeeddddddddddddddd"

Some people are saying he couldn't possibly have written the e-mail, but it was sent from The Chairman's computer, minutes before an ambulance came and took him away. The Chairman apparently came in late this morning feeling a bit under the weather, started working, and about an hour later paged his secretary, Barbara, on the intercom and asked her to call emergency. She ran into his office and found him slumped over in his chair, still holding on to the case file for Consolidated Industries, a company we're shepherding through Chapter 11 bankruptcy. She screamed for help, but no one responded. So she ran back to her desk, called 911, and then rushed around looking for the emergency defibrillator.

There's one defibrillator on every floor, courtesy of one of our clients (they make medical supplies; they've also provided an ample stock of gauze and bandages). But no one on The Chairman's floor is trained to use the defibrillator, so Barbara didn't know what to do. She just waited by his side until the ambulance came, making sure to check her watch so she'd know how much to bill to the client. The paramedics were able to revive him, and they lifted him onto a stretcher with an oxygen mask over his face. A small crowd gathered around. As they wheeled him out, he said, weakly, "Get back to work, everyone."

We're all waiting for news. Barbara went to the hospital to be with him and to tell his wife what happened. Just over two weeks on the job, and now a heart attack.

I'm torn as to my loyalties here. On a personal level, of course I hope he's okay. You'd have to be pretty heartless to see someone wheeled out on a stretcher and not hope he's okay. But from a different perspective, this could be a terrific boost to my career. An unbelievable one. There's no one else in line to be chairman. This was the plan of succession. He'd have it for a decade or two, and then it would be me, or it would be The Jerk. We're the stars of our generation. (One a little brighter than the other, of course.)

If you take The Chairman out of the equation this early, the executive committee is faced with a decision. They could go outside the firm and find someone with more experience, but if they do that, they risk losing me, and they risk losing The Jerk. Plus they make everyone else here a little nervous. People expect service to the firm to be rewarded. People expect to be promoted from within. A new chairman, who hasn't grown up as a lawyer here, could change the entire culture. People don't like regime change at a place like this. It would be very risky for the executive committee to turn elsewhere.

That means it would be one of the two of us. And that means I need to get clarity from The Chairman about what he meant at our meeting this weekend. If he was saying what I hoped he was saying—if he was saying The Jerk was on his way out—I need that in writing before he dies. A living will, not for himself but for the firm. And if it's not what he meant—if he told The Jerk the same thing he told me, and if in fact The Jerk is his choice for the future, then I need him to die before The Jerk gets to him.

I don't mean it that way. Of course I want him to be okay. I'm just saying that if he is going to die—and no one wants that, but it's a possibility we have to recognize—then I'd rather he die before he takes my career into the grave with him. His death would be traumatic enough for the firm. They shouldn't have to lose me too.

If he's not going to die, then I need to be there with flowers before The Jerk gets there. I can't have him waking up to The Jerk's face. For his sake, of course. If that's the last image he sees, he'll be haunted by it for all of eternity.

I've already volunteered to handle the Consolidated case while The Chairman's gone. I'll pass it along to an associate or something. It's just a gesture. But I'm hoping it's a gesture that'll send the right signal—that I'm next in line for his position, should he die. Not that I want him to die. Not that anyone wants him to die. Of course not.

#Posted by Anonymous at 12:17 PM

To: Anonymous Lawyer
From: Anonymous Niece
Date: Tuesday, May 30, 2:19 PM

I just read your post. Any news since then?

To: Anonymous Niece
From: Anonymous Lawyer
Date: Tuesday, May 30, 2:23 PM

No, nothing. I certainly thought by now there'd be some rumors about whether it would be me or The Jerk next in line, but no news yet at all.

To: Anonymous Lawyer
From: Anonymous Niece
Date: Tuesday, May 30, 2:30 PM

I meant news about The Chairman.

To: Anonymous Niece
From: Anonymous Lawyer
Date: Tuesday, May 30, 2:35 PM

Oh. No, nothing yet. I'm about to go visit him in the hospital and see if he'll support my bid to replace him. Only if he dies. It wouldn't make any political sense to try and replace him if he comes back to work, at least not right away. The game plan if he comes back will depend on his health and whether there are any aftereffects from this. But I probably have some time before I have to worry about that.

Tuesday, May 30

I drove to the hospital to see how things were going. I brought The Musician with me, and briefed him in the car about a new assignment I've got for him. I'm having him go through some old case files and come up with the skeleton of an argument as to why I'm a better candidate for chairman than The Jerk. I have some rough notes already written out, just from the advance planning I've been doing all along, but I didn't expect to need to put something together this early. My memory helps with this. Did I mention already that I have an excellent memory?

April 1993. The Jerk missed a meeting. These were the days before BlackBerries. No one could track him down. The client got upset. Ten points.

July 1995. The Jerk accidentally backed into a client's car in the parking garage. He paid for the damage, but the client got upset. Ten points.

November 1998. A terrible PowerPoint presentation by The Jerk. Too many graphics. The technology was new. We were still learning how to use it. He drew an animated file drawer graphic that danced around the screen and swallowed up all of the files. It was juvenile. We didn't win the account. Fifteen points.

The hospital waiting room looked like a portable workstation. Every partner of influence was there, the entire executive committee, The Tax Guy, The Jerk of course, and even some striving associates looking for brownie points. The Bombshell was furiously typing on her BlackBerry. Probably writing a grocery list, but the effect was that she looked busy, and that's exactly what she was aiming for. The Chairman's in and out of consciousness. It doesn't look good. Massive heart attack. I'll do a weeklong moratorium on the steakhouses, out of respect. Maybe get a nutritionist in, to talk to the summers. Free salad. I wonder if there are any salad-themed summer associate events I can squeeze into the schedule. We could rent out the Botanical Gardens at the Los Angeles Zoo for an afternoon and cater in some vegetarian food. I read somewhere that some musician named Moby is a vegetarian. I wonder what he charges for a private concert. That could be a noteworthy event they would talk about when they get back to school. Help with the recruiting for next year.

They gave me two minutes to go in and see The Chairman. Twenty-two-and-a-half dollars I could have billed, but it's worth it. He weakly squeezed my hand. Maybe that's a signal. I couldn't really tell. I told him we're all pulling for him. I noticed the Do Not Resuscitate order at the foot of his hospital bed. I'll have to tell The Suck-Up about that. He'll do anything to imitate The Chairman. I'm sure his parents would be extraordinarily grateful if the one accomplishment from his summer at the firm was that he signed a DNR order. The less effort made on The Suck-Up's behalf, the better for everyone.

Barbara's stuck in that waiting room, like her job depends on it. Which it does. If I'm The Chairman and I wake up and find out my secretary left my side during my hour of need, she's gone. Family emergency, full night's sleep, or bathroom break be damned. Heart attack at your desk is pretty much the only situation where you want your secretary to like you. You don't want them delaying that 911 call out of spite. Bad enough most of them are barely literate enough to read the numbers on the phone. You want them to at least be trying. Normally I tell the summers it's a mistake to be friendly to their secretaries. Being friendly is just an invitation for them to start talking. And once they start, they'll never stop. Every time you pass them in the hall—it'll eat up your entire day. You say good morning and they chew your ear off until lunch, about their shoes and their hair and their kids and the fungus that's growing on the bottom of their feet. You don't want to open that door. I made that mistake with my first secretary. I finally had to have her transferred to the records room. I tell the summers now: "Don't say hello, don't say good-bye, don't say anything. She's just a secretary. You make twice as much money as she does." Most of them don't listen. It makes me angry every time I see a summer talking to a secretary. I worry they're plotting something.

Barbara's plotting something, I'm sure. He dies, she's out of a job unless she can cozy up to the new chairman. She's probably the one to watch. She's talking to The Jerk. That's not a good sign. I said hello to her on the way out. Asked how her husband and kids were. Called them by name. She had no idea I even knew. Ten more points.

#Posted by Anonymous at 4:35 PM

To: Anonymous Lawyer
From: Chris Csefalvay
Date: Tuesday, May 30, 5:15 PM

I think you may work at my firm. Our chairman had a heart attack at his desk this morning too. Shipley Hoyer?

To: Anonymous Lawyer
From: Jessica Manley
Date: Tuesday, May 30, 6:51 PM

I knew it! You're Jack Tucker at Epstein Lajoie in Chicago. Our chairman had a heart attack this morning as well.

To: Anonymous Lawyer
From: M. Henry Lyon
Date: Tuesday, May 30, 9:44 PM

I don't know which partner you are, but our chairman had a stroke this afternoon, so I think you probably work just down the hall from me. I'll stop stealing your candy, I promise. Just don't fire me.

Wednesday, May 31

The Sweaty Guy couldn't even wait until we know if The Chairman lives or dies to let us know he's leaving. 9:05 in the morning and he sent a "departure memo" to the entire firm. He's stepping on The Chairman's moment. It's not a gracious gesture. But maybe that was the point. This is what people do when they leave, standard procedure. They send a note to the entire firm saying they're leaving, thanking everyone they've ever worked with, and explaining that it's not the firm's fault. The longer the memo, the more they hate the firm. People leaving on good terms send a two-line note. "I'm heading to Washington to work for the Department of Justice. Thanks to everyone who's been so helpful over the years, especially Greg and Frank." People being forced out write dissertations. The Sweaty Guy wrote a thesis. I've removed the names:

"Friday will be my last day at the firm. It's been an exciting six-year run, but the time has come to go elsewhere. I will miss you all, or at least a few of you. The firm I started at was a very different place than it is now, but everything changes. Thanks to [redacted] for taking me under his wing, [redacted] for his help on my very first document review, [redacted] for being an amazing secretary, and [redacted] for being the finest supervisor I've ever had. Of course, none of them are here anymore. So I give the requisite thanks to those who have worked with me since. To [redacted] for making me miss my honeymoon, to [redacted] for making me miss the birth of my daughter, to [redacted] for the ulcer, and to [redacted] for refusing to let me push three of my billable hours from calendar year 2004 to 2003 so I could qualify for the bonus and not have to take out a second mortgage on my vacation home. I'll miss some of you. I won't miss some of you. Most people write about how they're leaving the firm for a shorter commute. Well, I'll be working right here, three floors down, for [redacted], so that ain't the reason. I hope the clients follow me. Go to hell, everyone."

Well, The Sweaty Guy's certainly not leaving on Friday anymore. He's been escorted out of the building, and the e-mail's been recalled from the accounts of anyone who didn't open it in the first seven minutes. The response would have been faster, but we're distracted divvying up the client trinkets in The Chairman's office just in case. I'm taking the crystal fish to replace the one that my secretary cracked two weeks after we got the seafood chain out of bankruptcy. The Jerk's taking the desk chair embossed with the firm's logo. I've always thought the chair was a little bit gaudy anyway. So what if The Jerk won the coin toss? That chair will make his office look even smaller than it already does.

#Posted by Anonymous at 9:29 AM

To: Anonymous Lawyer
From: Timothy C. Kang
Date: Wednesday, May 31, 9:56 AM

You're despicable. I hope you have a heart attack at your desk and no one even cares. I hope you get food poisoning from the fifty-dollar sushi and all the summers take turns ripping off your toenails.

Wednesday, May 31

I went back to the hospital this morning for a status report and to make sure I showed my face. The hospital lobby was a mess, with photographers and screaming teenage girls. I heard someone say that Justin Timberlake was inside getting some elective surgery, and that was the reason for all the commotion. I thought about trying to track him down to get Anonymous Daughter an autograph, but I had more important things to worry about. Barbara was still there, in the waiting room, dizzy from lack of food. I asked her if she wanted anything from the cafeteria. She said that would be nice, but she didn't have any money with her. Given her precarious employment situation, I'm not sure she's the best person to be loaning money to right now, so I told her I'd just bring her some snacks from the office next time I visit.

Candyman arrived a few minutes after I did, breathless, holding a five-by-seven signed glossy of Justin Timberlake. "Can you believe Justin Timberlake is here?" he asked.

I pulled Candyman aside for a moment. "Can I count on your support?" I asked. "In the event The Chairman doesn't pull through, not that anyone is hoping for that outcome, I expect it'll end up coming down to the executive committee deciding between me and [The Jerk], assuming they don't choose to go outside the firm for a replacement."

"I think you're probably right."

"It would help to have some associates in my corner, spreading word through the grapevine that I'd be the more popular choice. Of course an associate's loyalty wouldn't soon be forgotten. I know it's only a few more years until you come up for partner. It certainly doesn't hurt to have the support of the chairman."

Candyman nodded his head. "I'm flattered you even think I'm potentially partner material. You know how much I respect you."

"Does that mean I can count on your support?"

"Sure. I think either of you would make a terrific chairman, and I'd be looking forward to working under whoever the committee chooses, should it come to that. Right now I just hope The Chairman wakes up from his coma and gets to come back to the office and do what he loves. It's a shame."

Yeah, a shame. I was getting nowhere with Candyman. No one else seemed to be showing up, and I didn't want to waste the whole day at the hospital, so I went back to work. I passed The Chairman's office, and The Jerk was inside, measuring.

"Just getting a head start," he said.

"He's not even dead yet."

"That's not what I hear. Check your sources."

#Posted by Anonymous at 11:47 AM

To: Anonymous Lawyer
From: Anonymous Niece
Date: Wednesday, May 31, 11:56 AM

He died?? That's awful. I can't imagine what would happen if a professor died like that, a heart attack at school, especially so young. People would be devastated.

To: Anonymous Niece
From: Anonymous Lawyer
Date: Wednesday, May 31, 12:06 PM

I don't know if he died yet. Barbara's not answering her cell phone and Candyman must not have his BlackBerry with him. I'm still trying to find out. I think The Jerk might have just been trying to get under my skin and make me panic. If he's dead, I need to move quickly to shore up support, but I can't be seen politicking out in the open if he's still clinging to life. So this is really ridiculous. I wish he would just pick one already. Live, die, it doesn't matter, just make a decision. We need a chairman who doesn't waver when it counts.

Wednesday, May 31

An e-mail came through about an hour ago asking everyone to meet in Conference Room 22A for an announcement about the firm. It was quiet as we all walked down the hall, knowing the news we were about to hear. Except for these two paralegals who wouldn't stop talking. I punched one of them in the face. That shut her up pretty quickly. They got some truffle cake in, on short notice, and put it out with some black napkins, for the somber news. The Chairman didn't make it. It was a heart attack, and the muscle suffered too much damage for him to recover. Fifty-eight years old and he's gone. And now I very quickly need to figure out how to take full advantage.

The Tax Guy, on behalf of the executive committee, announced that things will be proceeding as usual and that the firm is in good hands. He said the committee will be meeting to decide on a new chairman immediately, and hopes to have a decision by Monday. He said that later this afternoon the firm will be receiving its new stationery, without The Chairman's name on the masthead, and we should begin using that immediately. The Chairman's case files will be assigned by this evening. The funeral is tomorrow, followed by a reception. By Friday there'll be a portrait of him hanging in the main lobby. An artist has already been commissioned. I went back to my desk and e-mailed the associates who work under me to tell them that I won't be penalizing them for the hours missed if they choose to attend the funeral, but that they should be sure to make that decision with the best interests of their clients in mind.

There's a summer associate barbecue that had been scheduled to take place at The Chairman's house on Sunday. I told The Tax Guy I'd be happy to host it, but he said he'd already made arrangements with

The Chairman's widow and we're going to keep the location. One of the purposes of the barbecue is to show the summers the kind of luxury they can afford if they rise to the top of the firm. The Chairman's death doesn't change the fact that his house is gorgeous, so with his widow's cooperation, it makes sense to keep the party as scheduled.

A few summer associates have already e-mailed me asking whether or not they should come to the funeral. I've been telling them they should. I told the recruiting coordinator to get some commemorative T-shirts printed up for the summers, maybe a hat too. The secretaries aren't invited, but we're making an exception so Barbara can come. She needs to eat, after two days in the hospital waiting room without any food.

#Posted by Anonymous at 3:14 PM

To: Anonymous Niece
From: Anonymous Lawyer
Date: Wednesday, May 31, 6:19 PM

I'm meeting The Tax Guy for breakfast tomorrow morning before The Chairman's funeral to figure out a game plan. Is his son still e-mailing you? Has he said anything that you think might be useful to me—not necessarily something that could damage his father's reputation, but anything I'd be able to use to get him on my side would be great. Thanks.

To: Anonymous Lawyer
From: Anonymous Niece
Date: Wednesday, May 31, 7:02 PM

He e-mailed me the other day to ask if I had any freshman dorm recommendations. I don't think that's what you're looking for. Honestly I'm
not sure what you're looking for. Good luck with the meeting, I guess.
You seem a little bit crazy the past few days though.

To: Anonymous Niece
From: Anonymous Lawyer
Date: Wednesday, May 31, 7:29 PM

Of course I seem crazy. This whole thing has been crazy. I thought I
had a decade to prepare and I have a weekend. It's crude to have to do
this in the wake of someone's death, and I hope you believe me when I
say I'm really bothered by all of this and feel terrible about The Chairman. But if The Jerk isn't letting up, I can't let up either. It's going to be
him or me, if it's not someone from outside. I can't afford to get caught
up in what's polite and what's a little bit depraved. Someone's going to
be running the firm for the next decade, and I'm not going to step aside
and give up without trying my hardest.

   It's difficult for you to understand, I'm sure. But the thought of
being chairman one day is what keeps someone going at a place like
this. These chances don't come up all that often. I could never have
dreamed that as a Michigan graduate who failed the bar exam I would
ever rise to the point where I could even be considered for a job like
this. It's like an Alger Hiss story, from rags to riches. Then my life can
mean something. Then my kids can have someone to be proud of.

To: Anonymous Lawyer
From: Anonymous Niece
Date: Wednesday, May 31, 7:37 PM

I'm pretty sure you mean Horatio Alger, not Alger Hiss. Still, your life means something regardless. You have a family. You have a good job even if you're not chairman of the firm. I know you have a lot more experience than I do, and I feel silly giving you advice, but this is part of why I don't know if your path is the right one for me. I don't want to get caught up in office politics like this. Good luck tomorrow, but I don't think your kids will love you any less if you don't get the job.

To: Anonymous Niece
From: Anonymous Lawyer
Date: Wednesday, May 31, 7:43 PM

You'll look back at this someday and realize how naïve you're being. You're wrong if you don't think there's office politics at the homeless shelter. You haven't seen corporate battles until you've seen a fight to be on the board of directors of the ACLU. They send people rolling down the handicapped ramps.

Thursday, June 1

The executive committee is meeting after the funeral to decide on the fate of the firm. I'm about to head over to the burial ground, but first I had breakfast with The Tax Guy to try and talk myself up for the chairman's job. He owes me a favor. He seemed receptive, but you can never be sure with him. I found him looking at tax porn on his computer once. Naked women holding tax forms. I think it was a pay site. I can't imagine that stuff is floating around for free. I asked him if he was being considered as a candidate for the job himself. He laughed. They don't give it to tax guys, he said. He's right. They don't. I shared with him the list The Musician helped me compile, about the situations where The Jerk hasn't come through for the firm. There are a lot of them. I saw The Jerk double-dip a strawberry in the chocolate fountain at last year's Christmas Party. Excuse me—last year's Holiday Gathering. The Jerk didn't wash his hands once on the way out of the bathroom. September 1995. I've been taking notes. I knew this day would come.

#Posted by Anonymous Lawyer at 8:52 AM

To: Anonymous Lawyer
From: Jared Samson
Date: Thursday, June 1, 9:03 AM

I was arrested last week for shoplifting and I was wondering if you could be my lawyer. I found your Web site and it's very interesting. I can't pay you much but maybe you can help me?

To: Jared Samson

From: Anonymous Lawyer

Date: Thursday, June 1, 9:09 AM

Jared, I can't give you any legal advice over the Internet, and you shouldn't be writing to an anonymous character. You don't know whether I'm real or not. Maybe I'm the store manager where you shoplifted. Don't shoplift. It's bad. Good luck.

Thursday, June 1

Worst. Funeral. Ever. The crab cakes were cold, they ran out of sushi, and the chicken on a stick was shit. Everyone left hungry, plus we ran out of the firm-logoed handkerchiefs before we got halfway through. The whole thing was a mess, so let me just run quickly through the highlights and then I can end this post and get back to more pressing business about how I'm going to manage to push The Jerk down the internal staircase and render him unfit to lead the firm.

Got to the grave site. The Tax Guy gave a speech about The Chairman's devotion to the firm. The Woman Who Hugs Everybody gave a speech about how he reached out to embrace people of all genders. The Moron gave a speech about Virginia ham. I talked about The Chairman's vision of excellence that, for two weeks, led us to the top of the industry. The audiovisual guys taped everything so we can use it in the recruiting process this fall. Unfortunately, the sound is muddled because The Chairman's widow was standing right by the camera and the microphone picked up her sobbing. We asked her a number of times to be quiet, but she didn't listen. No one ever listens.

We wheeled a video screen outside and showed a highlight film: The Chairman's Tenure, in brief. Very brief. We only had a little bit of footage to play with. It was a forty-second film. Twenty seconds of him emceeing the charity auction last week, ten seconds where he introduced himself to the summer associates, five seconds walking down the hall to the bathroom, and we closed with a clip of him watching the maintenance guy change the nameplate on his office door. It would have been very inspiring if it hadn't come off like a big joke. It wasn't a joke. It was me, doing everything I could to show the executive committee I mean business here.

Buried him in the ground. His era—short as it was—is over. And now it's back to work. As it ought to be.

#Posted by Anonymous at 2:15 PM

––––––––––

To: Anonymous Lawyer
From: The Musician
Date: Thursday, June 1, 5:34 PM

I found a couple of old performance reviews in the database where partners called The Jerk "a bit overeager" and "somewhat cold." You want me to pull them?

To: The Musician
From: Anonymous Lawyer
Date: Thursday, June 1, 5:53 PM

Those are positives here. Leave them in the file. Keep searching. I appreciate your help on this. Pick your favorite restaurant in the city and
we'll go there next week for lunch, I promise. Make it a good choice.
Steak's off the agenda for a while, for obvious reasons, but there's a
whole world of food out there. Make it interesting. Organ meats. I want
to feel like a hunter, not a gatherer. I want to feel in charge.

Friday, June 2

The executive committee's deliberating. I'm not sure what else I can
do. I prepared a fifty-seven-page report on my qualifications, my vision for the firm, and why The Jerk should be stripped naked, tied to a
pole, and beaten with a whip by all of the associates he's tortured over
the years, rather than be appointed chairman. I'm sure he's prepared a
similar report about me; I only hope mine is longer. Length counts. It's
not just quality. Clients like to see stacks of paper, and I expect the executive committee as well will be impressed by the sheer size of my
submission. Word came out this morning that they've decided not to
look outside the firm, so it really is just the two of us, unless there's a
dark horse candidate I'm unaware of. If I stick around I'm just going
to drive myself mad, and send summers to hang out by the meeting
room with their ears to the door, so I know I have to get out of here.

I'm desperate enough not to be here right now that I told Anonymous Wife I'd go to parent-teacher conferences with her. For Anonymous Son, not Anonymous Daughter. At least he still talks to me. My daughter doesn't want anything to do with me, and I don't really have a solution to that problem yet. Two kids was too many. One kid is hard enough, but two is insane. There's a guy here with seven. He's Catholic. I don't understand how he handles seven kids, although obviously as a partner the economics aren't really the problem. Even more so, I don't understand how he reconciles what we do in the office with his devout religious beliefs. But that's his problem to deal with, not mine.

When Anonymous Son was born, my wife and I decided to split them up. She's responsible for the girl, and I'm responsible for the boy. Not in terms of day-to-day responsibilities, because obviously I'm too busy to deal with most of that, but in terms of ultimate outcomes. I'm allowed to blame her if Anonymous Daughter is pregnant at sixteen and living on the street, and she's allowed to blame me if it's Anonymous Son's child she's pregnant with.

I worry about him. I worry his mother's turning him into a moron. I worry about how little time I get to spend with him and how much time he's under her spell, sitting in the house staring at the television while his brain rots. He's a smart kid—did pretty well on the practice SAT I made him take last summer, and he can name all of the presidents, backward and forward—but she's going to let it all go to waste. I don't want him to be one of them. Like Anonymous Daughter's middle school classmates. Spoiled rich kids, in their own world, not understanding what's important in life. I grew up comfortable, but Mom and Dad never made us feel rich. I went to public schools. I had friends whose parents did all sorts of things: schoolteachers, council members, shopkeepers, my best friend's dad was a plumber. We weren't sheltered in the same way that children are now. Our kids can't go to public school here, and I don't have time to have friends. They're surrounded by other kids whose parents have money, and it's not the world that normal people live in.

Don't get me wrong, I'm very glad we have money, but I'm old. I'm allowed to be judgmental and elitist. But I don't want to force it on my kids. I've failed them, to some extent. I made a choice, years ago, and it's a choice I can't take back. At least if I'm chairman all the compromises are justified.

It's too easy to block out these thoughts when I'm in the office, surrounded by a couple hundred other people who've made the same choices I have. We validate one another's decisions, just by virtue of being at work. The Frumpy Litigator says she won't move out to a nicer suburb because it'll add fifteen minutes to her commute and those are the only fifteen minutes she ever gets to see her daughter. Her nanny quit and she doesn't have time to find a new one, so she's sending her four-year-old to live with relatives for the summer. In Russia. The Jerk calls it "babysitting" when he has to watch his kids. It's a foreign concept to him.

Okay, I have a round of golf to play and a parent-teacher conference to attend. And some tires to slash, but I probably shouldn't be writing that.

#Posted by Anonymous at 1:34 PM

To: Anonymous Lawyer
From: Marc Reiner
Date: Friday, June 2, 1:55 PM

You should see a therapist.

Saturday, June 3

The parent-teacher conferences were predictably disorganized. The teacher was running behind schedule, so we ended up having to wait in the hall for forty-five minutes and make small talk with the other parents. I hate having to talk to people. Anonymous Wife says she liked meeting the other parents. Maybe if she left the house every once in a while it wouldn't be such a special occasion. There was a misspelling on the bulletin board outside the classroom, which clearly means this teacher is incompetent, but even more so it's a reflection on the school system. A misspelling at the law firm is caught within three and a half minutes of when it's typed, under the regulations. But here no one notices, no one cares, and no one gets fired for it. It's a breath of fresh air. But it's also inexcusable.

Anonymous Son's teacher said he's "average." That's what I was afraid of. Although I'm not sure I should take what his "average" teacher says as the gospel truth. It doesn't take much to babysit a bunch of eight-year-olds. She should try babysitting some twenty-somethings like I do.

He's not average. Or if he is, it's his mother's fault. We have relatives who are average. They're horrible. We go to Thanksgiving and they talk about their average jobs and their average hobbies and their average kids, and it's all very frustrating to me that being average is all that some people aspire to. That's not what I want for my son. Kids are supposed to grow up thinking they're brilliant. And for my kid—it's supposed to be true.

It was true for me, up to a point. I've always expected great things to happen to me. I still think they will, but every year that passes makes me wonder. Perhaps part of becoming an adult is the realization that maybe you're not in fact as brilliant as you thought. But that should happen when you're forty, not when you're eight. At eight you should feel invincible. Otherwise at forty you're going to be serving food at Applebee's. I ate there once. There is no part of a pig called a riblet.

I used to hear about people I knew becoming great things—a CEO, a writer, a congressman—and I still can't admit that I'm never going to be one of those people. But when everyone who gets a profile in *The New Yorker* is younger than you, you start to feel a little less confident. When you turn 30, 32, 35, 38, you start to realize that the people making a difference are of a different generation.

It's my turn to be great. I have one more chance to make my case, and it's at tomorrow's summer associate barbecue. The Jerk can have a midlife crisis—I need a promotion.

#Posted by Anonymous at 2:01 PM

To: Anonymous Lawyer
From: Anonymous Niece
Date: Saturday, June 3, 3:18 PM

Jacob's a smart kid. You shouldn't worry so much about him. I'm sure he'll be fine.

To: Anonymous Niece
From: Anonymous Lawyer
Date: Saturday, June 3, 3:28 PM

That's easy for you to say. You're going to Yale Law School. Your cousins aren't like you. Even when you were a kid, everybody knew you were special. It's not like that for them.

To: Anonymous Lawyer
From: Anonymous Niece
Date: Saturday, June 3, 3:33 PM

I'm not that special. I've been lucky.

To: Anonymous Niece
From: Anonymous Lawyer
Date: Saturday, June 3, 3:39 PM

There's no such thing as luck. You get what you deserve. If I become chairman, it's not because I got lucky. It's because I've earned it. And if I don't become chairman, it's a cop-out to blame it on anything but my own failure to work hard enough to make it happen. Don't be like my associates and pass responsibility off on something out of your control. They come into my office after two or three years at the firm saying they're miserable and blaming the firm for doing it to them. It's not our fault if someone's miserable. People make their own choices and are responsible for what they decide. No one wants to make hard choices. But you have to do it, and you have to live with the consequences.

To: Anonymous Lawyer
From: Anonymous Niece
Date: Saturday, June 3, 3:48 PM

Maybe you're right. Maybe I haven't had enough life experience to know. None this weekend, anyway. I'm holed up in my dorm studying for finals. I'll probably do fine. But a big element of whether I get an A or a B is the questions on the test. I could get lucky and they could be the things I know best, or the reverse.

To: Anonymous Niece
From: Anonymous Lawyer
Date: Saturday, June 3, 3:56 PM

Or you could study hard enough that luck won't matter. Stop wasting time e-mailing me. Go study. You have to make sure you graduate.

To: Anonymous Lawyer
From: Anonymous Niece
Date: Saturday, June 3, 3:59 PM

Everyone graduates.

To: Anonymous Niece
From: Anonymous Lawyer
Date: Saturday, June 3, 4:02 PM

And that's a good thing?

Sunday, June 4

The Tax Guy was right to keep the barbecue at The Dead Chairman's house. Despite his death, the house is still amazing and exactly the kind of thing we need to be showing the summers. This can all be theirs—if they earn it. The Dead Chairman's widow was gracious enough to give us a tour of the inside of the house. I snuck a peek in The Dead Chairman's bedroom, just to see what he had lying around. I thought I might pick up some clues about how he got himself to the top. I opened the bottom drawer of his nightstand, hoping to find something useful. Instead, all I saw was a naked picture of his wife and his Ferragamo tie that I always liked. I made sure no one was looking and pocketed them both. He won't miss them.

The executive committee implemented a new system for the barbecue. Last year there were two food tents, one for lawyers and one for support staff. The lawyers' tent had lobster, gourmet desserts, and a fountain of chocolate, and the support staff's tent just had some hot dogs and hamburgers. So the support staff kept sneaking into the regular tent for the good food, and it became intolerable. This year, they went with different colored bracelets instead—red for lawyers and blue for non-lawyers—with color-coded tables and buffet stations indicating where people should sit and what they were allowed to eat. This worked much better.

There was a bouncy castle for kids and paralegals, who all enjoyed it a lot. I had to steer Anonymous Wife away, after she drank too much. I couldn't get my daughter to come, but Anonymous Wife and Son seemed to have a nice time. Although I had to lock my wife in the car for the last hour to let her sleep off the alcohol. I left the window open a crack so she wouldn't get overheated.

I noticed a couple of recent lateral hires, off to the side, pretending to carefully study the horizon. It's hard for a lateral to fit in. The majority of associates spend a summer with us, and get to know the rest of their summer class all too well, so when they come back the following fall after graduation, they have a network of acquaintances throughout the firm. But laterals get hired and thrown into an office and the only people they end up meeting are their assigning partners and whoever they happen to end up staffed on a project with. It's lonely work. Making friends isn't billable.

The Bombshell was lingering by the smoked salmon platter, talking to Harvard Guy. I guess she knows who's going to be important in the future of the firm, and she wants to get in on the ground floor. It never hurts to be one of the associates the summers look up to. Then again, he wasn't looking up. He was looking down. I think she borrowed her dress from Tara Reid.

The Frumpy Litigator was off to the side, by herself, like she usually is. I went over to her and asked how things were going.

"On my cases?"

"No, I meant more generally. We're not in the office. I'm just curious how you're doing."

"I'm a little stressed, to be honest. This stuff with [The Chairman] freaked me out a bit. It doesn't help that we're at his house right now."

"You should take Monday off. Relax for a day. It'll reenergize you."

"You're just testing my dedication. I'll be there extra early, don't you worry."

"No, I was serious."

"No. So was I. I'll be there."

She was right—I was just testing her. They can't bail when the going gets tough. Everyone feels the stress. It's how you handle the stress that matters. It's how well you can hide your feelings, for the good of the firm.

"This is like Easter," I overheard Candyman saying to a couple of the summers.

"What do you mean?" asked That Foreign Dude.

"I mean I was working on Easter, and now, here, another Sunday, I'm basically working. That they make us give up a Sunday for this is ridiculous."

"You were forced to come?"

"Not forced, but of course we had to come. They notice things."

The Musician came over to me just as I was showing Anonymous Son how to get the meat out of a lobster claw.

"An associate just told me it doesn't get any better than this."

"Any better than this food?"

"No. Any better than this summer. He said it's all downhill from here."

"Of course it is. You have no responsibility, you get to go home at six, you get free lunches, you don't have to do much work. This is as good as it gets. See those two associates standing in the corner?"

"Sure."

"The one on the left used to be interesting. The one on the right used to be a woman."

"That's . . . odd."

"That's life at a law firm."

"Is it worth it?" he asked.

"What's the difference? Go get some more lobster."

"You want your son to grow up to be a lawyer?"

I looked at Anonymous Son. "For now I just want him to figure out how to get the meat out of a lobster claw. Good skill to have. Important no matter what he ends up doing."

I got sixteen pledges of support today in my bid for the chairman's position. They probably said exactly the same thing to The Jerk, but still, I got a good vibe about things. I have a chance. Also, I slipped a sleeping pill into The Jerk's drink, so he was gone after an hour. Ten more points for me.

#Posted by Anonymous at 9:54 PM

To: Anonymous Niece

From: Anonymous Lawyer

Date: Sunday, June 4, 11:11 PM

I just got an e-mail from the executive committee, sent to me and The Jerk. They want us both in the conference room at 9 a.m. Wish me luck.

Monday, June 5

I arrived at 8:30 this morning, half an hour early for a 9:00 meeting that was called. This was supposed to be THE meeting—the meeting where I'd find out if I'm the next chairman. Well, it didn't take until 9:00 for the answer to become clear. I got off the elevator and decided to take the long way around and pass by The Dead Chairman's old office, just to check it out. I found Barbara, packing her stuff into boxes. Looked like she was stealing office supplies—I saw her grabbing a three-hole punch.

"They fired you?" I asked, surprised. "Before they even announce the new chairman?"

"He let me go half an hour ago," she said. "It's too late."

I peeked inside, and the chairman's office had already been cleared out. But there, in the center of the room, was The Jerk's wooden Harvard armchair.

I stormed down the hall toward The Tax Guy's office. He was finishing up a phone call. I stood outside his office, pacing back and forth. Finally The Tax Guy noticed me.

"You didn't even have the courtesy to tell me?" I said. "Did I even have a chance?"

"Of course you had a chance," he said. "Come in and take a seat."

I sat down on his couch. It's purple. It's really ugly. His whole office is ugly. It's like he's color-blind. Maybe he is. That would explain the suits too.

"I didn't mean for you to find out this way," he said. "It was very close, but ultimately the executive committee decided we'd rather keep you in your current role. You're very important to the firm—please don't take this as a slight."

"How can I not take this as a slight? You chose him, not me."

"I don't want you to be angry," he said.

"Did you even read my fifty-seven-page memo?"

"It wasn't long enough. I'm sorry."

Eighteen years of service. I've wasted MY ENTIRE LIFE.

#Posted by Anonymous at 9:39 AM

To: Anonymous Lawyer
From: Anonymous Niece
Date: Monday, June 5, 10:10 AM

I'm sorry you didn't get the job. Maybe they'll pick you next time.

To: Anonymous Niece
From: Anonymous Lawyer
Date: Monday, June 5, 10:36 AM

Next time? There won't be a next time. The Jerk is going to be in there forever.

Don't you get it? They just told me I'm nothing. They just told me everything I've done doesn't matter. I lost to the enemy.

Two weeks ago I was prepared to wait. It wasn't my turn yet. But this time I can't make that excuse. This could have been mine, and it's not. I have to figure out a way to get The Jerk out of there. I don't know how, but I will. I've got to do something.

Monday, June 5

This stinks. This was supposed to be the light at the end of the tunnel. I was supposed to run this place someday. That was the payoff for eighteen years of giving myself to the firm—of missing the chance to know my kids, or know my wife, or even know how to play golf. I'm okay on the golf course, but I could be so much better if I played more than once a week. But I haven't. For the good of the firm.

They strung me along the same way I string along my associates. I make them think they're going to make partner, and then, when they don't, they're crushed and I don't really care. They know the chances. They know we have to dangle partnership in front of their eyes, just to keep them here. It's been no different for me and the chairman's office. As long as I thought I was on the right track, I didn't have to worry whether this was what I really wanted to be doing with my life.

I don't know if there's a way for a good person to work at a place like this without losing whatever makes him good. Every choice you make is a choice that takes another piece of your soul. You sabotage another associate's work to get the credit. You miss your anniversary to demonstrate your commitment. You screw over everything else in your life because this has to be number one. You get caught up in it. Everything feels so critical. When you step back, it's not so critical. But who has the time to step back?

This isn't what I saw myself doing. This isn't the life I saw myself living. At some point I chose this path. I don't know when, but I must have. I started working, and this place started taking up more and more of my energy until . . . until this became IT. You tell yourself it'll just be for a few more years, until you finally make partner. And then the goal changes. You want to run the place. You want to be important.

I'm not important. I'm not even sure I'd be important if I were chairman. I just searched for myself on Google. I barely exist. None of us do. None of this matters outside these walls. I'm nothing in this world. I'm just an anonymous lawyer. A goddamned anonymous lawyer.

The Suck-Up came by for a new assignment. I was about to tell him to get on the next flight to Dubuque when he interrupted me and said he's tired of traveling and would appreciate a local project. So I sent him to the document room to sort papers. I don't even care anymore. The fun is gone. The Suck-Up is probably happy here. Eighteen years from now he won't be. Eighteen years from now he'll be me.

I can't sit here. I'm going home to figure this out.

#Posted by Anonymous at 11:01 AM

To: Anonymous Lawyer
From: Matthew Harper
Date: Monday, June 5, 1:09 PM

I graduated from a top law school a year ago. I took a job at a big firm just like yours. And from the day I started, I've hated it. Every second of it. But what else is there?

I don't know what I'm doing here. Every partner at every firm is scum. You lie to us to trap us in this indentured servitude forever. You did this to me. You do this to everyone. You rope us in and make us suffer. I hope you rot in the hell you've helped create. I hope you never get out. I hope your wife leaves you, your kids won't talk to you, and all you have is that fucking office of yours. That's all you deserve.

Fuck you. Fuck your wife. Fuck your kids. I'm dying here. I'm dying at my fucking desk and it's all because of you.

Monday, June 5

I left the office early. Anonymous Son saw me on the couch watching television when he got home from school. He jumped onto the armrest of the sofa and used it as a handspring to catapult himself into my lap, where he landed with a thud. He's getting too old for this. "Daddy, why are you home?" he asked. I told him I'm working. "You never work on the couch," he said.

I asked him if he wanted to go look for snakes in the trees behind the house. It's a thing we used to do. When he was three or four, I would sneak away from the office sometimes, for an hour or two in the late afternoon, quietly let myself into the house, and rescue him from his mother. He had this children's book about snakes that he loved to read, *The Great Snake Escape,* and I told him that if we look really hard in the trees, I bet we could find one. It was just an excuse to have him all to myself. We'd wander in the back for a little while, and then we'd find a log and sit down and talk, or play with sticks, or watch the ants, or eat the ice-cream pops I'd grab on the way out of the house as a surprise.

Then he started kindergarten. I got busier, and it became too hard to get away from the office. We stopped looking for snakes.

So this afternoon we went out back and poked around for a while. No snakes, but a pretty cool butterfly he chased for a couple of minutes. We found a nice log, brushed it off, and sat down. "This is fun," I said. We talked about his teacher, and why the creamy peanut butter is better than the chunky kind, and how the water gets from the ocean to the house. I promised him next time we go on vacation we can see a volcano. But mostly we just sat there, watching the tree branches sway back and forth. And looking for snakes.

#Posted by Anonymous at 5:53 PM

Tuesday, June 6

Two days in, and The Jerk's already screwing the firm. He just sent out a memo about some internal changes. I guess this was part of his pitch to the executive committee. He's figured out some ways to save the firm money. Maybe that's why they gave him the job.

He's consolidating office space by doubling up the fourth- and fifth-year associates again, like they used to be before we gave them their own offices. That'll make them happy, I'm sure. And he's deploying some senior associates to new project teams. The ones on the cusp of eligibility for partnership—Candyman, The Bombshell, The One With Food In Her Teeth. Instead of being the big dogs in charge of a team of associates, they're going to be under more layers of partner hierarchy and lose most of the perks of being senior. In other words, no more shunting work to the associates beneath them, no more marginal control of their own schedules, and no more power. From what I understand, he's doing this to light a fire underneath them, so they know they have to work for the partnership and it won't just be a given. And he's getting rid of the chair massage guy.

This isn't how to treat people. These things just make people feel angry and frustrated. They feel slighted. The little things are important. The ability to lead a case and feel like you're in control. Your own office. The chair massages. These are gumdrops we give them. Rewards that can provide a quick high and make them willing to sacrifice a few more nights for the good of the firm. A kind word, a note of thanks, a wink in the middle of a meeting—it all makes people feel valued. The Jerk doesn't think about that. He treats people like he treats dogs. He eats them.

I'm not joking—he really did eat a dog. He went to China once and came back and sent an e-mail to the partnership telling us all about it. The Beijing office got upset. He got a reprimand. It was in my report. How come the executive committee didn't take it into consideration? How come he still got the job? The whole executive committee eats dogs. They're puppy-eaters. Maybe I'll send out a firm-wide memo about that. See how they feel.

#Posted by Anonymous at 10:58 AM

To: Anonymous Lawyer
From: The Musician
Date: Tuesday, June 6, 11:40 AM

Sorry you're not the new chairman. I was rooting for you.

To: The Musician
From: Anonymous Lawyer
Date: Tuesday, June 6, 11:48 AM

A lot of good that did. And anyway, you should be working, not sending me e-mails.

Wednesday, June 7

Pointless. We got a last-minute e-mail this morning asking everyone to report to Conference Room 24A for a presentation. The Jerk brought in a psychometrics consultant to give everyone at the firm some sort of personality test. We don't know what he's using the information for, and everyone's pretty confused. I was talking to some other partners during the lunch break. They think he wants to identify potential rogues—people who might be likely to lead a charge against him, or refuse to take orders. We're not sure why on day three of his tenure he'd be doing this, but it fits the recent pattern.

The associates are worried. They're worried it's going to be an excuse to fire them, or replace them with robots. Their concern, not mine. I don't know how advanced robot technology has gotten, but robots could probably do a lot of the work that associates are currently doing. It worked out well when we replaced the shoe-shine guy with a robot. Much more consistent work, and you don't have to tip the robot. Still, there are more tactful ways of implementing these things. With the shoe-shine guy, we had him kidnapped in the middle of the night. We certainly didn't devote an entire morning to give him reason to worry.

My evaluation showed me to be choleric and melancholy, whatever that means. I'm not sure if that's a good thing for the firm, a bad thing, or what in the world The Jerk is looking for. It's not like he's going to be able to use a personality test to get rid of a partner. Maybe a paralegal.

The result of Candyman's test is that he's fat. But we knew that already.

The Bombshell is not fat. I don't even know why she needs to take this personality test. No one cares about your personality when you look like she does. Closet Lesbian thinks that somehow her test results are going to reveal the secret everyone already knows. Everyone's on edge.

If I were chairman we wouldn't be wasting time with personality tests. We'd be billing clients, improving our training program, increasing the quality of our work, and making sure our customers are happy with the job we do. Sitting in a room and listening to a new-age hippie tell us that we need to understand one another's "work temperament" is garbage. My work temperament is that if you do things right, I'm happy, and if you do things wrong, I'm not. I don't need a personality test to tell me that.

#Posted by Anonymous at 1:50 PM

To: Anonymous Lawyer

From: Anonymous Niece

Date: Wednesday, June 7, 2:19 PM

How are you holding up?

To: Anonymous Niece

From: Anonymous Lawyer

Date: Wednesday, June 7, 2:40 PM

Still seething, but trying to hold it in. I'm not just going to let this drop.
I'm going to figure out a way to get him out of that office. Maybe I'm
getting carried away. Maybe I'm too upset. I'll calm down. It's not that
bad. You're going to love it here.

Thursday, June 8

Tonight's summer associate event is our annual cooking school outing. This is one of the most popular events of the season, because it al-
lows the summer associates to get really drunk, really quickly. There's a
cocktail hour, then there's wine flowing freely while the summer associates cook the food, more wine while they eat, and then we take them
out to a bar at the end of the night for an afterparty. It's such a popular
event that all the associates want to come too, at least the ones who can
get out of the office in time.

The first year we did this cooking event, I was concerned that all
the drinking would mess up the food quality, but I was naïve. The food

they cook—the chicken they stuff, the vegetables they slice, the cheese-cake they bake—all gets thrown out, in favor of food that the real chefs cook in advance. The potential lawsuits regarding undercooked chicken or dirty fingers touching the string beans are too much to risk. The summers think they're eating their own food—they all act so surprised it came out well and talk about how they never knew they could cook. Well, they can't. Not their food. Big joke.

Even if we told them the truth, they wouldn't care. It's not about the cooking, it's about the drinking. As the summer associate programs have grown more and more lavish, the drinking has grown too. Last week I walked in on three summers vomiting in the stalls the morning after the summer associate dinner. (It looked like an episode of *Family Guy*. Anonymous Son loves *Family Guy*.) And if they're already drinking this much as summer associates, I can't imagine what it'll be like when they're actually in the office working. It's different with this generation. Back when I was a summer associate, the drinking was a secret. Your alcohol problem stayed behind closed doors. Like it does for the partners today. Just like your sexual dysfunction and the problem with your prostate.

I worry what the next step is for the summer program, beyond alcohol, and how much it's going to cost us. I fear by next summer we'll be buying cocaine for the summer associates to snort in the conference rooms and distributing amphetamines on orientation day.

I'm only half-kidding about the amphetamines. We have associates faking ADD to get prescriptions for Ritalin. We didn't need Ritalin in my day. We got by on pure grit. I've tried to get the firm to do something about it, but no one wants to criticize someone's productivity-enhancing lifestyle choices. It's like steroids in baseball. We should start testing. Maybe The Jerk's on something. I could live with a fifty-day suspension for him.

#Posted by Anonymous at 5:04 PM

To: Anonymous Lawyer
From: Associate X
Date: Thursday, June 8, 11:30 PM

Chicken breasts stuffed with pesto sauce, potatoes au gratin, steamed broccoli, and a strawberry swirl cheesecake. Free firm-monogrammed cooking aprons and chef's hats. Afterparty at The Ivar.

I was there. I know who you are.

To: Associate X
From: Anonymous Lawyer
Date: Thursday, June 8, 11:43 PM

That doesn't mean anything. Every firm does the same events. Just because you know what food we ate doesn't mean you know who I am.

To: Anonymous Lawyer
From: Associate X
Date: Friday, June 9, 12:01 AM

Your son's name is Jacob, your daughter's name is Lauren, and you have a teddy bear on your bookshelf.

To: Associate X
From: Anonymous Lawyer
Date: Friday, June 9, 12:04 AM

Who are you and what do you want?

To: Anonymous Lawyer
From: Associate X
Date: Friday, June 9, 12:10 AM

I think we can help each other out. I'm probably too drunk from the cooking school to be thinking straight, but the alcohol is making me bold enough to send this. "The Jerk" is getting a little unpredictable recently and it's making me uncomfortable. This promotion has gone to his head. I have some dirt on him. I've been saving it. I think we can make something happen.

To: Associate X
From: Anonymous Lawyer
Date: Friday, June 9, 12:12 AM

WHO ARE YOU?

To: Anonymous Lawyer

From: Associate X

Date: Friday, June 9, 12:26 AM

It doesn't matter. I'm an associate who thought I was better off in The Jerk's corner, but after the reorganization I'm thinking maybe I'm not. The Jerk's turning on me and I'm realizing I've been on shaky ground all along. I'm getting nervous.

I'm not trying to hide my motives. This is a power play. I want to put myself in the best position I can to ensure I rise as high as possible at the firm. I have dirt on The Jerk. And knowing about this blog means that now I have dirt on you. So with dirt on both of you, I should be able to make something happen for myself. I'm prepared to use my information to get The Jerk deposed and help make you the next chairman. That's what you want, isn't it? Fairy-tale ending. How does that sound?

To: Associate X

From: Anonymous Lawyer

Date: Friday, June 9, 12:32 AM

Of course I want to be chairman. That's no secret, on the blog or in real life. TELL ME WHO YOU ARE.

To: Anonymous Lawyer
From: Associate X
Date: Friday, June 9, 12:37 AM

I'm smarter than that. If I tell you who I am, then you have all the lever-age. You'll fire me for knowing about your blog, or you won't have the guts to take any real action so you'll turn me in to win brownie points with The Jerk, and he'll have me drawn and quartered like Evan in word processing, who stapled wrong the other day. You have to trust me. We can do this.

To: Associate X
From: Anonymous Lawyer
Date: Friday, June 9, 12:41 AM

Evan stapled very wrong. He deserved it. I'm uncomfortable with what-ever you're doing—I can't do this without knowing who you are and what you're talking about. If you tell anyone about my blog, I will track you down and have you fired, instantly. Be assured of that. For now, I'm going to pretend this e-mail exchange never happened. I don't know what kind of information you have about The Jerk, but I'm not going to risk that this is a trap of some sort. You're not going to get me. I'm too careful for that. I think we're done for now.

To: Anonymous Lawyer

From: Associate X

Date: Friday, June 9, 12:53 AM

I guess I was wrong. You don't really want to be chairman after all. Because if you did, you'd be jumping at this chance. This is opportunity falling from the sky.

In the meantime, rest assured you have nothing to worry about regarding the blog. I have nothing to gain by getting you in trouble for it, at least not yet. I want you to be my ticket to the top. But if you won't help me, I'll find some other way. I won't do anything stupid. Don't worry.

I'll tell you, though . . . and I know I'm going to regret writing this, but it's late and I can't help it . . . you're not just missing out on your best chance to be chairman, you're missing out on some great sex. For an older guy you're not bad looking. Especially given the sorry state of your colleagues. I bet you didn't know you're on everyone's top-ten list. The women talk about this. There's not much else to talk about. And the gay guy on 31 has a huge crush on you. He writes stories about it and sends them around. He says he thinks about you when he masturbates. In his office, with the door closed. While you're on the phone giving him an assignment. Sweet dreams, sugar.

Friday, June 9

Harvard Guy just stopped by to ask for some work. I don't have any assignments to give out, but I can always make one up. "Why don't you call up the insurance commissioners of all fifty states and find out their rules about car insurance minimums?"

He looked at me funny.

"Better yet, let's see if there are any county-by-county rules. That should keep you busy for a while, right?"

"I did that for [The Jerk] last week," he said.

"Oh."

"Anything else?"

"Well, I could always use a summary of the ninth circuit cases where employers tried to deny employees health care, and some recommendations for how our clients can potentially do this too. Just in case they ask."

"Did that one already."

"Okay. Help me out here. What else have you done?"

"Last week someone gave me twelve boxes of paper, a thousand pages in each box, with a number stamped in the corner of each sheet. They were all out of order. I needed to put them in the right sequence. It was tough."

"I sense some sarcasm." I don't like it when the summers use sarcasm.

"No, no. Sorry about that. I didn't mean it." He looked like he was getting upset. I don't like it when they cry either. Although crying is better than sarcasm.

"No, I'm not mad, it's okay. What's wrong?"

He sat down on my couch. Uninvited. But I let it pass. "It's just that I didn't come here to sort paper. I go to Harvard Law School. I can do more than sort paper. No offense, but I feel like this whole summer is kind of a waste of my time."

"And what wouldn't be a waste of your time?"

"I don't know. Helping to write a brief? Getting to watch someone go to court? Sitting in on a client meeting? I want to know what lawyers like you do, instead of just sorting paper."

"That's fair, I suppose. But a lot of what we do is sort paper. I hear what you're saying though. I know this can be frustrating. Here's what I have for you. We have a client who's trying to sell one of his factories. We're trying to figure out whether selling this factory is going to trigger any of the provisions in any of his loan agreements. It's an important assignment, and normally I wouldn't give it to a summer associate. But you're not just any summer associate. So I'm going to trust you with this. I'll have my secretary send over the stack of documents. It's about three feet high. I am sure there are paragraphs about contingencies in the event of the sale of an asset, like the factory. I don't know what the language will look like, or where in the stack this paragraph might be. Or if it's even there at all. But a multimillion dollar deal may hinge on this. It's very important work. Do you think you're up to the task?"

"Oh, I do. Definitely. I won't make you regret giving me this chance."

"Good. I expect great things."

And then he left. Thankfully. With another garbage assignment I was able to dress up to sound important. Victory for me. There's nothing I can do about kids like him. We need kids from the very best schools. The clients like them, it gives the firm prestige, it keeps the recruiting pipeline strong. But these Ivy League kids think too much about what we ask them to do, and the years of people telling them how smart they are have made them believe it.

Sometimes they're right and they really are brighter than everyone else. But sometimes they're wrong. We don't know right away, and we might never know. Even if I thought Harvard Guy was a legal genius, there's a system and he has to do the kinds of work that we give him to do. There's a limited amount of "good" work to go around.

Of course that's not what we tell them when we recruit them, especially not at places like Harvard. At the University of Minnesota, they'll accept anything we tell them. They'll kill for the chance to sort my papers into boxes, to break down my boxes for the recycle bin, to empty the recycle bins into the dumpster, whatever we have them do. They just want the job. Kids at Harvard are different.

Harvard Guy has a nice tie on today. He knows how to dress. It's a surprisingly important skill. I think it's getting him some summer associate action. I heard two of the female summers talking. They never have a crush on the ones from second-tier schools. It's always the ones with the high LSAT scores.

#Posted by Anonymous at 11:38 AM

To: Anonymous Niece
From: Anonymous Lawyer
Date: Friday, June 9, 12:44 PM

I got an e-mail from one of my associates yesterday. Or at least I think she's one of my associates. She knows who I am.

To: Anonymous Lawyer
From: Anonymous Niece
Date: Friday, June 9, 12:49 PM

You sure?

To: Anonymous Niece
From: Anonymous Lawyer
Date: Friday, June 9, 12:57 PM

I'm sure.

To: Anonymous Lawyer
From: Anonymous Niece
Date: Friday, June 9, 1:04 PM

This is bad, right?

To: Anonymous Niece
From: Anonymous Lawyer
Date: Friday, June 9, 1:12 PM

That's the part I'm not certain about. A week ago, I would have been really concerned about this, and probably would have tried to delete the whole blog. I know you said I can't, but I'd find a way. I have power.

But this associate said she wants to help me get rid of The Jerk. I'm not sure I can trust her. She could even be The Jerk pretending to be an associate, just to trap me. But if she's telling the truth, this could be just what I need.

I want to know what you can do with your computer to help me figure out who this is. Is there something you can trace, some way to know if there are people here who are reading this?

To: Anonymous Lawyer
From: Anonymous Niece
Date: Friday, June 9, 1:19 PM

There's not much I can do, but maybe a little bit. I can check the IP addresses of the user logs. I can do some Google searches to see if the
blog comes up anywhere. If you forward me her e-mails I can see if
there's any information encoded in them that can help me trace her.
But that's about all I know how to do.

To: Anonymous Niece
From: Anonymous Lawyer
Date: Friday, June 9, 1:26 PM

That sounds like a lot. I'd actually really appreciate that. I should probably ask you how your final exams are going.

To: Anonymous Lawyer
From: Anonymous Niece
Date: Friday, June 9, 1:29 PM

They've been going well, thanks. All I have left is this geology final, and
it shouldn't be too bad.

To: Anonymous Niece
From: Anonymous Lawyer
Date: Friday, June 9, 1:44 PM

Okay. Good luck with that. When you have a minute let me know what
you find out about the blog. I hope this isn't The Jerk playing a trick,
because if he finds this blog, it would probably kill my chances of ever
getting to run this firm or any firm.

   If I was smarter I wouldn't have even started this thing, but I feel
like it's given me some sort of connection with the outside world. I
didn't realize a lot of lawyers feel like this too—that this is as frustrating
for them as it is sometimes for me. It's bizarre—people have e-mailed
me and told me I'm at twenty-six different firms, I'm fifty-three different
people, I'm a chairman, I'm an associate, I'm a secretary, I'm a janitor.
And it's kind of a rush to take a risk. Is this how you felt passing up
Princeton to go to Stanford?

To: Anonymous Lawyer
From: Anonymous Niece
Date: Friday, June 9, 1:46 PM

Stanford's better than Princeton. I don't care what the rankings say.

To: Anonymous Niece
From: Anonymous Lawyer
Date: Friday, June 9, 1:59 PM

Of course you care what the rankings say. Everyone cares what the rankings say. Law students especially. They're all obsessed with rankings. It's a prestige thing. You'll see when you get to Yale. They talk about the *U.S. News* rankings for law schools, the Vault rankings for firms. At The Chairman's funeral I heard someone say it was the number-one-ranked cemetery in the Los Angeles area but that the coffin wasn't really prestigious enough. What does that even mean?

To: Anonymous Lawyer
From: Anonymous Niece
Date: Friday, June 9, 2:06 PM

I don't know. I think you might be getting carried away.

Saturday, June 10

Last night we threw the summer associates a party on the beach. When we did this last year there were some infiltrators—some ordinary beachgoers who stole some of our food—so this year we put up some fencing. I think next year we should just truck in some sand and do it in the parking lot. That way we'd have complete control over the atmosphere.

We set up some volleyball nets and hired a former Olympian to give a short clinic and warm everyone up. Karch Kiraly, a three-time gold medalist. Only a few of the kids knew who he was, but it makes us feel prestigious to have famous people come to our events. He did a few easy drills. Nothing too tough, since everyone's out of shape, but some simple sets and volleys. It didn't pay off. These were some terrible volleyball games. Karch would have left in disgust if not for the fee we were paying and the dinner we provided. He was a good sport. Maybe I'll get him for Anonymous Son's next birthday party.

Harvard Guy may have been good at bowling but he was completely inept at volleyball. Good for him. The most talked-about topic was the outfit worn by The Girl Who Dresses Like A Slut. It was almost a bikini, only smaller. Yellow polka dots. Well, one polka dot. There wasn't room for any more. I don't even know if it was designed as clothing or a napkin ring. But no one could take his eyes off of her. Or off The Bombshell, who could give The Girl Who Dresses Like A Slut a run for her money. Anonymous Wife can still wear a bikini, but not like that. Not like that at all. Not after two kids. Anyway, The Girl Who Dresses Like A Slut showed almost as much skin as The Fat Kid. He needs to keep his shirt on. We should fire him for taking it off. It's unsightly.

Unencumbered by clothing, The Girl Who Dresses Like A Slut actually played a solid game. She's sly that way. Does the unexpected. Amazingly, people say her work product is pretty good. The attractive ones never do good work. But she's the exception to that rule. She and The Bombshell. I remember The Girl Who Dresses Like A Slut's interview. Her résumé wasn't great. Her grades weren't stellar. Her LSAT score was a 178, which is okay but nothing special (or at least that's what we tell our candidates, just to keep them on their toes). But she wasn't wearing a wedding ring, and she had amazing legs up to the sky, and I knew she'd be an excellent addition to the summer class.

Pretty faces help office morale. They make everyone feel better about spending twenty hours a day here. It'll be my legacy as hiring partner. The last guy's legacy was opening the firm up to Jews. The overall diversity here has really grown in the past decade. When I started, there was hardly a minority. Now there are five. Well, four and a half. Remarkable progress.

We had the caterers bring a rolling bar to the beach, and after some pregame cocktails we were going to split the summers up into teams and do a round-robin tournament. But before we could get started, The Jerk wandered over, martini in hand, his fourth or fifth of the night:

"How about a rematch of that bowling disaster, champ? We'll each pick a summer associate to team up with. First to fifteen points wins." He was slurring his words. I figured this would be easy.

"Sure, if you want."

"Great. I'm the chairman. I order it."

I rolled my eyes and kicked off my dress shoes. The Jerk pointed to Doc, the six-foot-three summer associate who used to be a surgeon. He's about the only one who looks like he's made use of the discounted summer gym membership. I haven't worked with him yet, but the buzz is that he's this summer's star. We could use a star. He was also practically the only summer associate still sober.

"You're on my team. I'll give you five hundred bucks if we win. Cash from my pocket. Actually, make it a thousand. I'm rich." And completely wasted. Maybe the stress of the job is getting to him. A little incident with alcohol poisoning could torpedo his career pretty quickly.

"Have another drink," I told him.

I walked over to The Musician. "You play volleyball?"

"Not really. I write songs, remember?"

"Are you at least not embarrassingly bad?"

"I'm not embarrassingly bad. And I'm not half as drunk as your boss. I think we'll have a chance, if you're any good."

"Of course I'm good. I'm good at everything I do. Except bowling. Okay, let's do it. A hundred bucks if we win."

"You're not gonna match The Jerk?"

I took a deep breath. "A thousand bucks if we win." I didn't know if I wanted to win anymore. "You give me a thousand if we lose?"

"I don't think so. Worth a try, though."

We got out to an 11–6 lead. I played tennis in grade school, some intramural softball in college, but I was never really a jock. I'm a lawyer. Lawyers by definition were never jocks. Doc did his best to save The Jerk, but The Jerk's carrying fifteen extra pounds and was barely able to stand up anyway, so it was a struggle for them to keep pace. The Musician was right that he wasn't embarrassingly bad, but unfortunately he wasn't much better than that.

But then The Jerk turned on something extra. Doc started serving aces. The Jerk started staying out of his way. It's the hand-eye coordination that makes a big difference. Maybe Doc should be performing skin graft surgery on burn victims after all, like he was going to do before the law firm salary lured him away.

Before I knew it, we were tied at 13.

"We've got to win this," I said to The Musician. "It's important."

"It's just a game."

"No, it's more than that."

It was their serve. Doc got another ace. 14–13. They were one point away from winning.

But then we came back and beat them. Finally, The Jerk got what he deserved.

#Posted by Anonymous at 11:07 AM

To: Anonymous Lawyer
From: The Musician
Date: Saturday, June 10, 12:25 PM

Wait a minute—we didn't win! They won, 15–13. Why are you making up stories?

To: The Musician
From: Anonymous Lawyer
Date: Saturday, June 10, 12:32 PM

Creative license. Even if we couldn't stop him from winning again in real life, at least I can pretend. It's a better narrative that way. I get to be The Comeback Kid. Don't bring it up again and I'll give you the thousand bucks anyway. Or dinner with me and my family. Your choice.

To: Anonymous Lawyer
From: The Musician
Date: Saturday, June 10, 12:50 PM

I'll take the money. But keep in mind you're cheating your readers if you make up stories. What's the point if this is all just an exercise to lie about how cool you wish you were? Part of the charm of this—and I apologize if this sounds corny, but it's true—is that you come across a lot more real in your writing than you do in person. In person you're a little stiff.

Someone told me something about my music once. They said I write because I don't have any other way to express what I'm feeling. I'm clearly not the life of the party. Especially for a law student, I'm an introvert. Not to overstep here, but I think that's part of this for you. You're trying to keep up this image of being the perfect lawyer, but on the blog you're able to let that guard down a little bit. I don't mean to be overstepping my bounds. I'm sorry.

But even more practically—you don't write very realistically when you're making it up. All that detail about the real part, and then a throw-away line about the part you invented. I bet it'll be obvious to a lot of your readers.

To: The Musician
From: Anonymous Lawyer
Date: Saturday, June 10, 12:59 PM

I expect my readers don't much care if I won the volleyball game or not. They're not reading for that. They're reading to find out how they can get a job here. I lied about it because I didn't want to admit that I'd lost again. And he didn't have to announce to everyone that he beat me at volleyball like he beat me out for chairman. I know he was drunk off his ass, but that's no excuse.

I'll give you the thousand bucks on Monday. You can splurge on something fun. As if the damn $2600 a week we pay you kids isn't enough. Ridiculous.

To: Anonymous Lawyer
From: The Musician
Date: Saturday, June 10, 1:06 PM

Keep your money. We lost. It's not fair for me to take it. And cheer up. You're a hiring partner at a monster law firm. Everyone I know would kill to be in your position.

Saturday, June 10

Anonymous Wife decided this afternoon that what would make our marriage stronger is a remodeled kitchen. I don't know if she read this in one of her glossy magazines, if one of her thrice-divorced friends told her, or if she's just been drinking too much. But, however it happened, that's what she wants. Track lighting, new cabinets, an island in the middle, an industrial-strength refrigerator-freezer, a deluxe range. She never cooks, so I don't know what it's all for. She's been collecting catalogs. She says making the decisions together is part of the fun.

We have enough money for a new kitchen, but that's not the issue. We have enough money for five new kitchens. It's the principle of it. She doesn't earn it, so she shouldn't spend it the way she does. I never told her she had to stay home—she assumed that it was part of the deal. If she were a good mother, it would be a different story, but she's not.

She picked a bad week to bring it up—obviously. She doesn't care
that I didn't make chairman. She just wants a new kitchen. Whatever.
She's going to get a new kitchen. A new freezer with a built-in ice-
cream maker. She has a friend with one of those. We went over there a
few weeks ago and they'd made some chocolate ice cream with real
cocoa nibs. The bitter essence of the cocoa bean. That's to a Hershey's
bar what a Stanford graduate is to a high school dropout.

#Posted by Anonymous at 2:14 PM

To: Anonymous Lawyer
From: Associate X
Date: Saturday, June 10, 3:32 PM

WTF?? You didn't win the volleyball game. You're a liar!

To: Associate X
From: Anonymous Lawyer
Date: Saturday, June 10, 3:43 PM

You were there?

To: Anonymous Lawyer
From: Associate X
Date: Saturday, June 10, 3:44 PM

I'm everywhere.

To: Associate X

From: Anonymous Lawyer

Date: Saturday, June 10, 3:47 PM

I hate that he beat me again last night. I hate that he showed me up in front of everyone.

To: Anonymous Lawyer

From: Associate X

Date: Saturday, June 10, 3:49 PM

We can get rid of him. Are you in?

To: Associate X

From: Anonymous Lawyer

Date: Saturday, June 10, 3:51 PM

I want to believe you're being honest with me, but I don't know how I can trust you.

To: Anonymous Lawyer

From: Associate X

Date: Saturday, June 10, 3:55 PM

Okay. I understand. You need proof. Check the cabinet next to the copy machine on 19 East at 9:45 on Monday morning. It'll be a teaser to some of the evidence I've got. Only a teaser. I'm not giving you everything you need so easily. I'm only easy in the bedroom.

To: Associate X
From: Anonymous Lawyer
Date: Saturday, June 10, 4:22 PM

Make it noon. I'm going to my twenty-fifth high school reunion tomorrow and taking an early flight back on Monday morning. And if I find out you're The Jerk . . .

To: Anonymous Lawyer
From: Associate X
Date: Saturday, June 10, 4:28 PM

Wait, you think I'm The Jerk? If I was The Jerk, would I tell you I thought you looked awfully sexy playing volleyball last night? Jacket off, shoes off, I was hoping you'd take it all off.

To: Associate X
From: Anonymous Lawyer
Date: Saturday, June 10, 4:34 PM

Even if you're not The Jerk, you're probably something hideous—The Frumpy Litigator, or even worse—so this sex talk isn't really turning me on, I'm sorry to say. I'm picturing green face paint and warts—my wife dragged me to see *Wicked* when we were in New York, and the understudy we saw was not an attractive woman. She gave me nightmares.

Saturday, June 10

I'm supposed to be researching omelette makers. That's what I told her I'm doing on the Internet. She wants an omelette maker in the new kitchen. I don't even know if that's a pan or a whole device of its own. How often do we make omelettes?

#Posted by Anonymous at 4:40 PM

To: Anonymous Lawyer
From: Anonymous Niece
Date: Saturday, June 10, 4:45 PM

Congratulations on the volleyball game. It must feel really good.

To: Anonymous Niece
From: Anonymous Lawyer
Date: Saturday, June 10, 4:47 PM

It does. Thanks.

Saturday, June 10

I draw the line at a food dehydrator. We have never needed to dehy-drate our food. I like my food wet. The kids like their food wet. I don't understand the point of such a device. We don't eat jerky and we don't need to make our kids their own Fruit Roll-Ups. We can afford Fruit Roll-Ups. I am not letting her buy a food dehydrator. That's where I draw the line.

#Posted by Anonymous at 5:09 PM

To: Anonymous Lawyer
From: Matt Baxter
Date: Saturday, June 10, 6:02 PM

Am I The Fat Kid?

To: Matt Baxter
From: Anonymous Lawyer
Date: Saturday, June 10, 6:04 PM

What?

To: Anonymous Lawyer
From: Matt Baxter
Date: Saturday, June 10, 6:07 PM

I found your blog. Am I The Fat Kid from the volleyball post? Because I'm not really that fat. I've been on a diet. Maybe you haven't noticed.

To: Matt Baxter
From: Anonymous Lawyer
Date: Saturday, June 10, 6:09 PM

Matt, I don't know who you are.

To: Anonymous Lawyer
From: Matt Baxter
Date: Saturday, June 10, 6:10 PM

You're lying. I'm The Fat Kid. I know it. I hate you. I hate everyone at this stupid firm. Go ahead. Fire me. I'll tell everyone about your blog.

To: Matt Baxter
From: Anonymous Lawyer
Date: Saturday, June 10, 6:12 PM

I told you, I don't know who you are.

To: Anonymous Lawyer
From: Matt Baxter
Date: Saturday, June 10, 6:14 PM

You're not Rob Hendricks at Shaker Millstone?

To: Matt Baxter
From: Anonymous Lawyer
Date: Saturday, June 10, 6:15 PM

No, thank goodness. Your firm's a piece of shit.

To: Anonymous Lawyer
From: Matt Baxter
Date: Saturday, June 10, 6:19 PM

Oh, okay. I'm not fat. Just so you know. You hiring?

Saturday, June 10

Okay, maybe we can get a food dehydrator. But we don't need a vacuum sealer. She barely uses the regular vacuum. There is no need for more vacuum-based appliances in the house. What would we seal? She says we can store our clothing. We have closets. Lots of closets. A walk-in closet. Closets we barely use. And they're well-organized, thanks to another useless purchase she made a few years ago of some crappy hanger setup she saw on television. No vacuum sealer. That is where I put my foot down. I mean it this time.

Posted by Anonymous at 6:28 PM

To: Anonymous Lawyer
From: Mark Greenberg
Date: Saturday, June 10, 7:08 PM

I work in career services at Hastings College of the Law. I've stumbled across your blog and was wondering if I might be able to invite you to come speak on campus in the fall about your thoughts on the recruiting process and how our students can be more prepared for their interviews. We'd be willing to pay for your travel to campus and take you out for dinner. I appreciate your taking the time to consider this offer.

To: Mark Greenberg
From: Anonymous Lawyer
Date: Saturday, June 10, 7:47 PM

It's almost excusable when desperate law students e-mail me looking for a job even when they don't have any idea who I really am. It's inexcusable when an adult does it. Suppose I say yes, and I show up, and I give a talk, and it turns out I work as a baggage handler at the airport and I'm just making all of this up. Would you keep your job, or would they let you go? Best of luck helping your students become junior versions of me. May God have mercy on you for aiding in the process.

Saturday, June 10

What a sick job the law school career-services directors have. At least I only have to sell this job to these kids for a couple of months out of the year, and I'm doing it out of economic self-interest. These people have to put a smiley face on law firm life all year long.

The Suck-Up sent me an e-mail this evening. He's been doing document review all week and he's getting bored. He apologized for asking not to travel. He's worried he overstepped his bounds and I'm upset with him. I assured him I'm not, and I appreciate his willingness to step up and take one for the team. I've scheduled him on a flight to Burma to do some work for a pro bono case we've taken on. People think that when we say we have a human rights practice group it means we help prosecute corrupt governments. In fact it's just the opposite. Burma is our client. Myanmar, actually. Just like when we say we do asbestos work, we mean it's the companies who make it that we're helping, not the people "allegedly" harmed. Our environmental practice group is proud to have ExxonMobil as its biggest client. Our health and human safety group just settled a tobacco case last week.

I told The Suck-Up he should probably be a bit more deferential to his superiors at the satellite office we've set up in Burma than he's been to me. I don't think they offer second chances.

#Posted by Anonymous at 9:35 PM

To: Anonymous Lawyer

From: Lauren Bargholz

Date: Saturday, June 10, 10:09 PM

My firm sent me to Burma last month. I'm just now getting back. I've been reading your blog for a while now (Internet connection was surprisingly good out there). Just wanted to say you're describing my life exactly. I wish I worked for you.

Sunday, June 11

We're waking up at five in the morning to fly to my twenty-fifth high school reunion, back home in Michigan. I skipped the tenth and the twentieth because of work, but I promised Anonymous Wife we'd go to this one.

I'm eager to show my classmates what I've made of myself. I went to a public high school, and it's not every day people graduate and become partners at big law firms. Anyone can go from Exeter and Yale to a firm like ours, but to go from a public high school in Birmingham, Michigan, to a job like this—well, I'm pretty unique.

I had two friends in high school. I haven't stayed in touch with them, but I heard that one is now an accountant and the other one writes articles about boats for a specialty magazine. I don't know which one does which, but it doesn't really matter.

Actually, I'm sure I had more than two friends, I just don't remember them. I wasn't bullied or anything like that in high school. It wasn't torture, I had a good time, but I have to admit I wasn't one of the cool kids. Nobody at the firm was a cool kid in high school. The cool kids became the hedge fund managers and the venture capitalists, not the lawyers. Definitely not the lawyers. Some people are innately likable, from the moment you meet them. They have some sort of charisma that draws people in and makes everyone want to help them succeed in life. Lawyers realize early on that the way to get people to like us is by leveraging power. We can't rely on our charm.

There's a complete redefinition of cool at a law firm like this. I see it even in the summer program. It's a reordering of the universe. Almost none of these kids were cool before law school, and even in law school some of them aren't that cool. But it's all relative. You get here and even the barest degree of social self-confidence or a pleasant disposition can make you seem cool in comparison. People like me, who may not have been the big man on campus in high school, are suddenly the coolest people in the room. It's what retarded kids who can dribble a basketball must feel like at the Special Olympics.

Cool at the firm is based on a power index. The more power you hold, the cooler you are. It depends on control—control of your fate, and control of the fate of others. As an associate, cool is based on aligning yourself with those in power, and doing exactly what got you ostracized as a kid—sucking up to adults. What matters is getting the partners to treat you better than they treat your peers. The Suck-Up takes it way too far, but a lot of the rest of them have the right idea. It's not cool to volunteer your weekend just to show that you're willing to be a slave. That's pathetic. But getting a partner to trust you enough that he'll turn to you when there's important work to do—that's cool.

Tonight I get to show my classmates who I've become. The middle managers and the paper distributors and the door-to-door encyclopedia salespeople. The ones wasting their lives as "freelance magazine writers" and "jewelry makers" and "stay-at-home fathers."

#Posted by Anonymous at 12:19 AM

To: Anonymous Lawyer
From: Jed Goldfarb
Date: Sunday, June 11, 1:44 AM

I'm a law student at Hofstra with a weblog of my own. I was hoping you
might be willing to link to it. Also, I'm attaching my résumé. Do you
have any job openings?

Sunday, June 11

I hate the airport. I'm writing this on my BlackBerry—they just de-
layed our flight. I have a reunion to get to, goddammit! Luckily, I made
a contingency plan and I've got tickets on another airline. Contingency plans are a secret of partner life. If you need a cab, you order two
and take whichever one comes first. Always make backup restaurant
reservations in case you don't like the food at the first place. Get tickets
to two shows on the same night so you can bail on a lousy one at inter-
mission and still have something to see. We're taking the summers to a
comedy club in a few weeks and I picked up tickets to a sold-out jazz
performance, just in case. I'll probably stick with the comedy club,
since it looks bad if the hiring partner leaves early, but I'll have the jazz
tickets in my back pocket. I always buy tickets on a second flight,
whenever I fly. You never know when you'll be unavoidably late to the
airport. Sure, sometimes it flags me in the system and they want to
search me, but it's worth the inconvenience.

It's sad to wave goodbye to my fellow passengers who'll be stuck
here at the gate while I head over to Terminal 4 to get on my American
Airlines flight. I was going to fly Northwest nonstop, but now I'll be

switching planes in Dallas. It'll still get me there faster than waiting. I can't waste half my day in the airport.

#Posted by Anonymous at 6:47 AM

To: Anonymous Lawyer
From: Thomas D. Jackson
Date: Sunday, June 11, 6:53 AM

If you're the guy tapping on your BlackBerry about eight seats away from me—I'm the man working on his laptop and eating a breakfast burrito from El Cholo Cantina. I just wanted to let you know I'm reading your blog. My firm's sending me to Dallas to take depositions, on a Sunday. Life sucks. But the breakfast burrito is actually pretty good.

Sunday, June 11

I'm never flying American again. The guy next to me in first class smelled terrible. People in first class aren't supposed to smell terrible. If you smell terrible, you're supposed to be in coach. I asked the flight attendant and she said he'd gotten an upgrade. I begged her to do something about it. She said she didn't smell anything. I told her I'm reporting her. Obviously if an associate had been there I would have forced him to switch seats with me. Instead I made my wife switch. I don't know what I'd have done without her. She's in the hotel shower right now, washing the smell off. I told her she can't come to the reunion unless she scrubs herself clean.

#Posted by Anonymous at 2:25 PM

Sunday, June 11

The reunion was a nightmare—how did I delude myself into thinking it would be anything else?

We just got back to the hotel room. We're staying overnight and I'm returning on an early flight to get back to the office by lunchtime. Anonymous Wife is staying an extra day to spend time with my parents. Why shouldn't she? The nanny can be our kids' mother, that's fine. My wife can neglect her only job and the kids can be raised by a woman who doesn't even have a college degree and lets our daughter eat ice cream for lunch.

I thought it would be different twenty-five years later. But everyone immediately fell back into the same old cliques—the football team, the religious nuts, the idiots. I was stuck talking to the girl who has four kids with four different fathers and who looked like she was about to give birth to another one. That would have been great. Right there in the gymnatorium. The sanitation worker could have cleaned up the mess, and the nurse practitioner could have done a paternity test right then and there. I could have helped her file for child support, if I was inclined to volunteer any legal services, which of course I wasn't, and then the principal could have pretended he was a judge and executed the order. We could have had a whole minidrama under the basketball net.

No one had even heard of my firm. No one cared where I worked, no one knows anything about corporate law, what it means, and how important it is to a functioning capitalist society. People's eyes glazed over when I talked about it. They think lawyer means trial attorney. They wanted to know if I know Michael Jackson. No one knows what a partner is. I'm the guy who went to California and works in an office. No one gave a shit. It didn't matter at all.

There's a woman who was on the local news because she lived next door to a guy whose house burned down. Big stupid deal. There was a food service engineer, whatever that is. People were more interested in the sculptor than in me. Is his work in a museum? No. Is he on welfare? Probably. Does he need to stop with the ponytail, because it's obvious that he's compensating for male pattern baldness? Definitely.

I have a stack of business cards in my pocket. I don't even live here anymore, so I don't need lawn care supplies, a corporate account at The Home Depot, a family therapist, expert tax preparation, private investigation services, or the best catering in Oakland County.

Anonymous Wife stayed by my side and we mostly talked to each other. I'm sure she was tremendously unimpressed with my performance. I wasn't in touch with anyone from high school before, and I won't be in touch with anyone now. A waste of time, a waste of a flight, and a waste of this suit I'm going to have to throw out because it has the smell from the plane baked into its fibers.

#Posted by Anonymous at 10:54 PM

To: Anonymous Lawyer
From: Associate X
Date: Sunday, June 11, 11:45 PM

Don't forget—the cabinet next to the copy machine on 19 East at noon tomorrow. I expect you'll like what you find. I mean, it won't be me, naked except for some strategically placed "sign here" stickers, but I still think you'll find it pretty exciting.

Monday, June 12

I just got in to find an e-mail from a pregnant associate. I don't mean The One Who's Either Pregnant Or Just Fat. This one is definitely pregnant. She was in the office as recently as Friday, looking like she was going to burst at any moment and a baby was going to be expelled right out of her stomach, bounce off the wall, and make a real mess. All this pregnancy in my life lately. The pregnancy certainly affected the associate's performance at volleyball last week. We all gasped when the ball took a bounce off her stomach—although it was a good save, and frankly that's the price you pay for volunteering to be one of the summer program associate liaisons. I can't have people missing events or not participating, even if they're pregnant. They need to set a good example for the summer associates.

Her e-mail: "I just gave birth to a daughter, [name], this morning at 4:13 AM. Unfortunately, due to complications, I will not be in the office today. I expect to be back at work tomorrow at the latest. I will, of course, be checking my BlackBerry throughout the day, so feel free to let me know if you need anything. Thanks. I apologize for the inconvenience." I sent her a research request, urgent. Just for fun.

Things like this highlight how much has changed since they started letting women into the workplace. We never had to worry about pregnant associates until very recently. In some ways it's great that they want to be lawyers—they're certainly capable of doing the work. In fact, the women who overcome the gender stereotypes and make it to the top are usually better attorneys than the men. But a lot of them don't have the commitment you need to thrive here, and they end up wasting a few years of their lives working hard for no reward. If they want to have families along with careers, they're not going to make partner. And if you're not going to make partner, why bother?

A few years ago we stumbled on the perfect solution for the firm. Someone—and I wish it was me, but it wasn't—came up with the brilliant idea of letting them work "part-time" for a fraction of the salary. It's great. We get to cut their pay while merely pretending they don't need to work as hard as everyone else. Plus it lets us brag during the recruiting process about how "woman-friendly" we are. The Tax Guy and his porn habit—that's woman-friendly too.

What part-time ends up meaning is that the women work 100 percent of the time they used to work but for only 80 percent of the salary. It's a profit center. Technically, the part-timers don't come in on Fridays. That's the part-time part of it, the 80 percent. But their clients come in on Fridays, and the partners in charge of their cases come in on Fridays, and their meetings get scheduled on Fridays. So they end up coming in on the weekends to catch up anyway, and don't save any hours in the end.

Effectively, they spend 20 percent of their salary to be able to tell themselves—and everyone they meet, because it's all they can talk about—that they've made the sacrifice and work "part-time" to prove how much they love their children. It's self-delusion, but if it makes them feel better about putting their careers first, then that's fine with me. They can delude themselves however they want. The more women who want to work part-time, the better.

A man once applied to work part-time. Good thing we found out it was just a practical joke before we fired him.

#Posted by Anonymous at 11:37 AM

To: Anonymous Lawyer
From: Anonymous Niece
Date: Monday, June 12, 11:44 AM

Is that really what the firm thinks of the part-timers? That seems a little over-the-top. You have a family. Most of the people at the firm have families, don't they? Wouldn't you like to be able to be more involved with your kids?

To: Anonymous Niece
From: Anonymous Lawyer
Date: Monday, June 12, 11:56 AM

Maybe, but that's not the way it works. Raising the kids is the wife's job anyway. The men here are mostly happy not to be involved. The system's a problem, sure. But it's a problem everywhere. You think migrant farmworkers are spending a lot of quality time with their kids? Or salesmen who are on the road for nine months out of the year? The problem is that some people aren't realistic about it. You need to realize you can't always have everything.

We have one girl in the summer class who really wants to make partner one day. She was very up front about it during the interviews. It's unusual nowadays. Most of them just want to take the money for a few years and then go do something else. But she was very deliberate about telling us that wasn't what she was looking for. Of course my next question to her was about a family and whether that's part of her plan too. She looked me right in the eye and said, "I'm sterile." So there we had it. No worries there. She passed up lunch last week at Nishimura to finish up an assignment. She gets in early and stays late. She's the model of what all the summers should be. But most of them aren't that mature.

To: Anonymous Lawyer
From: Associate X
Date: Monday, June 12, 12:02 PM

You get the evidence yet?

To: Associate X
From: Anonymous Lawyer
Date: Monday, June 12, 12:12 PM

I just got it. I'm looking at it now. Walk me through this so I know why it's interesting. So far it just looks like half a bank statement.

To: Anonymous Lawyer
From: Associate X
Date: Monday, June 12, 12:48 PM

Look what bank it's from, and look at the withdrawals.

I used to work on one of The Jerk's big accounts, International Amalgamated. Instead of setting up the company's escrow account at the firm's regular bank, he set it up here. I didn't think anything of it at first. I figured it was the bank the client always dealt with, and that the client had requested the money be held there.

I would get to see the statements occasionally—statements like the one you're holding—and the account transactions weren't matching up with the client activity. The interest never seemed to accumulate for long—but on a balance of over eight million dollars, it was adding up to quite a bit of money.

There were large withdrawals that would sometimes get paid back, but sometimes not. I made a copy of some of the bank statements before The Jerk transferred me off the case. I didn't plan on telling anyone but I figured it couldn't hurt to have something on The Jerk, in the event I ever needed to use it.

Now that he's screwing with my career, these statements are looking pretty interesting. I think he's stealing money. I think he's withdrawing the interest and taking out principal. That's what I see when I look at the records. Have you seen his wife? He doesn't make enough money to afford all the work she's had done to herself. And his new house? It's about ten thousand square feet bigger than it should be.

To: Associate X
From: Anonymous Lawyer
Date: Monday, June 12, 1:19 PM

That's a serious charge. I certainly hope The Jerk is doing something like this and that we can catch him in the act, but I'm not sure these bank records prove it. I can't tell anything for sure from the small piece you've given me.

To: Anonymous Lawyer
From: Associate X
Date: Monday, June 12, 1:28 PM

It doesn't look like a normal escrow account though, does it? The number of transactions? The fact that it's not at the same bank as the rest of the firm's money? And you see how The Jerk spends. He has nicer things than you—his antique cars, his rare-book collection. Don't you wonder how he affords them? This is for real. Trust me.

To: Associate X
From: Anonymous Lawyer
Date: Monday, June 12, 1:52 PM

I need to see more records.

To: Anonymous Lawyer
From: Associate X
Date: Monday, June 12, 1:58 PM

Fine. I'll leave a couple more pages in the cabinet at five this afternoon. You just tell me when you're ready to proceed. I'll be waiting with bells on. And nothing else.

Monday, June 12

There's some gossip going around this afternoon that one of the summer associates is dating his secretary. He's going to ruin the reputation of his school around here. It'll make me add Hastings to my list of schools I'm wary of, simply because of the actions of one of its students. Vanderbilt, USC, Columbia, Virginia, Texas, UCLA, Georgetown, Penn, Cornell, Northwestern, Duke, Florida, and NYU are on the list too. I can't remember the details for most of them, but things happen and it completely spoils my image of a place. Someone wears an ugly tie, takes too many cookies, flubs an assignment, shows up late, sneezes too loudly, misses a deadline, or can't find a certain book in the library, and his school suffers for it in the recruiting process as a result. It's just a fact of life.

#Posted by Anonymous at 4:44 PM

To: Anonymous Niece
From: Anonymous Lawyer
Date: Monday, June 12, 5:28 PM

You find out yet whether anyone here is reading the blog?

To: Anonymous Lawyer
From: Anonymous Niece
Date: Monday, June 12, 8:50 PM

I haven't had much time—graduation is in two days, so I'm swamped. But I just did some research, with the IP addresses and everything.

You've definitely got a couple of readers at the firm, but it might just be The Musician plus the hits you're getting when you look at the site yourself. I don't know enough to know who this associate is. Is she still e-mailing you?

To: Anonymous Niece
From: Anonymous Lawyer
Date: Monday, June 12, 9:18 PM

Yeah, she's still e-mailing me. She showed me some papers. I think The Jerk is doing something illegal. I don't know for sure, but I'd bet money on it. The question is whether I'd bet my career.

Tuesday, June 13

I've just heard that The Girl Who Dresses Like A Slut has been sneaking food from internal meetings back to her secretary. This is against the rules. I've asked the recruiting coordinator to send out an e-mail informing the summers that the food at these events is for their benefit only, and all excess food belongs in the trash, not in the hands of other members of the firm. This is the same problem we had last year when a summer associate gave a cookie to a homeless person on the way out of one of the stops on our progressive dinner.

So I went to check up on her and her eyes were fixed to her computer screen. Her law school just released the list of which graduates had earned honors. I asked if I could take a quick scan to see if our incoming first-year associates from her school had made the list.

One of them had, and the other one hadn't.

We tell them it doesn't matter how they do in law school, but we're lying. I have a speech I give on the last day of the summer about how their employment is secure, it's okay if they get Cs, it's okay if they get Ds, it's okay if they get arrested for second-degree assault. As long as they graduate, and as long as the bar will admit them, we're okay, and we won't ask to see their grades.

It's not true. If they don't think we have preconceived notions of who the stars are, they're fooling themselves. We know whose names we eventually want on the letterhead (just a turn of phrase—we stopped putting all the partners' names on the letterhead a long time ago). And if they don't graduate with honors, then we start to second-guess ourselves. Maybe we made the wrong choice. Maybe they're slacking off.

And if they're slacking off in law school, maybe they'll slack off here too. Maybe a distinguished career in the law isn't as important to them as we thought. Maybe they're just like everyone else, and we should burn them out as fast as we can and throw their carcasses to the pack of dogs waiting out back (another turn of phrase—we got rid of the dogs a long time ago).

We want attorneys with good pedigrees, for the recruiting brochures. We want attorneys able to figure out how to get an A on a law school exam, because if they can't figure that out, how can we expect them to get a judge to buy their arguments?

So the one who earned honors gets a gift basket. The other one doesn't. They'll compare notes. It'll serve its purpose. They think things are accidents. Like office assignments. Think we don't know whose offices are bigger? Think we don't know who's near the important partners? Seven square feet. Well, before they made him chairman.

We've got a summer associate scavenger hunt tonight. We divide the summer associates into four teams and send them around the city looking for assorted detritus. A quarter from a homeless man. A take-out menu from a Vietnamese restaurant. A building code violation. A manhole cover. A street sign. It's a lot of fun. Last year someone got run over crossing the street. That's what we get for making it a race. Her teammates didn't even stop to pick her up. They couldn't spare the time. They just kept on going and met up with her at the hospital later. Just a few scratches. She was fine. First thing she wanted to know was if her team won. They did. But since she didn't finish with them, she didn't get to share in the prize. Oh well.

 # Posted by Anonymous at 3:45 PM

To: Anonymous Lawyer
From: Daniel Ray
Date: Tuesday, June 13, 4:39 PM

You're Sam Tannenbaum at Cole & Hartwick. The scavenger hunt post gave it away. I'll keep your secret though.

To: Anonymous Lawyer
From: Pamela Casey
Date: Tuesday, June 13, 5:20 PM

You're Ron Kenney at Mathis, I'm sure of it. I'd know your writing any-where. Remember me from summer at Lunberg? I quit three years ago and run a mail-order seed business. Blood pressure fell by half—I'm healthier and happier than I've ever been. Keep up the blog!

To: Anonymous Lawyer
From: Sara Gottlieb
Date: Tuesday, June 13, 7:45 PM

You can tell me now—you're the guy who fired me today, right? Tom? I knew it. You're a bastard and so is everyone else at Wechman Davis. Liars. You took the best twelve years of my life. I'm better off without you.

Wednesday, June 14

Last night's scavenger hunt was a wild success. No team found more than two-thirds of the items and they all went away feeling like failures. That's exactly what we aim for. A couple of the items were too easy. All of the teams found an associate who'd been in the office for thirty-six hours straight, and an unsent suicide note. A couple of the items were too difficult. None of the teams found a piece of sporting equipment in the office, or an ethnic minority. We'll know for next year.

#Posted by Anonymous at 9:50 AM

Wednesday, June 14

Candyman just stopped by to tell me he's leaving on Friday for his vacation to the Caribbean. His first vacation in five years. I told him I'm happy for him, and I hope he gets to go. I told him how brave he is to take off in the middle of all of these client deadlines we're up against. I told him to bring the Citicorp file with him and draft a motion while he's away. I told him it has to be filed by the twenty-third, so he won't have much time when he gets back. I told him I'd put The Frumpy Litigator on the case, but she'll already be swamped covering his other clients. I told him he'll need to make sure to call in for the daily meeting and keep in regular contact even while he's away, and to make sure he has access to a fax machine so we can keep him in the loop, and to make sure he's aware that we're evaluating everyone's commitment to the firm as we decide who to staff on the big case coming through the pipeline.

Suddenly he said he's not sure if he's really going to end up going. I told him that's too bad, and everyone should get to take a vacation every once in a while. He said this may not be the right time. I told him I'm sure the client would be happy to reimburse him for the plane tickets.

When associates do decide to go on vacation, we like to make sure the first day away turns into an emergency conference call. It's a rite of passage like fraternity hazing. If they get their first vacation day as planned, it's all downhill from there. They start to forget we own them.

#Posted by Anonymous at 11:34 AM

Wednesday, June 14

The Jerk just stopped by my office. "You're moving."

"Excuse me?"

"I'm reshuffling some partner offices around so that you're closer to the associates you work with. You're going to 2104. There'll be an e-mail, but I wanted to give you the courtesy of a heads-up. You move next week."

"2104 is on the dumpster side."

"Oops."

I started to get up from behind my desk. "You can't do that."

"Sure I can. I'm chairman of the firm, remember?" He smirked a little bit. "Your new office is also a little smaller than this one. I hope that's okay."

And before I could say anything else, he left. That's it. He's finished.

#Posted by Anonymous at 1:39 PM

To: Associate X
From: Anonymous Lawyer
Date: Wednesday, June 14, 1:56 PM

You read my latest post? I'm not moving to the dumpster side. I haven't worked my ass off for eighteen years to move to the dumpster side. He's done. Fuck this whole thing. If he thinks he can treat me like this, he's sorely mistaken.

I'm bringing him down. You're right. We have to act on this. I just called and set up a golf appointment with The Bank VP over at the other bank for next Monday, the guy whose name was on those statements. I told him I'm doing a review for the firm and trying to figure out if we want to stay with our current bank or move all of our accounts to a new one. There's nothing he wouldn't do to get all the accounts of a firm as big as ours.

While we're golfing, I'll coax whatever information I can out of him. I'll tell him I'm looking for a way to earn some money on the side and see if he has any ideas. The Jerk couldn't be doing what we think he's doing without The Bank VP's help. So he must know something. Maybe he's even getting a kickback. If I can get something out of him and combine it with your account records, I may have a case. So I'll need all of those records from you by Friday.

The Jerk is crazy if he thinks I'm moving to the dumpster side. This is not how you treat people. It's not how you treat partners.

To: Anonymous Lawyer
From: Associate X
Date: Wednesday, June 14, 2:03 PM

I'll look through the records and see what I have.

To: The Musician
From: Anonymous Lawyer
Date: Wednesday, June 14, 2:29 PM

You play golf? Change into some sneakers and come by my office in fifteen minutes. You're leaving early today. I have to make sure my game is at its best.

Thursday, June 15

I played golf with The Musician yesterday afternoon. I couldn't stay in the office. I have a coup to plan. I beat The Musician at golf. He's not a very good golfer. And then I went home and told Anonymous Wife that The Jerk wants to move me to the dumpster side, and she didn't understand. She didn't see why it was a big deal. Of course it's a big deal. And so I'm back in the office, at eleven at night, getting drunk on the half bottle of Grey Goose in my desk drawer.

The dumpster side. That's not where a chairman sits. That's where they put Old Yeller, and The Frumpy Litigator, and Black Guy. The people that don't matter. The people that aren't important. I'M FUCKING IMPORTANT. And The Jerk is not going to take all of this away from me. He is not going to ruin my life. I will not let him.

In a matter of days the course will be set. If I move to the dumpster side without a fight, he's won. He'll be entrenched in that office for the next twenty years and by the time it's my turn, it'll be someone else's chance. Another generation. And I'll die a hiring partner.

#Posted by Anonymous at 11:30 PM

To: Anonymous Niece
From: Anonymous Lawyer
Date: Thursday, June 15, 11:38 PM

Just wanted to wish you a happy graduation. I'm sorry I can't be there. I want you to know how proud I am, and how proud you should be of yourself.

Here's my graduation gift for you: I'm flying you down here for dinner on Sunday. Your aunt and cousins would love to see you. And I'll take you into work with me on Monday so you can see the office. It'll be fun.

To: The Musician
From: Anonymous Lawyer
Date: Thursday, June 15, 11:53 PM

Just a heads-up for this weekend—I'd like to invite you to my house on
Sunday for dinner. My niece is in town. I think the two of you would get
along nicely—she'll be at Yale Law School in the fall—and this way
she'll have someone to talk to.

To: Anonymous Lawyer
From: The Musician
Date: Thursday, June 15, 11:58 PM

Thanks. I'd love to come.

Friday, June 16

I can't get into the details here, but come Monday I'm taking a bold
step. The Jerk's going down, and I'm going to be chairman. He's done
something wrong, and I'm going to catch him. People do things wrong
all the time here and don't suffer the consequences. Three years ago, a
partner was accused of sexually harassing an associate. We paid the associate a small settlement, transferred her to the Lisbon office, the
problem went away, and the partner emerged unscathed. Two years
ago, a body was found in the trunk of a partner's car. After an investigation, the preponderance of the evidence indicated it was probably
just a prank. Good enough for us. Last year, a paralegal said she was

raped by someone at the firm, but since she was just a paralegal, no one cared.

No one is held accountable in today's world. So associates take risks and shortcuts without worrying they'll ever be caught. They skimp on the legal research and hope a precedent case doesn't turn up down the road. They skip a few boxes when doing document review. And it's true, usually no one notices. And even when we do notice we don't do much about it. We all advertise ourselves as humane, civil places where partners don't scream or spit or make the associates bleed. If someone makes a mistake, we get angry, but we don't do much damage. If someone begs to go see his baby's birth, he may feel the consequences down the road but it's not as if we're going to shackle him to his desk and beat him with the paper tray from the copy machine (legal size works better than letter size, incidentally— more torque). We ignore it when we hear an associate crying in the bathroom stall; we accept an apology for a missing comma.

Back when I was first starting out, the atmosphere was different. People yelled. People hit. People really held you accountable. I still have a scar near my elbow from the time I forgot to disguise the company name in the tender offer document I was putting together. That didn't happen a second time. It was a lot easier to reach for that letter opener when it was right there than to start fumbling through the desk drawers in a moment of passion. E-mail's ruined that. Nowadays I'm just as likely to grab a highlighter or a binder clip, and frankly there's a limit to how much damage you can do with those.

E-mail's ruined a lot of things. You can't mark up a document on the computer, and you can't carry it down the hall, wave it in some-one's face, and ask them what they were thinking when they screwed up the abbreviation of the source in footnote 114.

You can't walk into an associate's office, slam your laptop on his desk, and scroll down to show him his mistake. You need to have that brief printed out, you need to be able to tear those pages into tiny little pieces right before his eyes, scatter them wildly across the room, fill the sheets with red, crumple up the document, toss it in the trash can, light it on fire, and watch it burn. Sure, we could probably afford to destroy a couple dozen laptops each day just to make a point—but it's hard to argue that paper doesn't work quite a bit better.

We're soft these days. The Jerk threw a cup of hot coffee at a summer associate last year, after the summer accidentally sneezed during a meeting. We paid the summer associate fifty thousand dollars to keep the incident a secret. And The Jerk becomes chairman. I'm done doing it this way. Someone's going to pay for his actions, finally. And the loyal foot soldier who's been here eighteen years and has followed every rule is finally going to win. The Jerk thinks he's sitting pretty, but he's really sitting right on top of a land mine, and that land mine is about to explode.

#Posted by Anonymous at 9:55 AM

To: Anonymous Lawyer
From: Associate X
Date: Friday, June 16, 11:09 AM

I was up all night thinking about this. I'm sorry. I can't do it.

I promise you this hasn't been a trick. The evidence is real. But I can't go through with it. I can't give you all the account records.

There's a reason I came to this firm. There's a reason all of us did. It's safe. If you take action, and The Jerk catches you, he'll figure out

I'm the source of the records, and I don't know what happens after that. I'll be fired and blackballed throughout the industry. I can't take that risk. Especially without an appropriate reward.

There's nothing else I can do that'll pay me the salary I make here, or at least nothing that will let me keep my clothes on. That's why I'm here. I'm not here because I love the law. I'm not excited to wake up every morning and do the work we do. I wish I was, but I'm here because the money is good, this isn't manual labor, I'm smart enough to do the work, and it affords me the lifestyle I want. A nice house. A pretty car. A plasma TV. Even if I don't get much of a chance to enjoy them now, I will.

If I had some grand passion, or some great hunger to do something else, I wouldn't have gone to law school to begin with. It feels good to tell people I'm a lawyer. They've heard of the companies we represent. My parents are happy that I have a real career. My grandma loves to brag about me. I have a good life. I go through the motions, cash my checks, pay off my school loans, and I'm okay. People expect too much out of their jobs, and they don't find it. I have friends who are struggling. Ten years out of college and they haven't settled into anything. I don't envy them. At least I have a career.

I can live with what I have. We can pretend nothing happened. I'll forget all about your blog, and you can forget all about the evidence.

To: Associate X
From: Anonymous Lawyer
Date: Friday, June 16, 11:52 AM

You can't bail on me now—I need you! I started to trust you, and now you're pulling back?? You're a tease. I can beat this guy—I can nail him!

Sure, we could forget all about this. But you know what? I wouldn't just forget. I'd figure out who you are, and get rid of you. So there it is: You can't win. To use an analogy you'll certainly understand, you've made your bed, and now you have to lie in it—and take the risk that someone's going to crawl in there with you and rip your clothes off. You see? You're taking a risk no matter what. You give me the evidence, and we're taking the risk together. You keep it, and you're all alone—or at least until I find out who you are and I finish you off. And don't think The Jerk will come to your rescue. You already know that he won't.

To: Anonymous Lawyer
From: Associate X
Date: Friday, June 16, 12:02 PM

You're forgetting something. I know about your blog. You make a move, and I reveal it to the world. Where's your leverage now?

To: Associate X
From: Anonymous Lawyer
Date: Friday, June 16, 12:13 PM

Okay, you have a point. Fair enough. Time to make a deal. What are you looking for? How I can make this risk worth it to you? How can I get the account records?

I have a lot of leftover firm T-shirts I can give you. I have stress balls from recruiting season. I can get you a bigger office. I can get you a better secretary. We can work something out.

To: Anonymous Lawyer
From: Associate X
Date: Friday, June 16, 12:23 PM

T-shirts and stress balls? Even a bigger office doesn't cut it. I want to be guaranteed that I'm making partner. Guaranteed.

If you're going to rise to the top because of the evidence that I was smart enough to save for all of these years, I'm going to ride your coattails and get something big out of it. I don't want to wait ten years and then make partner. I want to be a partner immediately, with a full partner's profit share. That's the least you can do for me, Chairman. Because without my help, you'll be stuck on the dumpster side.

To: Associate X
From: Anonymous Lawyer
Date: Friday, June 16, 12:33 PM

Okay, you're right. If this works out, I will owe you, and I'll owe you big. So yes—if I become chairman, I'll gladly make you partner. You can even have my old office.

To: Anonymous Lawyer
From: Associate X
Date: Friday, June 16, 12:59 PM

Wait a second—not so fast. If I'm part of this plan, I want to make absolutely sure it succeeds—and I don't think your idea is going to work.

The Bank VP isn't going to give the information up so easily. The Jerk is chairman of the firm. Ultimately he controls the money, and The Bank VP knows that. He won't spill the beans about the illegal scheme they hatched just because you take him out to play golf.

I don't think you understand how much I'm bringing to the table. I'm not some moron in Trusts and Estates who's skating by on her pleasant personality.

So here's my other little secret. When I first thought something might be fishy about those records, I decided to see if I could get something out of The Bank VP on my own. We went out on a couple of dates. I really had him going, but then The Jerk found out I was asking questions and that's when he moved me off the case.

So I have a bit of a history with The Bank VP, and I think Monday may be the right time to rekindle that flame.

To: Associate X
From: Anonymous Lawyer
Date: Friday, June 16, 2:08 PM

Interesting. And potentially useful. But if we are going to work together, it's time to stop playing games. I need to know who you are.

To: Anonymous Lawyer
From: Associate X
Date: Friday, June 16, 3:14 PM

Ready? I'm The Bombshell.

You had no idea, did you? And now do you understand why I'll be much better at extracting the information from The Bank VP? Let me come over to your house on Sunday. We'll plot this out. And maybe connect a few other dots besides. I won't be seeing you on tomorrow's vineyard trip, and I don't want to be alone all weekend.

To: Associate X
From: Anonymous Lawyer
Date: Friday, June 16, 3:48 PM

You're The BOMBSHELL? Wow. Okay, I get it. I see how this could really work. And all of that other stuff, that sexy stuff? At some point maybe we can get back to that.

But getting together on Sunday can't happen. If you stepped foot in my house, my wife would divorce me in an instant. I'll take you golfing on Monday, you'll do your Bombshell thing, and I'll just stay out of the way. You get proof that The Jerk is stealing money, I'll take it to the executive committee, and they'll make me chairman. And then I'll make you partner—MY partner.

To: Anonymous Lawyer
From: Associate X
Date: Friday, June 16, 4:12 PM

Great. See you on Monday.

Saturday, June 17

I just got back from the annual summer associate vineyard trip. I love the weekend events. We do them under the guise of offering something special and exciting to the summer associates, but in reality we do them mostly to reiterate that their time is ours and we can occupy it however we like. We let them bring their spouses or significant others on a few events throughout the summer. This was one of them. It's always interesting to see who could possibly find some of these summers even remotely appealing. I had a number of thrilling conversations.

That Foreign Dude's girlfriend said he talks about me all the time. "Oh, interesting. I talk about him a lot too. Are you from the same country he is? You are? Is it nice there? Where is it exactly?"

Stanford Girl's boyfriend said they're getting married right after graduation. "That's good," I said, "because if you wait until she starts her full-time job at the firm, you won't have a chance to take a honeymoon until retirement."

Chicago Guy's girlfriend—or maybe it was his sister—said she's a law student too, working at a different firm for the summer. She named the firm. I told her to tell Jim The Functioning Alcoholic that I say hello.

The Prodigal Son came over with his girlfriend and asked if there's any way he can do real estate work. A lot of people want to do real estate work. I told him I'd think about it. His girlfriend works at a craft store. "Not very ambitious, are you?" I asked her.

I understand how The Prodigal Son is able to find a girlfriend. His family's well-off, he's not completely unattractive, he goes to a good school. I completely understand how Harvard Guy can find a girlfriend. Dresses well, full head of hair, almost six feet tall (a giant in this field). But when people like The Suck-Up show up with these magazine-cover attractive girls, I have to scratch my head. Does he not follow her around like a lapdog, constantly begging for positive reinforcement like he does in the office? He spent a good twenty minutes this afternoon—after three glasses of wine, I should add—asking me if he can work on the bankruptcy deal I'm currently on. He can't. He could if I liked him, but I don't, so he can't. Besides, he has another business trip coming up.

At the vineyard, Stanford Girl kept correcting the vintner, insisting that the proper temperature for storing grapes is this, and the proper way to grow the vines is that, and on and on and on . . . and her boyfriend just stands there, like an idiot, which he probably is. Even though he goes to Stanford. Idiots go to Stanford too.

Some people don't heed the instructions and bring people they hardly know, just to have someone to bring. We tell them to use their judgment. These events are expensive for the firm, and we're inviting significant others as a courtesy, not as a right. Marriage-minded relationships. Long-term, serious involvements. Some summer associates ignore that and bring someone they met the previous night in an Internet chat room. I know, because I read these Internet message boards, looking for people to cross off the interview list. You wouldn't believe what some students write on these message boards, and how non-anonymous they really are. I suppose I shouldn't be too critical, given this blog. I suppose.

First dates at a law firm event never turn out well. The date says something stupid that reflects badly on the summer associate, and then a decade later he doesn't make partner and it's all her fault. Even among the "legitimate" guests, many end up being even more bizarre than their partners. They wear ugly hats. A lot of ugly hats. I don't get it.

Mostly, the firm just wants to buy the affections of the significant others. Give them a nice day at the vineyard. In a couple of weeks we'll let them come to a barbecue on the beach. We'll let them come on the yacht cruise at the end of the summer. Maybe we'll even send their boyfriends and girlfriends home with a gift for them one of these days. A T-shirt. A canvas bag. A little stress ball with the firm's logo on it, that they can squeeze late into the night as they wonder when their partner will be home from the office, whether he'll make it for dinner, whether he'll make it by bedtime, whether he's cheating on her or whether he's really away on a "business trip."

The smart ones don't bring anyone. They avoid the stress of managing someone else's behavior, watching what they say, hoping they don't do anything stupid. At last year's barbecue, one of the summer associates' girlfriends wore a very revealing swimsuit on the beach. She didn't have the body to pull it off. It was not a pretty sight. He was embarrassed. We were all embarrassed for him. We gave him an offer at the end of the summer, but it was close.

The Musician came up to me as we were tasting the dessert wine after lunch and confessed to me that he'd never had a "dessert wine" before and that it tasted like cough syrup. I told him he shouldn't tell anyone else. It's bad enough his shoes didn't match his belt.

The Jerk was there. He bought five bottles of wine on the way out, at $37 each. So I bought six. The Suck-Up bought seven. Then I broke a wine glass in half and cut him with it. Okay, I didn't. But I wanted to.

I used to bring Anonymous Wife to these kinds of things, but she drinks enough as it is, and the last thing I need is my drunk wife at a wine tasting saying things to embarrass me. Instead, I brought Anonymous Son. He liked the barbecue, so I figured he'd have fun at this one too. It humanizes me for the summer associates to see me with my eight-year-old. He liked running around in the grass and tasting the grapes. All the female summer associates fawned over him, except for The Woman Who Wants To Be Partner, since she's sterile and lacks all maternal instincts. I let my son try a few sips of wine and it basically put him to sleep. Or maybe it was all the running around.

He liked the lunch they gave us. I'm teaching him to eat everything. I hate these people who don't eat certain kinds of food, or only like things that have a gravy, or won't eat fish, or vegetables, or spicy food, or whatever. It's such a pain, and food is so good that it's a shame to ignore big categories of it. I want to expose him to everything, so he grows up feeling like "exotic" food is normal and just like anything else. He really liked the morel mushrooms that came with the chicken. He kept asking the summer associates to give him theirs. They did. They were afraid not to.

#Posted by Anonymous at 5:25 PM

Sunday, June 18

Last night, Anonymous Wife insisted we have dinner at her friend Lisa's across town. She wanted to show me the new kitchen they've got. More kitchen talk. I can't stand it. Lisa's husband makes movies. They're rich in a way we're not. My wife is jealous.

Apparently when you're a movie mogul, you spend your days doing absolutely nothing. We watched a movie in their home theater. It wasn't very good. He produced it, so I couldn't tell him what I really thought. They catered in some food for dinner. It wasn't very good either.

The producer's wife's face has seams. You can see where it's been pulled back and sewn together. From a distance it's lovely. Up close it's like watching an accident on the other side of the highway—it's gruesome but you can't turn away. I was staring at her so much, she probably thought I was flirting with her. Or maybe she figured I was just struck by her beauty. The husband has apparently had some hair replacement work done, and not the best kind. It's hard to articulate how I could tell, but it was immediately obvious. The hair doesn't all go in the same direction. The hairline is jagged. The two of them are perfect for each other. Seamy and bald.

This is supposed to be the dream. To sit in your enormous house with your surgically enhanced faces and not have a care in the world. This is what my wife wants. She goes to the beach and does nothing, she goes out to lunch and does nothing, she sits in the house and does nothing. She wants me to earn enough money so that I can do nothing too. I don't want to do nothing. And spending the evening at Chez Face Lift isn't getting me any closer to the chairman's job.

#Posted by Anonymous at 10:09 AM

Sunday, June 18

The phone rang a little while ago. It was a former partner whose son is The Prodigal Son, one of the summer associates. His dad—I guess I should call him The Prodigal Dad—asked if he could come over and say hello. He said he was in the neighborhood, and made up some story about wanting to catch up. I said he could come over for coffee. Anonymous Wife ordered some in from The Coffee Bean.

The Prodigal Dad and I were always on friendly terms when he was at the firm—when I was an associate and he was a partner—but never close enough to see each other outside of the office. It's hard for an associate and a partner to ever find themselves on social terms. The gulf is too wide. An associate spends his free time venting about the partners; a partner spends his free time playing golf. A friendship could never work.

Associates become friends with one another out of necessity. You don't see anyone else all day, and you don't want to spend your birthday alone, so groups of two, three, four, five associates become one another's complete social network, complaining to each other about the work, and lamenting their life choices.

Partners become friends with one another out of necessity too. There's no one else to be friends with. No one else understands. And I need someone to sit next to at the partner dinner.

The Prodigal Dad walked in, we shook hands, and he sat down on the couch. As I suspected, he wanted to talk about his kid.

"My son's having a wonderful summer so far. He really is. You're doing a bang-up job as hiring partner. I always knew you would. Son."

I think he saw me roll my eyes. I can't stop myself from rolling my eyes. It gets me in trouble sometimes, but I can't help it.

"My boy loved the vineyard event yesterday. Oh, and he doesn't know I'm here."

"Really." That's a shock.

"But he's told me there are a lot of summers who want to do real estate work, and he hasn't done any yet, and he's worried he won't get the chance. I'm sure you understand how much I want him to follow in my footsteps. I don't want him becoming a trusts lawyer."

"The trusts department has changed since you left. There are some real stars in the trusts department, handling some cutting-edge issues."

"Don't give me the recruiting pitch. How much is it going to take? I wanted to get to you before the summer really gets under way."

"I'm not sure I understand."

"I have a blank check in my pocket. How much is it going to take to get my son in the real estate department?"

I was speechless. I stared at him for a moment. He stared back.

"I want to prove to my son that I can still move mountains. Twenty-five years working my ass off and I retire and no one knows what to do with me. This can be our father-son bond. Real estate law. It's all I want for him. Whatever it takes."

"Ten thousand dollars."

"Not a problem." He pulled out his checkbook and started to write the check.

"No. I was kidding. You don't have to pay me for this."

"No, I do. Just take it. It'll make me feel like I've done some good in this world."

"I can't."

"Take it."

So I took it. And The Prodigal Dad put his pen away, got up, shook my hand, and left. Just another business transaction. I heard Anonymous Daughter clomping down the stairs.

"Hey, honey, you want a pony?"

#Posted by Anonymous at 3:46 PM

To: Anonymous Lawyer

From: Bonnie Henderson

Date: Sunday, June 18, 4:30 PM

Did you really take a bribe? I thought I knew you better than that.

To: Bonnie Henderson

From: Anonymous Lawyer

Date: Sunday, June 18, 4:38 PM

I didn't really take it. He offered, but I couldn't say yes. It's a better story this way.

To: Anonymous Lawyer

From: Petere Fontes

Date: Sunday, June 18, 4:42 PM

How could you take that man's money??

To: Petere Fontes

From: Anonymous Lawyer

Date: Sunday, June 18, 4:49 PM

Oh, come on! You can't believe everything you read!

To: Anonymous Lawyer
From: Glenn Barrow
Date: Sunday, June 18, 5:06 PM

This is also the way we do business in Belize. If you have any work to send our way, I will be happy to send you a gift basket.

To: Anonymous Lawyer
From: The Musician
Date: Sunday, June 18, 11:09 PM

Thanks so much for having me over for dinner tonight. It was great to meet your wife, and especially your niece. I had a terrific time.

To: Associate X
From: Anonymous Lawyer
Date: Sunday, June 18, 11:34 PM

Are you ready for tomorrow? What are you wearing?

To: Anonymous Lawyer
From: Associate X
Date: Sunday, June 18, 11:47 PM

Are you finally flirting with me? Right now I'm wearing nothing. Tomorrow I'm going to wear a tank top and when I lean over to hit the ball, The Bank VP is going to have a view of everything. He's not going to even be able to swing his club, since he'll be too busy thinking about, uh, swinging his club. And yes—I'm ready.

To: Anonymous Lawyer
From: Anonymous Niece
Date: Monday, June 19, 1:25 PM

Hope you don't mind—I'm using your computer at home. Thanks for letting me check out the office this morning. I see what you mean about the paralegals. They're really terrible. And I have to admit, I didn't believe you about the summer who looked like he has Down syndrome, but I can totally see it now. Definitely Down syndrome, or at least something like it.

But you know what? Other than the paralegals, and that one summer, everyone seemed pretty normal. The part you never told me is that people at the firm—some people at least—are really working. Associates, partners, summers, in their offices, actually doing things. A few of them seemed to be enjoying it. I haven't seen what the public interest side of things looks like—I know you say it's going to be one desk for every twenty people, having to reuse staples and Post-it notes, fighting with wild dogs for the scraps of lunch meat they'll bring in once a week for a staff meeting—but, frankly, I think I could get used to life in an office like yours. The views out the windows are great, the furniture is all brand-new, everyone has beautiful artwork in their offices, they wear nice clothes, you have secretaries answering your phones . . .

The more I think about it, the more I could totally see myself doing this. I'm smart, I'm productive, I get work done pretty quickly. I think I could manage, and not be stuck in the office so late every night. And given the salary, for a few years it wouldn't be so terrible. People seemed nice. Even The Tax Guy—I know you said he's weird, but he seemed really pleasant, and he thanked me for helping his son and offered to take me to lunch next time I'm in town. The Suck-Up wasn't even as bad as you said. Sure, he's a little annoying, but he's cute and he seemed smart, and everyone sounded like they were working on interesting things, with clients that I've heard of.

Especially the third- and fourth-years, who said they got to talk directly to CEOs and had a little more control over their hours. And they're making over $200,000 a year with the bonuses! Plus they get to eat nice meals, and I'm sure if you really make an effort to keep the whole thing from taking over your life . . . maybe it's not as bad as the image I've been getting from your blog. I was pretty skeptical. But I think I could do this, I really do.

Monday, June 19

I don't know how much longer I can keep writing this blog . . . because it wouldn't be appropriate for me to be unmasked once I'm chairman of the firm.

I played golf today with some important people, and it will undoubtedly set some wheels in motion. I'm not at liberty to say much more, but it will be quite interesting here over the next few days. I expect to have some exciting news to share, very soon.

#Posted by Anonymous at 5:17 PM

To: Associate X
From: Anonymous Lawyer
Date: Monday, June 19, 5:38 PM

You were terrific today. The way you sucked him in was brilliant. E-mail me as soon as you get this and let me know how things went afterward. When I left the two of you in the parking lot, it seemed like things were going really well—that's why I made up the excuse about having to get to the bar crawl. Did you get any information out of him? Do we have what we need?

Monday, June 19

I've got to get ready for the summer associate bar crawl tonight—five bars in five hours. This is usually the one event I skip, because there's nothing worse than watching the very few summers I haven't come to detest, and actually hold some amount of respect for, get sloppy drunk and throw up all over one another. Then they come back to the office, late at night, sneak into a conference room, and have an orgy. Law students are not the most attractive people. And when they start including the late-night maintenance staff, the after-hours word-processing people, and the muffin guy from the lobby, here early to set things up for the next day—and then you walk in on them first thing in the morning, naked, sweaty, and sleeping in their own bodily fluids, it's really a sight you don't want to behold. I'd pledged to never let myself witness it again, but tonight I have something to celebrate.

#Posted by Anonymous at 5:58 PM

To: Anonymous Niece

From: Anonymous Lawyer

Date: Monday, June 19, 6:14 PM

I knew a visit would change your mind. I'm so pleased. I'll be chairman, you'll be a summer associate, it'll be perfect. Someday soon you'll be a true member of the corporate elite. There's nothing better.

    Are you coming to the bar crawl tonight? You should—I think you'd have a lot of fun, before you head back home tomorrow.

To: Anonymous Lawyer

From: Anonymous Niece

Date: Monday, June 19, 6:19 PM

I think I'm going to skip the bar crawl—I made some other plans. But I'll see you when I get back tonight, or otherwise in the morning before you leave for work, I hope.

To: Anonymous Lawyer

From: Associate X

Date: Tuesday, June 20, 7:58 AM

Sorry I didn't get back to you sooner. This is the first time I've been able to check my e-mail in private. I think I got to The Bank VP pretty well. We're seeing each other again tonight, and that's when I'm going in for the kill. I've started to hint at the fact that I'm getting to the point as an associate where you and the rest of the partners start looking at me and thinking about whether I'm partnership material. And to get there, I need to demonstrate that I can add real value. If only there were some secrets I could share with a discreet partner about how to make some extra money on the side, to prove my value to the firm. I didn't dwell on the point, but I definitely made him aware that if he happened to know something—some way he could help me curry favor—there'd be something in it for him. That there's nothing I wouldn't do. Then again, there's pretty much nothing I didn't do last night. Well, one thing. He asked, but I said we'd have to wait until I'm ready. Hopefully we can make a fair trade tonight. I'm taking the day off from work, if that's okay. I'm—well, to be honest, I'm a little bit sore.

To: Associate X
From: Anonymous Lawyer
Date: Tuesday, June 20, 8:35 AM

That's fine. Take the day—take the week, if this works out. I'll make sure no one catches on that you're not here. Great work—this is going to pay off in a big way.

Tuesday, June 20

I left the bar crawl a little earlier than usual last night. This morning I have an e-mail telling me that a number of the summers ended up at a strip club at two in the morning and one of them has submitted the receipt to the recruiting coordinator for reimbursement. When I left, we were at the last bar and everything was fine. The recruiting coordinator had cabs all ready to take the kids home, and I don't know what happened after that. These are all adults, and, at least as long as they're summers, officially we don't care what they do during their time off.

But to ask the firm to reimburse a visit to a strip club, as an "informal summer associate gathering," may finally cross the line. Their argument, according to the e-mail, is that the firm pays for all sorts of events the summer associates have, and that since this activity was made up entirely of summer associates, and it was a bonding activity to help them get to know one another better, and it came after a firm-sponsored alcohol event, they think the firm should pay. This may be a problem.

Last year there was an instance where a full-time associate took a handful of summers to this same strip club, submitted the receipt as a generic summer associate entertainment expense, no one bothered to check what the expense was for, and he got reimbursed. So to not reimburse the summer associates this year would be inconsistent. Or at least that's the recruiting coordinator's inclination, as expressed in her e-mail.

My inclination, on the other hand, is to fire everyone who went (that includes The Suck-Up, The Prodigal Son, Stocky, Stinky, Doc, and, uh, The Woman Who Wants To Be Partner). Not because they went to a strip club, but because by asking to be reimbursed they're expressing a sense of entitlement that's a little ridiculous. That kind of entitlement is for partners, not summers. It's true that we pay for a lot of drinking over the summer, and it's true that we pay for a lot of meals, and it's true that we paid the drunk driving fine and legal fees for someone who was pulled over by the police on the way back from a summer associate event last year. But those were firm-sanctioned events that we planned, not just something that a group of summers decided on their own to do. When we pay, we want control. We want ultimate authority. This was something they chose to do alone. So why should we pay for it?

Of course we're not actually going to fire the summer associates involved. That would be a public relations disaster, in part because if we did, it would get out that we reimbursed the strip club trip last year, and in part because firing anyone, for anything short of murder, is a PR mess. We'll give them a stern warning, and write them a check. It's important that they realize there's a limit to the excesses we're comfortable with, although I suppose writing the check won't send that message. But we need to draw a line. The fifty-dollar lunches are okay; an eighty-dollar lunch would not be okay, except of course on Fridays or if they asked nicely.

The bigger problem is that I really don't want us to end up as the strip club firm when I go back to these campuses in the fall. I know they have a shorthand for all of us. There's the racist firm and the sexist firm and the firm that's filled with assholes and the lifestyle firm and the bad suits firm and the ugly offices firm and I don't want to be any of those. I need us to stand out for something positive or not stand out at all. It's not like the racist firm has any fewer minorities than any other firm, but they acquired the reputation and it's hard to shake. I'd hate to be them. The last thing I want to talk about is why we don't have any minorities. We try. We did an event last summer but it got all screwed up when the invitations announced we were serving "Latino food." Apparently it's Latin food. But these are recruiters who do this, barely college educated. We're lucky when they spell "food" right.

#Posted by Anonymous at 9:09 AM

To: Anonymous Lawyer
From: Anonymous Niece
Date: Tuesday, June 20, 9:45 AM

I'm sorry I got back so late last night and we didn't get a chance to talk.
I just wanted to say goodbye before I head to the airport. I had a really
great time visiting. I hope I get a chance to see you and my cousins
again soon. I'll be back at Stanford to move out, and then on Friday I
go home to Michigan to start my job at the homeless shelter next
week. I was really excited about it until seeing your office yesterday. Oh
well—it's only for a summer.

To: The Musician
From: Anonymous Lawyer
Date: Tuesday, June 20, 9:58 AM

Where were you last night? I was surprised you didn't come to the bar
crawl. You haven't missed any other events. You know how important it
is to go to all of the events. They're not optional. The firm spends good
money on them.

To: The Musician
From: Anonymous Lawyer
Date: Tuesday, June 20, 10:01 AM

Never mind that last e-mail. I pushed "send" and then two seconds
later I figured it out. You were out with my niece, weren't you? I could

tell there were sparks there. That's terrific if that was the case. I had a feeling the two of you would hit it off.

To: Anonymous Lawyer
From: The Musician
Date: Tuesday, June 20, 10:14 AM

Yeah, I was out with your niece. I should have told you before. She didn't think you'd mind. We had a very nice time, I really like her. But I need to talk to you. Can I stop by your office?

To: The Musician
From: Anonymous Lawyer
Date: Tuesday, June 20, 10:16 AM

Sure. Come by at about eleven. But can you give me some sense of what this is about? Just so I can get the police involved if I need to.

To: Anonymous Lawyer
From: The Musician
Date: Tuesday, June 20, 10:24 AM

It's nothing, it's just that your niece was so excited about the firm last night. She said that after finally seeing the office, she thinks she could work here . . . and we were talking and I probably said some things I shouldn't have said, and I don't want you to hear anything from her without hearing it from me first. I'd feel terrible about that. And it's nothing really about the firm—it's about me, and my own ambivalence about this job. I'd feel a lot more comfortable to just have a face-to-face conversation about it, so I don't have to worry that I'm doing anything wrong.

To: The Musician
From: Anonymous Lawyer
Date: Tuesday, June 20, 10:37 AM

Come by at 11:00.

Tuesday, June 20

Maybe a sign of maturity is realizing that sometimes practical concerns need to trump the feelings of the heart. It's amazing to see how shortsighted some people can be, and how easily they can choose to pass up opportunities that most people would die to have.

The Musician just came by my office to tell me that he's probably not going to take our offer at the end of the summer. He wanted to tell me himself because he was worried I'd find out another way. The details of how I'd find out aren't important. What's important is that he's not as smart as I thought he was.

He explained how he's afraid that if he doesn't pursue his music, he'll live his life regretting that decision and always wondering "what if." For some reason, no one ever wonders "what if" they don't pursue a career at a big law firm. I imagine he'll regret not making the kind of money a good corporate lawyer makes more than he'd regret not pursuing the music, especially five years from now when he hasn't succeeded and he can't get a job doing much of anything.

He painted it as a real dilemma and talked about how he's struggled with it for a long time. How he went to law school knowing he probably didn't want to become a lawyer, but feeling like he didn't know how to become a musician right after college and wasn't brave enough to take the risk. People like The Musician have the concept of bravery all wrong. It's not brave to pursue impossible dreams. It's brave to put those dreams aside and suck it up and choose a real job instead. It's brave to fight through the imaginary "crisis of the soul" and realize that most people don't love their jobs but they do them anyway.

He said he feels like the law degree is a great thing to be able to have "just in case," and now he's finally comfortable taking the risk that the music involves. And that his salary this summer will certainly help him with that. But what he doesn't appreciate is that he's essentially stolen that money from us, and stolen a job at the firm from someone who really wants it. He lied to get the job. He lied in the interviews when he said he was finished with the music, and he lied when he said he was serious about a legal career. He said he wanted to tell me today because he wanted to do the "honest" thing. It's too late to do the honest thing. He's been lying all along, and wasting everyone's time.

I don't hold any of this against The Musician personally. I wish him well. But if he thinks I respect what he's doing, he's absolutely wrong.

#Posted by Anonymous at 11:38 AM

To: Anonymous Lawyer
From: The Musician
Date: Tuesday, June 20, 11:46 AM

Do you mean all that? I'm sorry if that's how you feel. I didn't come into this looking to screw you over. I could probably be happy as a lawyer. But there'd be something missing. It's not my calling. I wanted to use this summer to make sure. I don't think anyone here is wasting their lives. It's just that it's not for me. And I shouldn't have said anything to your niece, and I shouldn't have said anything to you, and I'm sorry I did. But I felt like we were becoming friends, and I didn't want to be less than honest. I know you're a hiring partner, but I felt like you might also be a human being.

To: The Musician
From: Anonymous Lawyer
Date: Tuesday, June 20, 11:59 AM

We're not friends. I'm your boss. You have some growing up to do.

To: Anonymous Lawyer
From: Anonymous Niece
Date: Tuesday, June 20, 4:08 PM

I just got home and saw your post. Please don't be mad at The Musi-cian! It's all my fault for going on and on about how much my visit changed my mind about the firm, and how lucky he is to be there. I made him feel guilty. He really likes you, and he respects you. Don't be mad at him, please. I really like him.

Wednesday, June 21

I got here about ninety seconds earlier than usual this morning and went to the attorney lounge. There was only one bagel left, so I took it. Just then, The Jerk walked in. "Split it with you?" he asked.

I laughed. "I don't think so."

"You sure about that?" he said. "We've started with the move to the dumpster side, but I can keep piling on. Less influence, less power, less everything. I'm not threatening you, but I am a bit surprised at your casual attitude."

"I'm fine with the dumpster side," I said. "I'm fine with anything you want to do to me. How you're going to marginalize me is not keeping me awake at night."

"Well, maybe it should. You're a critical part of the firm right now. I know that. But there are young people waiting in the wings. Good associates I'd love to groom to take the place of people like you. But for now, it's in your interest to make sure we see eye to eye—and I know you can be a productive member of my team."

"You're looking too far into the future," I said. "If you'll excuse me, I have to go enjoy my bagel and get to work on some client matters. Have a danish. They're not as bad as you think."

And I walked right out. I hope he ate a danish—they're absolutely as bad as he thinks, and maybe even worse. Especially the cheese danishes. It's like eating tile grout.

#Posted by Anonymous at 9:55 AM

To: Anonymous Lawyer
From: Associate X
Date: Wednesday, June 21, 10:19 AM

I had an excellent night. I told The Bank VP my sob story—about how I stay up nights, worrying how I'm going to get a partner to champion me and help me become a partner too. I told him I've always felt like once I make partner, I can really focus on the personal side of things—that I could never enter into a relationship until now, but once I'm partner all that becomes possible. That's mostly true. I made a deal with myself. It's all business until I'm forty. I can be miserable, I can be happy, it doesn't matter. Until I turn forty, it's all about building up the security so that once I get there, I can focus on the rest of my life.

But that's not the point. The point is that he bought all of it. He swore me to secrecy—ha!—and told me that he has some ideas about how a partner can skim some money off the top, out of the escrow accounts. I feigned complete ignorance and asked for more details. He described exactly what we'd suspected. He didn't mention The Jerk by name, but he said there's a partner here who he's been working with, and who's made some nice money on the side, completely undetected.

He said he could write up an outline of how he's structured that other situation, and that I could take it to a partner, if I thought it would help me. I told him I'd be eternally grateful, and that I was sure no one would get in any trouble for it. "After all," I said, "we steal money from our clients all the time." He was a bit relieved when I said that. I think he feels a little guilty.

I'm having lunch with him this afternoon and he's going to give me the outline. Combined with the bank statements, I think we have enough to get The Jerk. I really do.

To: Associate X
From: Anonymous Lawyer
Date: Wednesday, June 21, 10:31 AM

That's great. How about I come with you to lunch?

To: Anonymous Lawyer
From: Associate X
Date: Wednesday, June 21, 10:48 AM

No. I've gotten us this far by myself. I don't want to spook him and make him think something's going on. He'll tip off The Jerk and we'll be dead. I'll get the document, and I'll come right to your office, hand you everything, and you can go to The Tax Guy. You'll take it to him, he'll take it to the rest of the executive committee, you become chairman, I become partner, and life will be good. Sound like a plan?

To: Associate X

From: Anonymous Lawyer

Date: Wednesday, June 21, 10:54 AM

Sure. Good luck at lunch.

Wednesday, June 21

The Jerk just sent out a memo. Hopefully it'll turn out to be his last official act. He's taking the associate photos off the Web site. "Associate turnover is such that maintaining the Web site in its current state requires a full-time administrator. We are looking to save costs and will as of this afternoon feature associate names only. The partner biographies will remain as they are. We appreciate your cooperation in this minor adjustment."

For once, I think I agree with him. Why do the associates think they have the right to be featured on the Web site? They're lucky we put their names on there at all. The firm is not just run by the partners; it IS the partners. We're the partners OF THE FIRM. I hate how petty associates can be. They want their photos on the Web site? Thirty percent of them leave every year. They're not invested in this place; why should we invest energy into making them as much a part of the firm as the partners are? Everything bothers associates. How many hours they work, how much responsibility they're getting, how much their bonuses will be. They should feel fortunate they have a secure job at a good firm where they make a lot of money and barely have to think. This is the reward for being smart and well-educated and suffering through law school. Why can't they appreciate that and stop complaining? What are they doing studying the Web site anyway? Who even looks at the Web site? Who cares?

 # Posted by Anonymous at 12:05 PM

To: Anonymous Lawyer
From: Associate X
Date: Wednesday, June 21, 3:30 PM

I'm back. I have everything. I'm coming to your office.

To: Associate X
From: Anonymous Lawyer
Date: Wednesday, June 21, 4:48 PM

I just got through with The Tax Guy, and I think everything's working out perfectly. I explained what I'd found (well, what you found—but I didn't tell him that), and what I'd gotten from The Bank VP, and he said he's really concerned and he'll start an immediate investigation. He was sober and serious about it—a little scared too. The Tax Guy understands how chaotic and dangerous this is—one chairman retires, the next one dies, and the next one is potentially stealing money?

So now we wait. He couldn't stop thanking me for quietly bringing this to him instead of taking everything into my own hands and potentially letting things leak to the media. I told him I wouldn't do that. But I think he knows that if he just brushes this under the rug, I'm not going to be satisfied.

Thursday, June 22

The Suck-Up was loitering outside my office when I got in this morning. "I've got no work," he said. "I haven't had anything to do since yesterday at 3:00. I've been going nuts. I'll go anywhere. I just don't want any downtime. I know it looks bad if we're not working on anything. Please give me an assignment. I went to ask [The Jerk] but his secretary said he's in meetings all day."

"Well, you're in luck. I just got a message on my BlackBerry about a case we're working on that needs a smart summer associate like you. Are you up for the challenge?"

"I certainly am."

"Terrific. Pack your bags. You're off to the Sudan for a week of desert document review. Don't forget your sunscreen."

#Posted by Anonymous at 9:34 AM

To: Associate X
From: Anonymous Lawyer
Date: Thursday, June 22, 2:51 PM

Come by my office. Now. I'm breaking out the $400 bottle of Château Margaux I've been saving for something special. We have reason to celebrate. I just got word from The Tax Guy—the executive committee investigated this morning and The Jerk is leaving. They're not making the official announcement until tomorrow. They want to wait until there's a new chairman in place. But The Tax Guy told me I'm under serious consideration and they'll let me know in the morning. Who else is there anyway?

To: Anonymous Lawyer
From: The Musician
Date: Thursday, June 22, 4:30 PM

Should I be congratulating you? Rumors are flying all over the place.
One summer told me that his secretary said she talked to someone
who saw The Jerk packing up his things and leaving the building. The
Girl Who Dresses Like A Slut said she thinks The Jerk got caught
sleeping with a summer associate. I didn't ask what she's basing that
rumor on. That Foreign Dude said he thinks The Jerk got deported. I
don't understand that one any better than anyone else. So is this it?
Did you get it? I know you're probably still mad at me, but I'd be really
happy for you if you get the chairman's job. I know it's what you want.
Your niece will be so thrilled too.

To: Anonymous Lawyer
From: Anonymous Niece
Date: Thursday, June 22, 5:10 PM

The Musician just told me about the rumors—is The Jerk really leaving?
Are you the new chairman? So exciting!

To: Anonymous Lawyer
From: The Musician
Date: Thursday, June 22, 5:35 PM

Someone saw someone in the bathroom who said The Jerk shot his
secretary when she lost a phone message and that's why he's leaving.
Is that true?

To: The Musician
From: Anonymous Lawyer
Date: Thursday, June 22, 5:39 PM

As far as I'm aware, that's not true. But I wouldn't put it past him. Look,
I'm not mad at you. If I do become chairman, I'll be giving you an offer
to come back here, and I hope you'll accept it. You'd be smart to do
so—but if you don't, I'll expect a signed copy of your first CD.

To: Anonymous Lawyer
From: The Musician
Date: Thursday, June 22, 5:45 PM

Thanks. I appreciate that. Latest rumor is that The Jerk stabbed you
with a letter opener. Just so you know.

Thursday, June 22

There are rumors racing around the firm that The Jerk is gone. I can't comment any more than that. I should know more in the morning.

#Posted by Anonymous at 5:57 PM

To: Anonymous Lawyer
From: Christopher J. Perras
Date: Thursday, June 22, 6:23 PM

I know where you work—rumors of our chairman leaving are all around the firm too. He punched his secretary when she lost a phone message, or at least that's what I'm hearing. So you've really been here in Chicago all along? That's incredible.

To: Anonymous Lawyer
From: Kristin Beals
Date: Thursday, June 22, 6:41 PM

I hear rumor about your chairman this evening. News spreads fast. I live in Nigeria, where law firm life is very similar, and I get a great deal of joy in reading about how terrible it is to have life in America. I am sorry for my English. It is not my main language I know. Good luck in all that you do.

Friday, June 23

The Tax Guy just called me into his office. I expect the next time you
hear from me, I'll have some very big news.

#Posted by Anonymous at 8:45 AM

To: Associate X

From: Anonymous Lawyer

Date: Friday, June 23, 10:08 AM

The Tax Guy can go to hell, along with all the rest of them. He's
chairman—THE TAX GUY IS CHAIRMAN! And the whole world will
know at 4:00. After all of this, the firm makes HIM chairman instead of
me??? He said that there's such turmoil they wanted stability. He said
he was as surprised as I am, and he never expected to be chairman—
he wasn't even considered last time, when The Jerk was appointed. He
was too old, too quiet—but the rest of the executive committee felt like
with the third change of power in only a few weeks, they didn't want
someone "young and inexperienced" like me.

I've been here eighteen years! How inexperienced does that make
me? The Tax Guy is fifteen years older than I am! He said they wanted a
voice of stability and wisdom, that it was critical to stop associates
from quitting because of uncertainty about the future of the firm. Instead, they have a voice of the elderly!

He said the executive committee was very grateful to me for bringing this to their attention, and for figuring out that The Jerk's been
stealing money. "We live or die on our client relationships," he said. He
said I'm important to the firm, and my day will come—it's just not right

now. He wants me to stay, and not be too upset about this decision. He wants me to understand.

He said he can give me a bigger office, back to the window side, and he'll knock down a wall and give me my own connecting conference room. He said he'll give me a bonus. He said he'll give me anything I want—except for the one thing I really want!

To: Anonymous Lawyer
From: Associate X
Date: Friday, June 23, 10:37 AM

Hold on a second. So you get a bigger office and more power—you get to be the guy who saved the firm from a chairman who's stealing money. What do I get? I held up my end of the bargain. I did everything I said I would do. I still get to be partner, right? You promised. That was the deal.

To: Associate X
From: Anonymous Lawyer
Date: Friday, June 23, 10:46 AM

That was the deal if I got to be chairman. But I'm not chairman—yet. I can't make you partner. I'm sorry. The Tax Guy is old. His run can't be that long. I can hang on five, eight, ten years—it's not perfect, but I never thought things would happen this quickly anyway. I think I can hang on and wait—he made me think I'll be next, he really did. And so you need to wait too. You'll come up for partner in a few years. I'll fight for you as best I can. I'm sure I'll have enough influence to be persuasive. And if you don't make it, there'll be other opportunities. Other firms, other years. We'll figure it out.

To: Anonymous Lawyer
From: Associate X
Date: Friday, June 23, 11:08 AM

That's not good enough. You promised partner. And it's not fair that you get all of the credit while The Tax Guy barely even knows I exist. I'm going to him and telling him that it was me—as much if not more than it was you—and getting some of this glory. I want to be the one with the bigger office and the promises for the future. You're not in power. You can't guarantee me anything. He can guarantee me something. He can make this all worthwhile.

To: Associate X
From: Anonymous Lawyer
Date: Friday, June 23, 11:12 AM

NO! YOU CANNOT DO THAT! He doesn't realize the extent of what we did. He thinks I stumbled into this information somehow. If you tell him how we really got the dirt on The Jerk, he'll know we were plotting a coup. That would make him very uncomfortable.

I may not be chairman yet, but I'm in a good position now, all things considered. The Tax Guy trusts me and he's grateful. The Jerk is gone. I don't need you ruining that. You CAN'T ruin that—and you'll regret it if you do. That's a promise.

To: Anonymous Lawyer
From: Associate X
Date: Friday, June 23, 11:18 AM

After all this you're threatening me? After all that I've done for you,
you're threatening me? You're taking all the credit for something I did.
You're getting all the promises. I can't have that. I'm going to The Tax
Guy, and there's nothing you can do to stop me. I'm telling him every-
thing. I want to be the one with the bigger office, on the window side.
You can't keep the credit for yourself.

To: Associate X
From: Anonymous Lawyer
Date: Friday, June 23, 11:28 AM

Okay, okay—calm down. I'll split my bonus check with you. He said
he's paying me a bonus, and I'll give you half. Three-quarters. Give me
time. I can make you partner. I just need time.

To: Anonymous Lawyer
From: Associate X
Date: Friday, June 23, 11:36 AM

Not good enough—the deal was I make partner now. You lied to me
and I refuse to be stuck in this hellhole for another day without becoming partner. I'm leaving for The Tax Guy's office right now. And by the
way—that secret blog of yours? Kiss it goodbye.

To: Associate X

From: Anonymous Lawyer

Date: Friday, June 23, 11:42 PM

Seriously, you've got to calm down. Don't do this. You'll regret it. We both will.

To: Associate X

From: Anonymous Lawyer

Date: Friday, June 23, 11:52 PM

Where are you?? This discussion is NOT finished. I'm coming to your office.

To: Associate X

From: Anonymous Lawyer

Date: Friday, June 23, 12:03 PM

You're not in your office—and The Tax Guy's door is shut and his secretary won't let me in. Come find me as soon as you get this!!!

Friday, June 23

I called my wife to let her know the big news. I think this will be good for our marriage. All of these years she's had to compete with the firm for my time and for my energy. But now she knows—I know—that I'll still have to work hard, but it's all paid off. I can finally breathe out.

#Posted by Anonymous at 2:17 PM

To: Anonymous Lawyer
From: Anonymous Niece
Date: Friday, June 23, 2:25 PM

I'm assuming the big news means you're chairman. Congratulations! I'm so happy for you.

To: Anonymous Lawyer
From: The Tax Guy
Date: Friday, June 23, 3:08 PM

I don't have Asperger's syndrome, I'm not allergic to people, and you shouldn't criticize naked women holding tax forms until you've looked a little closer.

Your "friend" was just in my office, and she shared a lot of very interesting information with me. I see I gave you a little too much credit for uncovering "The Jerk" and his transgressions. Your friend informed me that the information didn't just fall into your hands. You plotted to take him down, and almost got very lucky. Question: How long before you begin plotting to take me down as well?

True, I'm very appreciative for the chance to be chairman, and recognize that without these revelations about "The Jerk," it wouldn't have happened. That doesn't mean I'm going to tolerate open revolt against power. Your friend thought that by coming to see me, she would be rewarded. She was wrong. I don't look kindly on associates who plot against partners. As of thirty minutes ago, your sexy friend no longer works here.

Had that been all I learned, I would have invited you to lunch and we would have tried to iron out our differences. Perhaps we would have put in place a succession plan. Perhaps we would have put into writing your future appointment as chairman, on the condition that we work in tandem for the next few years and help make my goals for the firm become a reality.

But it's too late for a conciliatory lunch, because that wasn't all your friend shared with me. Once she realized that she was finished here, she made it very clear that if she was going down, she would be taking you with her. She directed me to a site on the Internet that you've been maintaining. I'm sure you recognize the details I began this e-mail with. I must admit at first I was somewhat amused reading through your writing. I enjoyed creating this new e-mail address, for one use and one use only.

So let me be clear. I don't appreciate being mocked. I don't appreciate having someone write about the firm in this appalling fashion— and on the Internet no less. Your friend told me that lots of people are reading this. That is intolerable. After such an egregious transgression, you cannot possibly expect to continue working here. I have a responsibility to the firm, as do you, and there are limits to what kind of behavior is allowed. Do you understand? I will not let you destroy my tenure as chairman, and I will not let you bring down this firm.

I didn't tell you the entire truth this morning. It was a surprise to me that I was the committee's choice for chairman, but it was not a surprise that you were passed over. You are too young, you are immature, and you lack judgment. We were hoping that over the next decade you would grow into the role. But now you will not get that chance.

We had an emergency vote of the partnership. It was not close. Effective immediately, your association with this firm is over. Security will be at your door by the time you read this. They will watch you pack up your things and they will escort you out to the parking garage. And you will never show your face here again.

Monday, June 26

If I look outside the window of my new, much larger office, I can see tiny people on the sidewalk, walking to their mediocre buildings filled with mediocre people. I wish I could break their legs. They're taking up space on this planet. Space that belongs to me, and the handful of other people who deserve to share that space. Ridiculous.

It's nine a.m., and I note that at least a few of our employees haven't arrived yet. That's unacceptable. Under my reign as chairman, this firm will be returning to glory. The first step toward accomplishing that is making sure people are here on time. Over the years, the typical arrival time has drifted later and later, and I haven't been able to do anything about it. I don't care how late someone is stuck at the office the night before. If they can't get here by nine in the morning, they should find another job.

I have a team of locksmiths changing the locks on every empty office this morning. When the associates arrive, they'll be directed to pay me a visit, where I will explain to them that this is the last time they will be late. I will give them a new key. One time. The next time I change the locks, the only keys they'll need are their car keys.

The attorney lounge is now off-limits to associates. Their access cards won't open the door. There are privileges to partnership. The hierarchy has gotten soft over the years. That's something I'm changing. Same thing with the bathrooms.

I've had the maintenance staff slow down the clocks in the hall, and the IT staff do the same with the computers. We're turning twelve-hour days into sixteen hours and seeing if anyone notices. And if they do notice, they should keep quiet about it if they know what's good for them.

Tonight's summer associate event is bungee jumping. One of every three cords is frayed. I'll be setting the order in which the summers will be jumping. It should be a fun evening. Too bad The Suck-Up isn't back from the Sudan.

I'm keeping my secretary. She's been pretty good to me. She'll have a fresh bowl of candy on her desk every morning. I just saw The Tax Guy walk past. He took a Junior Mint. The candy's not for him. My secretary. My candy. MY FIRM.

#Posted by Anonymous at 9:00 AM

ACKNOWLEDGMENTS

I owe a debt of gratitude to Sara Rimer at *The New York Times*, without whom this book would not exist; to lawyer-blogger Evan Schaeffer, who encouraged the book project before it became a reality; to Howard Bashman, Ernest Svenson, and all of the lawyers and bloggers who helped spread the word about Anonymous Lawyer; to Michael Giordano, who provided valuable advice along the way; to Web Stone and Shawn Coyne, who helped me get my feet wet as a writer; to Professor Elizabeth Warren, who showed me that there are brilliant people in this world who love what they do, and that a law degree doesn't necessarily have to mean a life at a law firm.

I'm also grateful for the useful feedback on structure, character development, plot, and more that I received from some very talented friends: David H. Turner, Rebecca Ingber, Eric Bland, Zach Pincus-Roth, Nate Allard, Chris Sharp, Gerry Moody, Iris Blasi, Elizabeth Greenberg, Roger Pao, Chris Geidner, Katie Sewell, Lorraine Lezama, Mike Laussade, Pallavi Guniganti, and Jesse Liebman. I'm confident I'll get the chance to return the favor for many of them in the not-so-distant future. Look for their names in bookstores, on theater marquees, in newspapers, and on defense briefs at courthouses near you.

My editor and publisher, John Sterling, asked all the right questions and gave me the encouragement to find the answers. Even when I wasn't sure I could write this book, I never felt his confidence waver. Thanks, John, for taking a chance on me. And thanks to everyone at

Holt for their enthusiasm and work on behalf of the book—Flora Esterly, Meryl Levavi, Erica Gelbard, Maggie Richards, Lucille Rettino, Claire McKinney, Richard Rhorer, Jason Liebman, Denise Cronin, Jennifer Barth, and Sarah Knight.

Thanks as well to Suzanne Gluck and her entire team at the William Morris Agency, especially Erin Malone, along with Stuart Tenzer, Cara Stein, Scott Lonker, Lauren Whitney, and Anna DeRoy. I couldn't be in better hands.

Scheherazade Fowler has been a generous friend, a sounding board, and a lifeline throughout this project. She read more drafts than anyone should have to, and had smart and helpful things to say each time.

During my freshman year of college, I auditioned for a student-written musical put on by the Princeton Triangle Club. Triangle awakened in me a passion for writing that I didn't know I had, and provided a mentor of sorts in its music director and trustee, Jay Kerr. I continue to benefit from Jay's guidance and friendship, and thank him especially for teaching me the importance of rewrites.

Finally, thanks to my mom, Arlene Blachman, who couldn't be more supportive; my dad, Richard Lines; and my grandmother Anne Brooks, who has the soul of a writer and the heart of a grandma, and who provided terrific critiques of the material and an always-willing ear. My grandfathers, Julius Blachman and Emanuel Brooks, would have gotten a kick out of all this.